JET IV

RECKONING

Russell Blake

First Edition

Copyright 2012 by Russell Blake. All rights reserved. No part of this book may be used, reproduced or transmitted in any form or by any means, electronic or mechanical, including photocopying, recording, or by any information storage or retrieval system, without the written permission of the publisher, except where permitted by law, or in the case of brief quotations embodied in critical articles and reviews. For information, contact Books@RussellBlake.com.

ISBN: 978-1484814918

Published by

Reprobatio Limited

PROLOGUE

Papua, Indonesia

Hulking yellow ore trucks sat quietly in a sprawling gravel lot, their huge, battered carrying bins empty. A bored guard lounged in the gatehouse, listening to a CD on a small portable stereo as he sat sentinel over nearly two hundred vehicles. After a long day of grinding routine, the shifts had departed and the incessant roar of motors and machinery had subsided, leaving the area eerily quiet compared to the daytime cacophony.

The torrential rain had finally slowed to a drizzle, a remnant of a monsoon that had blown in earlier during the afternoon and dumped six inches of water on the mountains in as many hours, making the access roads muddy but manageable, as was frequently the case in September.

The largest gold mine in the world was shut down for the night, awaiting the return of the nearly twenty thousand workers who would arrive at dawn to operate the machines that had stripped the top off a nearby peak, methodically extracting the precious ore that held gold, silver, and copper – natural resources that should have made the region one of the wealthiest on the planet. In reality, the prosperity was almost entirely leached off by the Indonesian government and the company that operated the mine. The jewel in that corporation's crown, it was responsible for unimaginable profits, while the majority of locals lived in primitive tribal conditions, much as they had for thousands of years.

That lifestyle was doomed, the toxic sediment from the open pit mine having clogged the rivers and poisoned the animals, intruding into every area of the ecosystem and sullying everything it touched. Fishing, hunting, and virtually any endeavor that required clean water or land were finished in the region – an acceptable cost for the conglomerate that earned billions each year, though not for the natives whose land was forever ruined.

A roaming sentry shined his flashlight beam in the direction of the man watching the silent vehicles from the guardhouse, then swept it over the huddled silhouettes before returning to the path in front of him. The security force was equipped with pistols and shotguns, but there hadn't been any problems at the site for several years, so the men were relaxed about their duty – one of near-endless drudgery.

Headlights bounced up the rutted access road toward the entry gate, and a pickup truck pulled to a stop. The bed was filled with laughing local men whose chocolate skin glistened from the rain, a nuisance to which they were inured, having grown up with the monsoons – the periodic storms as routine as the sun setting into the sea that surrounded their island.

A guard welcomed the graveyard shift maintenance men with a wave and exchanged a few words with the grinning driver, then raised the barricade and motioned for it to pass. The vehicle lurched off with a groan, its springs straining with the human cargo. The guard lowered the barricade back into position, his sole task for the next six hours completed.

The local islanders didn't mix with the transplanted immigrants from Indonesia, preferring to keep to themselves in one of the company towns that had been built to house the workforce. The islanders were bitter that they had gone from owning the island to being a minority, the influx of immigrants having swelled the non-indigenous ranks to over fifty percent of the population, encouraged by the Indonesian government, which was anxious to minimize the power of the natives.

Efforts to create an independent nation had been stymied when Indonesia effectively annexed the western half of New Guinea and imposed its rule, a move ratified in a sham election in 1969 in which the population was prevented from voting, except for one thousand twenty-five 'representatives' of the New Guinea people, who were instructed by their governors to vote for an Indonesian regime or be slaughtered. Unsurprisingly, the vote was unanimous – and approved by the United Nations in a shameful acceptance of the shotgun wedding election.

Consequently, over a third of the locals lived on less than ten dollars a week and subsisted on primitive farming in conditions of misery and squalor. Malaria killed a huge number of the islanders each year, largely because of inadequate health care and basic infrastructure.

The night air was thin at fourteen thousand feet, so the mercenaries were winded after the long trek from their base camp. Bright spotlights illuminated the barren mine production area, operations having ceased hours before, and only a security detachment remained to guard against vandals or theft. The outline of the massive open pit gashed into the heart of the mountain was just visible in the gloom, the yawning expanse stretching for over a mile.

The leader of the group of six men pointed to his right at the aerial tramway that ran down the side of the mountain. A short, muscular man with a large backpack strapped securely in place nodded, and then broke off from his companions and made for the control area. The others watched him disappear into the dark before turning their eyes to the leader, who pointed at the buildings below them.

"You know the drill. Let's get this over with. I want to be out of here in half an hour, tops," he said, then gestured at the buildings – a hospital, a school, and the production facilities.

The men had run simulations on the most efficient way to achieve their objective and were prepared for what was to come. Each was equipped with a modified M4 assault rifle with a sound suppressor, visible laser, infrared illuminator, and PVS-17A mini night vision sights. But in spite of the firepower, the goal was to penetrate their objective, place explosive charges throughout the facility, including on the sluice pipelines and all communications wiring, and then slip away – not to get involved in a full-scale gun battle if they could avoid it. If they did have to fight their way out, however, they had come prepared. In the end, it didn't much matter to the men either way – they'd all seen more than their share of combat and were as used to it as humans could be.

The leader motioned to the men to split up, and they made their way to their pre-assigned targets, melting into the night like ghosts.

A truck carrying two security men crawled along the perimeter road, the engine barely turning over, the patrol rounds obligatory. Everything seemed in order. Which it had been every night for as long as either of them could remember.

"Hey, you thinking about what you're going to do once you get a little time off?" the driver asked, making conversation, trying to kill the boredom that was a constant of the job.

"No, not really," his partner said. "I mean, I have to worry about the kids, and my – wait, did you see that? Over by the sluicing pipeline?" He pointed a wavering finger at the big pipes.

"See what? You hitting the bottle early tonight?"

"I saw something."

"*Something*. What was it?" the driver asked, slowing further and cranking the wheel to the right, bringing them closer to the huge pipelines that carried the slurry – a mixture of gold, silver, and copper concentrate – to the port at Amamapare seventy miles away, where it was filtered and dried before being shipped all over the world.

"I don't know. I thought I saw someone."

"At the pipes? What would they be doing there?" the driver asked caustically. "There's nothing to steal."

"Can't hurt to take a look."

The truck crept towards the pipelines.

"I don't see anything, do you?" the driver asked again, and his partner shook his head.

"No. Wait a second. What's that over by that seam? Can you make it out?" The guard aimed his LED flashlight at the pipes.

"What are you talking about?"

"Over there. I see something."

"I don't. This is a waste of time."

"You're probably right, but let's check it out on foot. You never know."

The driver rolled to a stop and both guards got out, the passenger carrying a twelve-gauge pump-action shotgun in addition to his sidearm.

They moved around the concrete wall that separated the pipeline from the access road, the beams of their lights playing along the freshly painted metal surface of the three pipes. Both men stopped at the same point twenty yards away. Two rectangles protruded from the surface, near a welded seam where the sections had been joined.

"What the hell is—"

The driver's chest exploded in a bloody pulp as three silenced rounds tore through it, his exclamation cut short by a gurgle as he flew forward and landed face first in the wet dirt. His partner swung the shotgun back towards the road where the truck sat idling, but never made it. Two slugs blew off the side of his face and the top of his skull with a wet *thwack* before he could find a target to shoot at.

A figure in black stepped from the shadows adjacent to the nearby maintenance shack, leading with the silenced snout of his M4, and hurried to the two corpses and removed the radio from the driver's belt before glancing up at the rectangles. A small red LED blinked at him. He double-checked his watch before tapping his ear bud and murmuring into it.

"This is Jupiter. I took out two guards. I've got their radio, but we need to presume they'll be missed. Where are we? Check in. Over."

A whispered voice responded in seconds. "Tram's wired. I'm five minutes out from getting my secondary target finished. No interruptions so far. Saturn out."

"This is Mars. Ten minutes away from my target being completed. One patrol came by, but I didn't engage."

The others checked in. They'd be ready to boogie in twenty minutes, tops.

"Pluto here. I'm headed to the communications center. See everyone at the rendezvous point in twenty. Check in if there are any more casualties. Don't leave any survivors."

The group's leader considered the latest and shook his head in silent disapproval, then returned to sighting through the night scope at the guard standing under the overhang of the darkened building that housed the cables and communication equipment connecting the mine to the outside world. They had always known there would be collateral damage, but the more of the security detail that went missing, the greater the chances that the operation would be interrupted before all the charges were placed.

He made a quick judgment call and lightly squeezed the rifle's trigger. His weapon spat death into the night, and the hapless guard collapsed in a bloody heap. It couldn't be helped. He'd been watching the man for five minutes, but the drizzle had kept the sentry glued to the building, and now he was short on time. There was no room for failure or partial completion of their mission. The orders had been unambiguous: cripple the mine so that it would be out of commission for months. It had been made clear that payment hinged on the success of their work, and no qualms had been voiced about any casualties that resulted. The objective was paramount, and anyone who got in the way was expendable.

He trotted to the building and, without glancing at the dead guard, moved to the locked door and affixed a small charge to the deadbolt. Ten seconds after he flipped the switch, the small detonator gave a dull thump and the door blew open, the noise muffled by an incoming cloudburst. He swung around, checking to verify he was still alone, then edged into the gloom of the darkened interior, taking care to swing the door closed.

Four minutes later the leader stepped back out and scanned the area, then sprinted to the dead man's security truck and pulled away, pausing to give the rest of his group an update as he drove towards the main gate. The guards there would also have to be executed, but he'd planned to do so anyway once all the charges had been placed, signaling the conclusion of the night's work.

His ear bud clicked and another report came in – four of the group were now done and ready to roll. The fifth man murmured a terse update – he would be finished shortly.

The truck's headlights swung towards the gate that protected the mine's primary entry road, and just as the leader was drawing near it the distinctive roar of a shotgun boomed from one of the buildings near the crushing area. He stiffened as the radio he'd lifted from the dead guard crackled to life.

"We have at least one intruder in sector C. He's shooting at me. David got off one with the shotgun, but he's down. Doesn't look like he's going to make it." The voice sounded panicked, and then two smaller caliber shots echoed from the same area, followed by three more. Pistol, by the sound of it.

One of the two guards at the main gate squinted at the approaching truck and swung his shotgun towards it as his partner fumbled inside for his. The ruse the leader had hoped would get him close enough to take them both out had just gone down the drain. He gunned the gas and then cranked the wheel hard left as he stomped on the brakes, sending the truck into a controlled skid as it drew closer to the gate. The shotgun's baritone detonation sounded from the guard shack, then the explosion of the windshield and passenger side window showered him with glass as the truck slowed to a stop. He jumped out, rolling onto the ground while he fought to keep the protection of the wheels between himself and the guard.

Another deep boom; buckshot tore into the gravel next to him, and both rear tires popped. The leader took a breath, dodged to the side of the wheel, and cut the first guard in half with two staccato bursts from his rifle; then paused, waiting for more shooting. He was rewarded by another explosion and rolled clear of the truck, firing as he did. The second guard flew backwards and slammed against the wall, dropping his weapon in the process. The leader let loose another burst for good measure, obliterating the man's head. He heard another few pops from below – the pistol again – and then the mine fell silent as his ear bud came to life.

"This is Neptune. I'm hit, but the charges are in place."

The leader tapped his bud. "How bad?"

"Shoulder. Not terminal. I can still make it to the rendezvous. Took down two guards." Neptune's voice sounded strained but calm.

"Any more near you?"

"Negative, but I see lights approaching, so we can expect pursuit."

"We can't wait for you if you get stalled." The leader's voice was flat, emotionless.

"Roger. I'll be there."

Another glance at his watch told him they had three minutes until rendezvous. He reached into his backpack, removed a can of red spray paint, and approached the fallen guards, eyes scanning the periphery, his M4 at the ready. Once at the shack, he pulled on a pair of latex gloves and popped the cap off the paint, tossing it onto the floor, and then carefully sprayed the message that would be found on the shack walls. Finished, he took a towel from the sack, wiped down the can, and threw it outside onto the gravel, next to the first butchered security guard's corpse. Stepping back to inspect his work, he nodded to himself, and then extracted a phone from his pocket and took several photos.

If the company or the government tried to hush up the attack on the mine, the images would go live on the internet within twenty-four hours, leaving them with no option other than to acknowledge that the unrest in the area had grown to the point where the sustainability of the operation was in question. Two similar painted messages had been left by his men in other strategic locations, so there could be no doubt about the apparent motives of the attackers.

The sound of powerful truck engines revved from within the grounds as the night security force rallied, and he spotted two vehicles heading his way. Quickly calculating that he had no more than thirty seconds, he jogged five yards from the gate and withdrew three grenades from his bag, waiting for the trucks to come within range. When the headlights played across the bed of the truck he'd abandoned, he pulled the pin on the first orb and threw it as hard as he could, watching with satisfaction as it sailed beyond the truck and onto the road.

The explosion slowed the approaching guards, and when he lobbed the second and third grenades they stopped, any appetite for engagement quashed by the blasts. He didn't wait to see the results of the next detonations but instead ran to the blackened edge of the road that led down the mountain and made his way steadily into the darkness, the mine entrance receding behind him. His com line crackled into life again – his second-in-command quietly informed him that all the men were now at the rendezvous point. He acknowledged, then turned and withdrew a remote transmitter from his pocket as he faced the entrance. In a lightning motion he lifted it over his head as he flipped away a small plastic protective cover with his thumb and depressed the button.

A shuddering blast shattered the night as the explosives were triggered simultaneously from locations around the complex. The sky over the mine became an inferno as fire sailed into the air from the eight carefully chosen areas. The pipeline that carried the precious ore was ruined in two different spots, the communications facility destroyed, and worst of all for the operation, the crushers were hopelessly mangled by the strategically placed charges. Secondary explosions from fuel tanks and flammable liquid drums sounded from further down the ridge, but he had already turned and resumed his run.

They needed to get clear of the mine. The hard part was done. In a few minutes three more of his men would detonate their assigned targets nine miles down the mountain, further crippling the pipeline. He wasn't worried short-term about pursuit from the mine's remaining guards – his designated team members had placed spiked anti-tire countermeasures on the road to incapacitate any chase vehicles. When he reached the rendezvous spot two minutes later, the men were all accounted for, Neptune with a field dressing on his shoulder, and the engines of two dark-colored vans purred softly in the high-altitude atmosphere. All eyes followed him as he walked to the driver's door of the lead van and shrugged off his backpack, then tossed it together with his rifle into the cargo area. He climbed behind the wheel and gestured to his men.

"Let's get the hell out of here."

Two more explosions echoed from far down the mountain. The pipeline had been ruptured, right on schedule. The mercenaries clambered into the vehicles, requiring no further encouragement, and within seconds they were rolling down the road, lights extinguished, navigating through the drizzle using night vision goggles until they were five miles away, near the closest company town. Once in Tembagapura they'd ditch the vans and switch to motorcycles, then disappear, their work on the island done.

Gravel crunched under the oversized tires as they headed away from the chaos they had caused, the glow of Tembagapura below them beckoning through the haze of light rain. Three other attacks had been launched against the Indonesian military's nearby outposts, concurrent with their assault on the mine, ensuring confusion and mayhem to cover their escape. By the time the full extent of the damage was understood, they would be aboard the helicopters that awaited them in a secluded field and on their way to Mopah airport, where two prop planes would whisk them to the New Guinea side of the island, and from there onward to Australia, where they'd lie low in Sydney and await further orders – richer by five million dollars for a single night's bloody work.

CHAPTER 1

Alan watched from his window seat as the jumbo jet lumbered through the rough air on final approach to the international airport in Buenos Aires. He rubbed a hand across the two-day growth on his face and stretched his arms overhead, trying to compensate for ten hours wedged into an economy seat on the red-eye flight from Mexico City. Sleep had been impossible, and he reconciled himself to another long day of travel; while delayed on the ground in Mexico, he'd booked a fare on the ferry from Buenos Aires to Montevideo, Uruguay, for later that day.

The runway lights appeared below him and the wheels smoked on the tarmac as the huge plane rolled down the long strip, decelerating as the landscape rocketed by. A stewardess came over the public address system, welcomed them to Ministro Pistarini International Airport, and advised the passengers to remain seated. Alan checked his watch and reset it to local time, calculating how long it would take to get from the airport on the farthest outskirts of the sprawling city to the ferry terminal near the domestic airport on the waterfront. If customs wasn't too much of a problem, he could make it. Just.

The flight was three and a half hours late due to a mechanical problem before takeoff, and the uneasy, packed plane had been forced to return to the gate while a maintenance crew scrambled to fix a faulty warning sensor. Nobody had been allowed off, and every half hour the pilot had calmly assured them over the speakers that it wouldn't be long now – a transparent lie that had increased everyone's annoyance as each hour rolled into another. When the plane finally took off, the air was stagnant and the passengers restless, their already long flight turned into a marathon by a faulty piece of wiring.

The big plane pulled into the gate and things moved faster, although Alan was at the rear of the cabin and so one of the last to disembark. Fortunately he only had his carry-on bag, and Argentine immigration was efficient, so within half an hour he was instructing a taxi driver to take him to the ferry as quickly as possible.

A slum near the city fringes, constructed from tarpaper and old pallets, marred the landscape, and a cloud of exhaust and smoke lingered over the area like a noxious fog. The taxi raced past it on the modern highway, and soon they were in Buenos Aires proper, where a seemingly endless procession of dingy high-rise apartments cluttered the skyline, indifferently built to provide affordable housing in one of the world's most populated cities.

Alan found his cell phone and powered it on, and once it acquired service he saw he had seven missed calls. He checked his voice mail and there were two messages from Jet: brief, as was her style, the second tinged with concern that he hadn't picked up yet. He checked the timing – the last attempt had been twenty-five minutes ago, but when he pressed redial, the line just buzzed faintly, with no ringing. It could take a while for his phone to be able to place international calls, he knew from experience, and he made a mental note to try Jet one last time before he got on the boat – her flight should be just taking off, but if it had been delayed it was possible she would still have her phone on, and he could check in and verify that everything was okay.

It wound up taking over an hour to arrive at the ferry building, by which time Alan's stomach was rumbling – the food on the plane had been marginal, at best, and it had been all he could do to force himself to choke it down. He looked at his watch again and hoped he would have enough time to grab lunch; even the worst Argentine diner would be light years ahead of the plane's fare.

He handed the driver a wad of local currency, walked quickly to the ticket windows, and claimed his place on the ship with another slug of bills. The attendant advised him that the ferry was boarding – that he should hurry – it would be taking off in twenty minutes, and the late afternoon run was especially crowded, even though the company was running a much larger boat than usual while the smaller catamaran that ordinarily did the trip underwent maintenance.

Alan moved to the line and stood patiently with the rest of the crowd waiting to go through security and embark the huge vessel. As he shifted from foot to foot, he had a distinctly uneasy feeling, and he swung around to scan the boarding area. On the far side of the long main hall two men turned to look at the ship, but not before Alan caught one staring at him.

The shorter of the two said something to his partner, who laughed and then pointed at the boat. Alan's eyes continued roving over the crowd, aware that after so much time in the air, sleep deprived, his sensory warning system could be misfiring. A woman near the magazine stand was looking at him, then glanced away as his eyes caught hers. She returned the copy of *Vogue* she'd been browsing through before selecting another and going to pay.

"Hey, buddy. Move up, eh?"

The man behind him, stocky, dressed in a cheap suit, gestured with his head at Alan, who was now ten feet from the person in front of him in the boarding line. Alan met his gaze with red eyes and mumbled an apology before shuffling forward. Another scan of the salon, and the woman was gone, as were the two men by the window.

Alan sighed and scratched his face. His mind was playing tricks on him. Nobody knew he was in Buenos Aires, much less traveling to Uruguay via boat. The stress of the last forty-eight hours was messing with his head – and the blow to his skull wasn't helping. It was still hurting, and he reflexively touched it, then winced. The Russian mystery man had clobbered him with his pistol butt, and when he'd dropped to the ground, he'd hit his head again. The examining doctor had advised Alan to stay in bed for a week – counsel he'd immediately ignored, preferring to get as far from Los Angeles as possible.

The line proceeded forward, and he placed his carry-on bag and phone onto the conveyor belt so security could be reassured he wasn't smuggling guns or heroin to Montevideo. The process was cursory and superficial, more for show than anything. If he'd wanted, he knew from experience that he could have carried on a carbon fiber knife that would have never shown up. What he would have done with it on the ferry was a different story – it wasn't like a plane, which could be used as a flying weapon.

Once aboard he found a seat by a window and looked back at the terminal. The two men had returned and were looking at the ship. A tingle of apprehension tickled his stomach, and he fought down the anxiety. He needed sleep, not paranoia. So there were two men watching the ferry. There were probably hundreds throughout the day, waiting for passengers to get off, or to wave at departing loved ones.

As if sensing his thoughts, both men turned and walked away from the oversized glass windows. The engines increased in volume once the lines were detached from the dock and secured onboard.

Then they were underway, the steady thrumming of the engines at idle turning into a dull roar as the revs increased, heading out to what appeared to be open ocean but was in reality a huge bay created by the Rio de Plata meeting the Atlantic. A hundred and twenty miles north across the water, Montevideo, their destination, awaited his arrival.

He fished his phone from his pocket and placed another call. This time it rang, but then a message announced that the recipient was out of the service area – so Jet was now in the air, winging her way to Buenos Aires. He texted her that he'd gone on to Uruguay, and then sent a brief email to her blind account to the same effect, asking her to call his cell once she arrived in Argentina and explaining that he'd meet up with her in Montevideo.

The boat gathered speed, and soon it was flying across the bay at over thirty knots. Alan watched Buenos Aires recede into the distance as they headed northeast, parallel to the coast, the current in their favor in this direction as the river's contents spilled towards the sea. The ride was nearly flat, and once the snack bar was open he bought a sandwich and soda and took a seat near another window.

His intention was to get a hotel in Montevideo and sleep overnight, and then the next day meet with Jet once she'd made the trip...*and then what?* The truth was that he didn't have a plan beyond that. He'd decided spontaneously to leave Los Angeles after the terrorist strike and turn in his retirement notice to the Mossad once he understood what his future held. Beyond getting to South America and waiting for Jet, he hadn't thought through the rest of it. A lot depended upon Jet and what she wanted to do. They'd need to find someplace new in which to start over with Hannah after disappearing off the radar...but after that, the future became cloudy.

His thoughts turned to Jet. His brother's ex-girlfriend, the mother to his brother's child, as beautiful as any woman he'd seen, and as deadly as nightshade. Alan shared that quality with her; he was an expert at only a couple of things – search-and-destroy missions and undercover operations where he was in constant peril. What would he do now that he had quit the Mossad? Open a convenience store? Get a factory job? Sell insurance?

Alan wasn't too worried about his immediate financial future; he'd managed to sock away a fair amount of money in his operational accounts while he was in Yemen, and never spent any of his salary, so he was okay for a few years. And of course, Jet was loaded now – but that wasn't his money, and he was conflicted over being dependent upon her. One way or another, he'd need to find a way to earn a living. But that would take care of itself, he supposed. First he needed to understand where he would be in a week; then he'd worry about long term.

There was definitely chemistry between them. She was an intoxicating collection of contradictions, and after years of being alone he was powerfully drawn to her. It seemed like the attraction was mutual, but he wasn't going to force anything. Whatever happened, if anything, would happen at its own pace.

His food eaten, he returned to his seat and dozed, the gentle rocking of the ship bringing the fatigue from all the travel home. He was just beginning to dream about captivating emerald eyes when a hand shook his shoulder. He started, and instinctively grabbed the shaker's wrist and prepared to deliver a strike, then relaxed when he saw it was one of the crew.

Alan released him and forced himself to full awareness.

"What is it?" he demanded groggily.

"I'm sorry, sir...we're looking for Angel Perozzi," the crewman asked.

"And?"

"Are you Señor Perozzi?"

"No. Why are you looking for him?"

The crew member looked conflicted, then shrugged. "We're matching up travelers with vehicles, and he's the only one unaccounted for – his truck is onboard, but he hasn't submitted his paperwork. It's not a big deal. Thank you for your time," he said, turning to go to the next row of seats.

"Oh, okay. What kind of vehicle?"

The crewman checked his clipboard. "Just says a truck."

"Do you often have this kind of thing happen?" Alan asked, the tickle of apprehension returning.

"Actually, it's my first time. I've only been working here for six months, though."

"Well, good luck. Where are the cars located, anyway?"

"They're on the lowest level, but the area is locked until just a few minutes before we get into port, so nobody can go down there. Company rules."

"Ah. It's not like he could go for a swim, so you'll find him. Why don't you just announce something over the public address system?"

"It's on the blink. Oh, well, have a good nap, sir. Again, sorry I disturbed you."

"No problem," Alan said, then closed his eyes again, his brain racing.

It was probably nothing. The driver was in the bathroom or asleep somewhere on the huge ferry. Still, a buzz of anxiety did a gymnastics routine in his stomach. His operational training had taught him to never overlook even the smallest anomalies. They could be the difference between life and death.

But you're not on a mission anymore. You're done, out of the game. This is just residual tension from the terrorist near miss, or a by-product of being slammed in the head.

He tried to go back to sleep, but his mind wouldn't let him. He shifted to get comfortable, but his thoughts were whirring, playing out scenarios. What did it mean? Could there be danger? If so, from whom and why?

After ten minutes of fruitless non-sleep, he resigned himself to the restless fugue state that now defined his reality and cracked an eye open. The steward was returning, having completed his search of that level. Alan caught his glance, and the man shook his head with another shrug, then approached the stairs to the next level and ascended.

Alarm was now more prominent in Alan's awareness. Maybe everything was fine. Or maybe something was badly wrong.

He groaned audibly, then made his decision.

One way or another, he needed to get to the lower decks and find the truck belonging to the missing driver. Just to reassure himself. That was all. It was probably nothing, and he was just projecting, looking for an emergency, a threat where none existed. He knew that was a side effect of living in constant danger, undercover in the field, as he had for years with the terrorist cell in Yemen. You got home and were mowing the lawn, and then became convinced that the neighbor had you under surveillance, or that every car rolling down the street carried gunmen out to terminate you. It went with the territory.

Still, it couldn't hurt to look.

Alan stood, shouldered his bag, and moved to the stairs that led down to the main deck level. He checked his watch – they'd been underway for a little over an hour, so he still had two and a half to go before they arrived in Uruguay.

A little peek would take hardly any time at all.

Just a glance. Nothing more.

To put his mind at ease.

He just needed to figure out how to get into a locked cargo hold, possibly under guard, on a boat plowing through the water at high speed, so he could chase phantoms.

Piece of cake.

CHAPTER 2

On the main deck, Alan wandered the length of the boat, trying to get a sense for the traffic as well as the number of crew members patrolling the area. At the halfway point he spotted the stairwell leading to the car transport area, but it had a chain across it. Fortunately, almost all the passengers were on the upper levels watching the distant shoreline race by, so after a few moments of skulking nearby, he ducked beneath the chain and made his way silently down the steps.

Deeper in the ship's bowels, the steady rumble of the engines was more pronounced. Thirty feet from the stairwell, a set of double doors with a sign over it announced the parking area, and he edged towards them, alert for any signs of life. As far as he could tell, there was nobody on this level other than he.

The doors were locked, but the bolt was an older model, primitive, and would pose a slim deterrent. The angle of the latch made jimmying it with a credit card a cinch, so he retrieved one from his slim wallet and had the door open within seconds.

The interior of the vehicle hold was dark, and Alan had to use his cell phone screen for illumination, holding the phone in front of him, looking for the trucks. The distinctive odor of gasoline and motor oil blended with rubber and stale exhaust, creating an oppressive atmosphere he would be happy to escape as soon as he set his mind to rest.

Near the bow, he saw several distinctive outlines of truck cargo boxes and moved to them with deliberate purpose. A dark blue truck with the logo of a multi-national heavy equipment manufacturer was the closest, but a cursory inspection yielded nothing suspicious. He'd been afraid that he might need to deal with padlocks on the boxes, but there were none – likely some sort of customs requirement.

The next truck was empty, returning from Argentina without anything inside.

The third truck's forty foot cargo box had a lock on it.

The hair on Alan's neck prickled, and the sense of mild anxiety in his gut blossomed into a full-blown attack. None of the other trucks had locks. The anomaly was a bad sign.

He studied the padlock. An industrial model, fairly hard to pick.

But not impossible.

The only problem being that he didn't have a set of picks.

Alan moved to the cars and scanned the interiors for anything helpful. After rummaging through five vehicles, he started popping the trunks, hoping for a toolkit. The law of averages said that at least one vehicle would have some sort of tools he could use.

His efforts were rewarded by an older Ford. A red box rested in the trunk with a full set of what looked like plumbing and electrical-related tools. He quickly found several that would serve his purposes, along with some stiff wire, and set about creating a set of primitive picks, bending the heavy-gauge metal with two sets of pliers and snipping off the lengths with wire cutters when he was done.

Three minutes later he was back at the truck, slipping the crude implements into the lock, hoping to get the tumblers to cooperate. A bead of sweat ran down his forehead and hung off the tip of his nose as he concentrated on the task, and after several false starts the mechanism sprang open with a snap.

He slid the lock out of the lever's hasp and placed it to one side of the bumper, then rolled the door up with a heave. The noise sounded like cannon fire in the enclosed space, echoing off the metal walls. Alan cringed, then forgot his caution when a powerful stench hit him. The apprehension in his gut exploded into a supernova of alarm as his inadequate cell phone illuminated the sacks, stacked high. He knew that smell all too well.

The door to the hold opened with a loud clatter and he ducked below the level of the surrounding cars. The harsh glare of the lights came on with a flicker, and then a voice called out.

"We know someone's in here. Show yourself. There's nowhere to go – only one way out," a man's voice warned.

He peered up at the cargo box. It was just a matter of time until they spotted the open truck door and the cars with their trunks open. He debated doing as instructed and explaining what he was doing, but quickly rejected it. He had to figure out a compelling way to warn the crew without being personally involved and drawing attention to himself. Which meant that he needed to get to the other side of the bay. If he could slip by the crew when they were occupied with the truck, he had a chance.

"Come on. It's no good. Show yourself," another voice urged. So there were at least two.

Footsteps rang out from the metal floor, approaching cautiously. Hoping he wouldn't be heard over the din, Alan inched away from the truck and moved to the nearest wall, then slid behind a sedan, using the vehicles as cover. He would have to time it perfectly to get to the door as they reached the truck, and it was a lot of ground to travel – at least a hundred yards.

The only positive was that the crewmen were not trying to conceal their approach. The sound of their boots on the deck rang out like drumbeats, even over the engine noise. Alan slipped along the wall on the opposite end of the bay, crouching behind the cars, peering through the windshields to see where they were.

"Hey. Sergio. Look at this," one of the men whispered from ten yards away, and then two more sets of footsteps moved towards him. They'd seen the open trunks. It was time to make his move.

He scurried in the direction of the doors, and was three quarters of the way there when his bag bumped against one of the vehicles with an audible thump. His breath caught in his throat as he froze, waiting for an indication that they'd heard, and then after a few seconds he relaxed. He'd have to be more careful – the fatigue was making him careless.

The exit in sight, Alan picked up his pace. He was almost there when a voice called out from behind him.

"Freeze."

Alan weighed running, but stifled the impulse. He slowly set his bag down by his side, then raised his hands over his head. Boots approached, and he listened intently, trying to time his turn – it would be child's play to disarm the crew member, assuming he had a gun, which was a good bet based on the shouted order.

His body tensed, ready to spin and knock the crewman's legs from under him, and then everything went black, the distinctive *thunk* of a wooden nightstick on the already brutalized back of his injured head Alan's last impression before he lost consciousness.

Alan came to lying on the floor of a small room with metal walls and a tall, rectangular window. The entire chamber was painted a dingy gray and reeked of mildew. Three men stood near the steel door, their arms crossed, watching him warily. He reached around to his head and gingerly probed the new bump, then looked at his fingers. There was a small amount of blood, but it could have been worse.

"He's conscious," the smallest of the crew members said, his hatchet face cruel in the dim light.

"Doesn't look so good, does he?" the man next to him asked, shaking his head, and then addressed Alan. "You're under arrest. You'll be taken into police custody once we dock in Montevideo, in…" – the speaker checked his watch – "one and a half hours."

The room swam as Alan tried to sit up. He waited a few seconds and tried again, this time successfully. He didn't say anything, remaining silent while he gathered his wits.

The third crew member tossed him a white towel. "Hold that against your head. It's not too bad, but you'll want to clot the blood."

Alan reached for where it had landed on the floor, and his entire being radiated pain. He balled the towel up and held it against the bump, then studied the men with bloodshot eyes before speaking.

"This isn't what you think," he began.

"Sure it isn't. I mean, maybe we need to call Sherlock Holmes, or something. Let's see, we have a bunch of cars broken into, a truck broken into, a lock picked…no, it's a tough one to figure out, all right," the smaller crew member spat. His companions chuckled.

"The cars were all open. I didn't break in."

"Save it for the police. Maybe they'll care about the technical distinction. I don't."

"You don't understand. We're in danger. Everyone on the boat. The truck–"

"Danger? What the hell are you going on about?" the middle man interrupted.

"The truck. It's filled with fertilizer. It's a bomb."

"Sure it is."

"I'm serious. The ammonium nitrate in the fertilizer acts as an explosive if the right combination of ingredients are used. That truck has a bunch of fertilizer in it. I'd bet anything there's a detonator and a shitload of fuel or maybe Semtex stored inside. If I'm right, then it would be a big enough blast to destroy this ship."

The men exchanged glances.

"Ah, so you're not a thief at all. You're actually saving mankind from...from what, again? A shit truck? Please."

"It's true."

"Work on your story for the cops."

Alan shook his head in frustration. A bad idea – nausea reminded him why.

"Then how did I know to look in the truck?" Alan countered.

"Gee, that's a tough one. We've been asking everyone whether they were the driver of a truck in the hold. So let's see. You concocted a story, on the fly, using this preposterous scenario as a cover for being a thief? Works for me." The men laughed again.

"You need to listen."

"No, I think you need to realize the game is over. We caught you red-handed breaking into cars. You had picks. And you have three passports in different names. If that doesn't sound like a criminal, nothing does. So save the cock and bull story. Nobody's buying."

"This is a huge mistake. Everyone's in danger."

"I know. I feel it. The world is going to end soon. It's the Mayans." More laughter.

Alan's voice strengthened. "Let me talk to the captain."

"Why, sure. We'll escort you to him shortly. Meanwhile, can I get you anything? Some sorbet? Champagne, perhaps?"

"Listen–"

"Enough of this. I'll go down and look at the truck, just to confirm you're full of shit. But don't bore me with these fantasies any longer."

"No...if you don't know what you're doing, you could set off any device–"

"Oh, right. Because the truck's a bomb. Someone wants to bomb the ferry to Uruguay. For what reason, exactly?"

Alan turned his head too quickly and winced from pain. "I...I don't know..." he confessed. Even to his own ears it sounded weak.

"Riiiiight. Just because." The shorter man looked at his companions. "We're done here. Lock him in," he said, then turned and opened the door. The other men followed him out.

"You're making a mistake—" His protestation was cut short by the clank of the steel hatch slamming shut, followed by the scrape of the deadbolt locking.

Alan knew he was right. The fertilizer, the lock, the missing driver… And the fools were going to let it happen, killing everyone.

He had to get out of there. He'd done his best and tried to warn them. Alan had no doubt the truck was a bomb, and if these idiots wanted to wind up murdering everyone on board with their recklessness, he might not be able to stop them, but he certainly wasn't going to be one of the statistics.

Rising unsteadily to his feet, he moved to the large rectangular window and studied the glass and the surrounding seal, then was overcome by a dizzy spell and had to sit again. Judging by the distance of the wake and the engine noise, he was near the waterline towards the stern. What he could do with that information remained to be seen, but one way or another, he would have to do something.

CHAPTER 3

"He's right – it's fertilizer," Gustavo, the crew chief, muttered to his subordinates. The two hapless crew members exchanged troubled glances.

"So it's possible that this is a bomb?" one of them asked.

"I don't believe that for a second. I think he just made up a story with whatever was at hand, so he didn't look like he was doing exactly what he was doing," Gustavo said. "Didn't you ever see that movie? *Keyser Söze*," he groaned the name in a hoarse voice. "A pathological liar."

"But why? It'll all fall apart when the cops interrogate him. What happens when they confirm it's not a bomb once we get to port?"

"He can use that as his defense – he thought it was, and was afraid it was, but turned out to be wrong. That way he can claim he was being a hero; only a misguided one."

"Why don't we just go through the truck now and show it to be false?"

"It's not our truck. We don't have authorization to go through it – it's someone else's property. We have no probable cause. And most of all, because I don't feel like trying to dig through twenty thousand pounds of poop." Gustavo shook his head. "Speaking of which, have we found the driver yet?"

Both crew members shook their heads. "No. We sort of got sidetracked by this."

"That's the only troubling piece. Find the driver, and I'll stop being even slightly worried," Gustavo instructed.

"We'll get back to it." The first crewman hesitated. "What should we do now?"

"I'll tell the captain and we'll radio ahead to port so they have a couple of police there to take him into custody. The multiple passports in different names has to be illegal. Whatever he's doing, he's up to no good. That's undeniable. He got into the auto hold in the first place, which means he picked that lock too. No, this is a bad guy. I just wish we'd found the damned truck driver…"

"Should we close this back up?" one of the men asked, motioning at the truck cargo door with his head.

"Might as well. The stink isn't doing anything for my appetite."

≈≈

After forty-five minutes of stripping it away, sliver by sliver, the window seal was almost entirely removed. Alan's hands were cramping from the effort, but he kept at it, keenly aware that he could be blown into another galaxy at any moment. The amount of fertilizer in that forty-foot cargo container was enough to vaporize even a ship of this size. The thought spurred him on. His headache was still bad but the dizziness and disorientation had passed, and he felt stronger than when he'd regained consciousness.

Ten minutes later the glass gave, and he was able to kick the heavy inch-thick pane into the sea. He stuck his head out and immediately realized that the ferry was still at least twenty miles from shore and moving at a tremendous clip. It would be suicide to jump into the water from the side of the ship – he'd be sucked into the props and chewed into hamburger if he couldn't get far enough away from the boat.

If he was lucky enough to avoid the propellers, the water temperature was probably too cold to stay in for the dozen hours it would take to swim to shore. He knew from prior experience that if it was fifty degrees Fahrenheit, the best he could expect absent a flotation device would be to stay alive for five to six hours – and he'd be virtually useless for the last three, even though he was in peak physical condition.

That didn't leave him many options.

But at least he now had a means to escape the locked room.

He pulled himself halfway out the window and looked up. There were small cavities in the ship's hull that would make easy holds, although with a nearly forty-mile-per-hour wind buffeting him, it would be tough. Glancing out one last time, the wind lashing his face, he reached overhead, grabbed the first hold, pulled himself up. All he had to do was make it twelve feet and he would be just below the main deck level, where there appeared to be a small ledge he could traverse to get to the rear of the ship.

Salt crusted the exterior of the hull from where sea spray had dried, leaving a slippery film. It was all he could do to maintain his grip as he pulled himself higher, and then his feet found an indentation and he was able to use his legs. He realized that he was completely exposed, a flyspeck on the side of the mammoth ship, and that the slightest miscalculation could end in disaster.

When his fingers finally curled around the edge of the main deck ledge, he felt a return of the dizziness, and it required every bit of his strength to haul himself the last few feet. The slim lip he found himself clenching led back thirty feet to an exterior deck on the stern, where he could just see a lifeboat on a crane, as well as other emergency equipment. Inch by inch he crept back until he was crouched under the lifeboat. His watch told him that he was twenty-five minutes from port, which meant he was probably still fifteen miles from shore, but he didn't want to risk being on the ferry for another second.

Alan groped at the lifejackets and hurriedly pulled one on, grabbed a second vest for additional buoyancy, and climbed over the railing. With a final look behind him at the ship, he faced the wake trailing the big boat and threw himself into space.

The icy cold hit him just after the shock of striking the surface feet first jarred his spine. Water rushed over him, and then he was bobbing in the four-foot swells, batted around in the white froth that trailed the ferry cutting its way through the seas. The extra life vest was floating twenty feet away. He pulled himself towards it with measured strokes, eyes following the boat as it continued to Montevideo.

༺༻

"Man overboard! We have a man overboard," the crew chief shouted at the captain on the bridge.

"How is that possible? We're completely enclosed."

"One of the passengers saw a man fall in from the stern platform and reported it just now."

"Shit. All right. I'm going to put the drives in neutral, let her come to a stop, then circle around. Prepare to launch one of the lifeboats," the captain ordered, and then pulled the two transmissions from their forward position and disengaged them, allowing the momentum to slow.

※

Alan watched as the ferry seemed to lose power, the wake from the stern stopping as it continued to move forward, and then the ship began to slowly turn, perhaps a half mile ahead of him. He realized that his escape must have been noticed, and registered the change of course even as he weighed his options. He could jettison the life vest and start swimming – a lousy choice, but one that would ensure he was far enough from the bright red vests so he couldn't be seen. The problem would be surviving while he stayed afloat – the clock was already ticking on hypothermia.

But there was another way, he realized, and he hastily pulled off the vest and removed his jacket. He slid his arms through the straps and then donned his jacket again before zipping it over the vest; now he blended with the surrounding water, the red completely concealed. It would take a while for the boat to alter its course and make its way back, by which time he could be a quarter mile away. As long as he didn't splash around and increase his profile in the water, the deception might work.

The ferry was beginning its turn when its sides exploded outwards, the metal distending and then blowing open with a massive fireball that hurled debris and black smoke into the sky. Alan watched in horror as the ship seemed to break in half even as the blast continued rippling through the hull as if in slow motion. The stern pointed straight into the air as the hull cracked at the midpoint, and then pieces of debris came sailing through the air, splashing into the sea between him and the sinking vessel. He was shocked at the speed with which the two sections disappeared into the depths, and in less than a minute there was nothing left but pieces of floating wreckage.

The mainland was just visible in the far distance of the horizon, but even so he knew that the smoke would be caught by the Montevideo authorities and a host of boats dispatched to hunt for survivors. There were actually a few pleasure craft in the distance, maybe five miles away, and he was confident they would soon be near enough for him to flag one down.

Fifteen minutes later the first made it to the vicinity – a ninety-foot commercial trawler with a bright orange hull, rusting through in patches. The captain saw him waving from the relatively calm seas, and in a few more minutes the crew dragged him onboard, the life vest already jettisoned once he was sure they'd spotted him.

The captain spent a half hour searching in the water, but didn't find anybody else, and seemed genuinely concerned when Alan described an explosion that had capsized his small boat and how he'd struck his head somewhere in the process. One of the crew inspected the bloody bump and the captain made a course for the mainland, anxious to get Alan medical attention. He radioed the Uruguayan authorities to let them know he was coming in, and they agreed to meet him at the dock to rush Alan to the hospital and take his statement.

The boat lumbered towards land at eleven knots, and soon the crew was stowing the lines and preparing to dock for the evening before heading back out the following day for another try at the ocean's bounty. Alan sat near the pilothouse watching their progress, and when they were a mile from port amidst the container cargo vessels, awaiting clearance to enter the harbor, he slipped to the stern, unseen by the captain and crew, who were focused on their nearing destination. He took three deep breaths and dived into the water, figuring that now he could easily swim the distance to land and disappear, an unidentified survivor who would forever remain a mystery.

He treaded water until the boat was a couple hundred yards away and then struck out for the shore on the western side of the port. An hour later Alan dragged himself onto a small beach as the sun set over the city. He was dripping, cold, and had little more than the clothes on his back – the sole witness to the worst disaster in the port's history.

CHAPTER 4

Jet waited in line at customs in Buenos Aires, the long flight from Europe finally over. The queue inched forward as the tired travelers shuffled like chain gang prisoners toward the bank of immigration officials working at a snail's pace. Even with the excruciating delays, she was happy to be on the ground, and once her passport had been stamped and she was allowed to use her cell, she powered it on and waited for service.

The little phone beeped at her, indicating she had a text. She pressed a series of buttons and studied the screen intently. Thank God. Alan was okay, and hadn't answered before because of a flight delay. But he'd decided to skip Buenos Aires and proceed to Montevideo, which changed her plans, too. There was no point in staying overnight if he'd already left, so she proceeded to the taxis and took the first car, instructing the driver to head to the ferry building near downtown.

She checked the time and saw that it would be dark fairly soon – customs had taken almost an hour, which might mean that the last ferry of the afternoon had already left. But she seemed to recall from her perusal of the schedule on her last boat ride from Uruguay that there was a late one that departed after dinner. If so, then she would catch it. If not, she was only a few blocks from some of Buenos Aires' best hotels, and would spend the night and take the first ferry in the morning.

Jet tried Magdalena's phone again, but there was no answer. Her agitation level increased, but nothing like before – just as there had been a perfectly good explanation for Alan not answering, there was doubtless one for Magdalena not picking up. Unlike at the airport, she didn't feel the same sense of dread she'd had when boarding her flight – Alan's message had calmed her nerves.

All of the rush hour traffic was headed out of the city, but even so, once they approached downtown things slowed to a crawl, and the final three miles took as long as the first fifteen from the airport. When they finally arrived at the terminal, Jet couldn't wait to get out of the cab. She handed the driver a fistful of pesos and hauled her bag out of the back seat.

Soldiers toting machine guns ringed the ferry building – odd, as they hadn't been in evidence when she'd been there less than two weeks ago. Perhaps some sort of civil disobedience or protest had occurred since then – a perennial problem as the Argentine economy continued its slow-motion train wreck since the financial crisis. The stone-faced soldiers barely glanced at her as she moved through the oversized doors and approached the ticket booth, where a noisy throng milled. An old woman sobbed as her family stood around, trying to comfort her. Jet pushed her way through the agitated crowd until she reached an open window and greeted the young woman behind the bullet-proof glass.

"*Buenas tardes.* Is there another ferry going to Montevideo tonight?" Jet asked.

"No, and because of the incident, probably not tomorrow, either," the woman curtly informed her.

Jet did a double take.

"Incident?"

"Ah, you haven't heard. It's the ferry. There's been an explosion."

"What?" Jet's blood froze. "Which ferry?"

"The one to Montevideo. It exploded an hour ago near Uruguay. They're saying it was a terrorist attack, but nobody really knows. It just happened, so it's all speculation."

Jet's heart rate increased to trip hammer speed, and her pulse pounded in her ears. She choked back bile, the wave of nausea coming over her as the woman finished pronouncing the last syllable.

She cleared her throat. "What time did that ferry leave?"

"It was the one that took off four hours ago. The afternoon boat."

"Good Lord. That's terrible. What about survivors?" Jet asked woodenly.

"I don't have any official information on that, but you can listen to the news for updates." The woman pointed to a flat-panel television suspended above the nearby bar that a large group was standing near. A sincere anchorman was talking to a reporter in Uruguay, whose face was somber. Jet edged closer to hear the broadcast.

"…explosion was heard all the way in Montevideo, and the smoke from the blast could be seen with the naked eye. The Uruguayan navy is in the area, as are a host of other boats, but so far it doesn't look good. There's no trace of the ferry, and no known survivors," the reporter intoned.

The scene flipped to an aerial view of floating wreckage in the dark water, barely visible as the sun set, spotlights from the nearby ships and helicopters playing across the surface.

Five more minutes of coverage yielded no new information. The ship had exploded, the authorities had nothing definitive but were treating it as a terrorist attack, and the experts had ruled out an engine or fuel explosion due to the speed at which the vessel sank – if it had been a naturally occurring calamity, at least some passengers would have had time to move to the relative safety of the water and the lifeboats, so there would have been survivors.

Nine hundred and forty-seven people were believed dead – the number double what it would have been if the smaller catamaran that usually did the trek had been operating. The TV switched to interviews with gasping family members of passengers. Jet had seen enough. She pulled up Alan's text message again and looked at the time stamp – he'd sent it about the time the ferry would have been pulling away from the dock.

Her senses overloaded from the news of the explosion and the realization that Alan was dead. She shuffled to the exit doors like an automaton, hardly registering her surroundings. Alan had survived Yemen, countless hazardous missions, the Los Angeles bio-attack…only to die on a supposedly safe ferry ride across the bay?

It seemed surreal.

And yet the news was reporting real-time about the disaster, so it wasn't a mistake. He'd been in the wrong place at the wrong time. Sometimes life was like that – brutal, sudden, disastrous for apparently no reason. But why now? Why Alan?

Outside on the sidewalk she dialed Magdalena's phone again, automatically, only to have it ring before disconnecting. Jet swung around, looking at the boulevard that ran in front of the terminal, and forced herself to think. Now what?

Hannah. She needed to get to Hannah. That was the overriding priority.

But how could she get across the bay with no ferry service?

She knew there was a road that ran across the Rio de Plata and then across Uruguay to the coast, but that was an eight or more hour drive – she'd looked into it before, and while it was possible to do, it was unwieldy and time-consuming. It would mean renting a car and driving all night to get to Maldonado, a daunting proposition after having spent a dozen hours in the air and being disoriented from time changes.

Jet flagged down a taxi and asked to be taken to the nearby domestic airport – her best shot at chartering a plane. They arrived in eight minutes, and once she found herself standing outside the departure terminal, it struck her how chaotic and inefficiently she was behaving. She moved inside and asked the information kiosk for information on air charter companies, but was greeted with a blank stare. Not surprising – she'd realized the error of her assumption that the charter companies would be at the airport as the cab had pulled away.

An internet café sat at the side of the departure hall, and she strode to it and took the nearest open computer to do a hasty web search. There were three companies she could quickly find. She dialed each on her cell, but only got recordings. Given that it was after business hours, that made sense. She was screwed until the following morning, unless she wanted to drive.

Jet paid the attendant and approached a car rental booth on the arrivals side of the airport, and was informed that vehicles were available, and that, yes, she could take the car to Uruguay, but that it would require a significantly higher rental rate as well as additional insurance.

Now she had to choose – drive until dawn, or spend the night and try to get a plane the following day. She thought about it, then decided to drive. She could always find a motel en route if she became too tired, but at least she was guaranteed to see her daughter tomorrow; whereas if she had to arrange for a plane, it could realistically take most of the day, especially since any others with pressing business in Montevideo would be competing for the few available airplanes. Neither prospect was appealing, but she was too filled with nervous energy from the news of the explosion to just sit in a hotel all night hoping she could get some rest. Doing something, even if it was only driving, would keep her occupied.

Alan's face came unbidden to mind, and her eyes welled as she signed the requisite forms. She turned from the agent and blotted them with a tissue, then got ahold of herself. There would be plenty of time to mourn Alan's passing on the road; no need to put on a display for the passers-by.

The car was a red four-door Ford Mondeo, almost new, and the helpful lot attendant did his best to explain how to get out of Buenos Aires, using the complimentary map the agency provided. It took her an hour to negotiate her way to the city limits, but once she was clear the area became verdant and rural, mostly dark, the only illumination that from the highway lamps and the occasional other vehicle.

She stopped in the small town of Zarate and grabbed dinner at a local *parrilla*: a small outdoor restaurant with a wood-fired grill that specialized in every imaginable cut of meat, forcing herself to eat in spite of her lack of appetite. One thing she had learned in the field was to grab sustenance when you could – you never knew when you might be required to go days without a meal.

Once fed, she pointed the car north and pulled onto the two-lane highway that led to the border, resolved to keep going until she couldn't keep her eyes open. When she got to the frontier, the Argentines were courteous and efficient, but after crossing the river bridge that defined the natural border between the two countries she wasn't so lucky, and had to endure a seemingly endless search of her car. The Uruguayan officers apologized, but warned that since the ferry explosion she could expect periodic checkpoints and random searches – the entire country was on alert.

In the early hours of the morning she was nodding off, the incessant coverage on the radio failing to hold her interest as the same information was repeated over and over, and when she arrived at San José de Mayo, a few hours west of Montevideo, she found a simple hotel staffed by a cranky night clerk and rented a room.

As she drifted off to sleep, tossing and turning on the hard mattress, her final thoughts were of Alan and her daughter, Hannah. Now that Alan was dead, she and her daughter were truly alone in the world again, their brief connection to another human being severed by a random and chaotic universe's fickle nature.

CHAPTER 5

A raven peered down from its leafy perch at the large southern-styled home in Wolf Trap, Virginia, before the sound of a leaf blower startled it into flight. The tops of the trees rustled in the stiff breeze, the first signs of approaching autumn only just beginning to show in their color.

A quiet enclave of moneyed power, the area was among the most desirable real estate in the United States, a community of discretion and subdued wealth, where bankers rubbed shoulders with the power elite of the nation's capital over lattés, amid talk of polo and votes.

The nearest neighbor was an eighth of a mile away, and from behind the shoulder-high black-lacquered wrought-iron and stone perimeter wall, the immaculately manicured grounds spoke of precise attention and subtle good taste.

An unobtrusive gatehouse stood just inside the grounds, two men on twenty-four hour duty inside and another ten patrolling the property on round-the-clock shifts. No expense had been spared on the highest technology security measures, and the palatial plot was bristling with motion detectors, infra-red, and counter-surveillance jamming equipment. None of this raised any eyebrows in the low-key community, where dignitaries and high-powered movers and shakers routinely employed bodyguards and private security forces.

A landscaping crew was working on the hedges that lined the long drive as the electric double gates opened and a black American sedan pulled onto the cobblestones and rolled around the small bend before coasting to a stop near the front entrance. The driver leapt from behind the wheel and hurried around to get the rear passenger door. A heavy-set man in his forties got out, his gray suit slightly rumpled, and ascended the three steps to the colonial portico, eyeing the security cameras discreetly mounted under the porch eaves as he pressed the black doorbell. As he waited, he turned and surveyed the compound – it was park-like, completely private, and he wondered for the twentieth time what it was worth.

The door opened with a squeak, and a short, slight man in his fifties regarded him, his face flushed, his closely cropped salt-and-pepper hair slightly mussed – at odds with his impeccably tailored black suit, white shirt, and black tie.

"Sloan. Thanks for coming," the smaller man said.

"Standish. My pleasure, as always. I have nothing better to do than drop everything when he calls," Sloan said, his tone friendly, but his humorless blue eyes cold as glaciers.

"Ah. Just so," Standish murmured noncommittally.

"How's he doing?"

"He's not having a good day."

"Does he ever?"

"No."

Sloan entered the foyer with its gleaming hardwood floor and noted the incredible collection of antiques that adorned the living room off to the right. It was like an early American museum, some of the pieces worth multiples of the price of a luxury automobile. Standish motioned to Sloan to follow and led the familiar way to the elaborate stairway. The wheelchair lift was still at the top, and they stepped around it as they arrived at the landing.

"Is he now wheelchair bound?" Sloan asked.

"It's more comfortable for him. He can walk, but prefers not to."

Sloan took in that piece of information without comment.

"We leave the lights low all the time in his room. Your eyes will adjust," Standish warned.

"They were low last time I was here."

"They're lower now."

"How is he? He's added to the security detail," Sloan commented.

"About as well as can be expected, under the circumstances. And yes, he's got a small army around here. It makes him feel better. I think he feels exposed…"

"Paranoia?" Sloan asked.

"Hard to say, isn't it? Given what he's been through, do you blame him? The way I see it, it's always paranoia until something bad happens – then it's prudent planning."

"Fair point."

Standish approached an eight-foot-tall door at the end of the hall and knocked softly, then twisted the antique brass knob and swung it open. Sloan followed him into the room and closed the door quietly behind.

The air was warm and moist — a tall humidifier sat in a corner of the spacious room — more a suite, easily twenty-five by eighteen, with an attached bathroom. The windows were covered with heavy curtains, and the lighting was barely sufficient to illuminate the furniture. A ventilator and sundry medical machines sat in a bank at the far end, next to a custom king-sized bed with a reclining section that was raised so that the occupant could sit up comfortably. Oxygen tanks rested near the night table on the other side of the bed, and tubes and a hose for the mask that covered the occupant's face stretched to the machines.

"You wanted to talk to me?" Sloan asked, ignoring the gloom and the odd circumstances.

Standish cleared his throat. "He wanted to compliment you on a successful operation in Papua," Standish began. "He wants to make sure there are no loose ends, and that you have full faith in your men's discretion."

"Maybe he can tell me that?" Sloan suggested.

"Talking any more than necessary causes...complications. He asked me to speak for him, but he's anxious to hear your answers."

"I see." Sloan turned to the figure in the bed. "Everything went well. We had one wounded man, but he was tended to. The team's now in Australia, lying low, awaiting their next assignment. It might be difficult to use them again in Papua, but if we absolutely had to, we could probably find a way to insert them without raising eyebrows. The border between New Guinea and Indonesia is a joke, as is most everything there, from what I hear."

"There are no plans to use them again in Indonesia, but we'll want to keep that card in case we need to. There will be more to follow as we see how the situation develops," Standish said.

"Fair enough. They're at your disposal."

The figure in the bed motioned with one hand, a tentative gesture. Sloan came two steps closer, but Standish stood his ground.

"He wants to know about the other matter," Standish said.

"Yes. I suspect he does. There's nothing new to report. I have a group on the ground, waiting. But so far there's nothing going on. They have their instructions, though, and the men are the best. I'll get in touch with you the second I have something more."

The figure in the bed seemed to deflate, and waved weakly before stabbing at a button. The bed back reclined to a slightly less-than-flat position.

"Very well, then. We have a meeting in the next few days that will determine the next step in the Indonesian matter. The island is in chaos, and the Indonesians screwed the pooch on their response. The separatist movement is gaining traction even as the usual suspects are condemning the violence. But shutting down the mine was a masterstroke. They don't even have an estimate of when it could re-open," Standish said.

"Based on the damage we inflicted, not any time soon." Sloan wiped away a bead of sweat that was working its way down the side of his paunchy face from his hairline.

A croak emanated from the bed, which Standish seemed able to interpret.

"We need to keep the momentum up. The locals seem ill-prepared to do the minimum to keep the ball in the air."

"No surprise there."

Standish cleared his throat. "He wants to thank you for coming, and apologizes for not using the phone. You know how he feels about phones," Standish explained, as much for the figure's sake as for Sloan's.

"No problem. I'm not a big fan of them either."

Standish held out a hand, signaling that the meeting was over. Sloan nodded and walked to the door, careful to make as little noise as possible, sensitive to the precarious condition of the invalid to whom he'd just reported. Standish stepped around him and opened the door, and then they were out in the hall, the cool air refreshing after the jungle-like humidity in the bedroom. The door closed with a whisper, and they retraced their steps back downstairs.

"Try not to waste my time like that anymore, would you?" Sloan hissed, annoyed at having interrupted his day to give a three-minute summary.

"Shall I pass that sentiment along?" Standish asked, his tone conveying nothing.

Sloan thought better of it. "No. I'm just blowing off steam. A lot of crap on my plate."

"And a lot of money in your bank account. Let's not forget that."

Sloan's eyes narrowed. "Speaking of what we shouldn't forget, don't you think you're getting a little arch for a personal assistant? I don't work for you. You're just the go-between," he cautioned.

Standish smiled to himself. "My apologies. Sorry if I came off as...what was the word you used...*arch*? I didn't mean to. We're all under a lot of pressure, and I can assure you that I have my challenges to deal with attending to our friend, just as you have yours carrying out his...wishes. But I'd suggest you remember that I'm the closest person to him in the world, and he places a lot of weight on my views. You don't want me as an enemy. I'm not your adversary. Let's not go down that road, shall we?"

Sloan considered pushing the little shit down the stairs and jumping on his back and snapping his spine like a twig – but remembered the stakes and affected a neutral tone.

"And you don't want me as one, either, Standish. I think you know why."

"We're all aware of your position, Sloan. So let's play nice with each other, make the best of this situation, and press on to better days, okay? I don't need any more shit in my life than I already have. I'm just following orders. Don't make it any more than what it is."

They reached the ground floor and Standish led him to the front door.

"You want anything for the road? Soda? Water?"

"No, I'm good. Is it just my imagination, or is he getting worse?"

Standish stared at the scowling face of a naval officer in one of the dark oil paintings in the foyer and considered his words carefully. "I think he's about the same. Stable. Taking one day at a time. No worse, no better."

"Kind of a purgatory, then."

"Very much so. But we all have our crosses to bear."

Standish swung the door open and Sloan moved out onto the porch.

"I'll touch base as soon as I have something for you," Sloan said.

"That's all we can ask. Safe travels."

The door shut with a solid *thunk*, and Sloan frowned as he descended the stairs and approached his car, the driver waiting by its side. He turned and saw two of the security men watching him, the bulges of their shoulder holsters obvious under their windbreakers. He knew that hidden cameras tracked his every move, and somewhere an operator sat watching screens that captured almost every corner of the property.

All par for the course; but still, the place gave him the creeps, and the invalid was even creepier now than he had been before – which was hard to believe given his circumstances. But somehow, hooked up to machines, he still radiated a quiet menace that was palpable.

If Sloan had been in the same position, he would have swallowed his Glock and finished it. There was no way he would want to go through whatever remained of his life like that. Sloan knew enough of the story to get a chill whenever he thought about it, and he exhaled with relief when he settled back into the cushy leather of the back seat and took a final look at the mansion.

Be careful, old boy, he thought. *There are worse things than dying.*
Far worse.

As he knew all too well.

CHAPTER 6

Morning light streamed through the thin motel curtains, forcing Jet awake the hour after dawn. For a brief moment she didn't know where she was, and then the sound of a heavy truck driving by on the road brought her into the present. Everything came rushing back at her – the trip to reunite with Hannah, the uncertainty over the phone not answering, and…Alan, dead in the ferry explosion.

Jet switched on the ancient television and found a news station, where the ferry was the main story. The authorities now had no doubt that it was a terrorist attack, with the only uncertainty being which terrorist group had perpetrated the unspeakable act of savagery. Speculations abounded, but nobody had claimed responsibility, so there was nothing to fill the airways but possibilities and fanciful notions.

She quickly tired of the vacuous coverage and switched the TV off, then took a fast shower before hitting the road. Breakfast would be something grabbed from a market on the way out of town, and then, with any luck, she'd be with Hannah by lunchtime.

Jet tried Magdalena's cell number again before setting off, but only got the now familiar endless ringing followed by the line going dead. Nothing had changed. She switched off the phone to conserve battery power, shouldered her bag, and made her way out to the car.

A cup of strong, rich coffee and a breakfast pastry later, she was rolling across the bridge that spanned the Rio San José, and then found herself on a two-lane rural highway lined with palm trees, incongruous with the surrounding farmland but somehow fitting with the quirky nation, a confluence of conflicting influences that came together harmoniously. Jet smiled as she pulled past an old man and woman in a horse-drawn wagon, on their way to market with their crops loaded in the back. For some, life was filled with consistency – planting, sowing, reaping. They worked the land the same way their forefathers had, and would go to their graves without experiencing the stresses of modern life.

Part of Jet felt a pull to that simplicity, for herself and for her daughter. She knew that the world she had inhabited was an ugly reality that most were unaware of, and she longed to escape it once and for all. When she'd faked her own death she had thought she'd put that all behind her, but it wasn't meant to be. But now that she had eliminated the final threat from her past – the Russian's son, Grigenko – she could finally imagine a new future, a better one where she and Hannah could live in peace and tranquility, the ugliness left buried in a past she would spend the rest of her life trying to forget.

And it would definitely be better to leave the dead buried. David, with his betrayals and their incredible connection; Matt, his magnetic pull unexplored beyond a few kisses; Alan, and the promise of a different future in the company of a kindred spirit…so many dead, cut short by the brutality that was her old stock in trade.

A solitary tear rolled down her cheek, and she brushed it away. She was no stranger to death, had invited it along on countless missions and opened the door for it in more instances than she could count. But those she'd sent into the afterlife had been professionals who knew the risks of the game they were in, or had been cancers of humanity – terrorists, criminals, threats to her country. The loss of the only three men she'd ever cared about seemed unfair. As the landscape raced by, though, she reasoned that life wasn't fair, which was why it was important to enjoy the good when it came – there were no guarantees it would last.

The roads were marginal as she wound her way through the flat farmland. Then, as she turned onto a highway that would bypass the capital of Montevideo and take her to Maldonado, they suddenly improved, and she was able to increase her speed. Calculating the remaining distance, she figured she'd be at Magdalena's condo by half past twelve. Jet's desire to see Hannah was like a physical pain, and as she drew closer her sense of restlessness grew stronger with each mile of pavement.

She made better time than she'd hoped, and at noon she was on the outskirts of Maldonado. She reached the condo a few minutes later and did a cursory circuit around the building before parking across the street. Glancing at the back seat, she decided to leave her bag in the car – she had no idea what she would find at the condo, and didn't want to get bogged down carrying luggage if she needed to move quickly.

When she reached the lobby, the security man recognized her from her previous visit to look over the place on the day she'd dropped Hannah off and Magdalena had moved in.

"*Buenas tardes.* Could you please ring condo 2D?" Jet asked the man.

"*Si.* Of course. Go on up. I remember you," he said with a wave, in a typically informal South American manner.

"Thank you. Nice to see you again." Jet beamed a brilliant smile at him, and she caught him blushing. No question he remembered her – probably had for many days after she'd last visited, judging by his response.

She ascended the stairs to the second floor and knocked on the door, then pushed the doorbell. After a few moments, she heard footsteps inside and Magdalena opened the door, a look of delight on her face.

"*Señora!* You're back! Welcome. What a wonderful surprise!"

As she stepped through the door, a small bundle of frantic energy raced down the hall and threw herself at Jet, giving her just enough time to drop down to one knee and spread her arms wide. Hannah's wet hair rubbed against Jet's chest as they embraced, the springtime smell of her floral shampoo the most satisfying odor Jet had ever encountered.

"Mama! You home!" Hannah exclaimed.

"Yes, sweetie. I am."

They held each other for a small eternity, and then Jet leaned Hannah's head back and studied her face.

"So did you miss me?"

"Yes. Hannah miss you!"

"Have you been good?" Jet shifted her gaze to Magdalena. "Has she been good?"

Magdalena smiled. "Of course she has. She's a little angel, sent straight down from heaven."

Jet regarded her daughter, who smiled innocently. "Is that right?"

"Yes, Mama."

Jet hugged her close again, and then Hannah pulled away and went running back into the living room, where a battery of toys were scattered across the floor. Jet stood and faced Magdalena.

"I've been calling for a couple of days…"

"Oh, *Señora*, I'm so sorry. The phone…well, Hannah decided she was going to see if it floats. So when I was doing the dishes, she did an experiment in the bathroom."

"Ah. I suspect they don't make them with full immersion in mind."

"No. But I'll get another one tomorrow. I just didn't see any point if you didn't have the new number."

"You know there's a chip inside the old one I could remove and you could put into the new phone, so you still have the same number."

"Really? *Mierda*. After it wouldn't work for the second day in a row, I threw it away. I'm sorry."

Jet sighed, and moved into the living room. "It's no problem. As you said, we can get a new one for you tomorrow."

Magdalena followed her and busied herself in the kitchen. "So, did everything…are you back for good now? Did you sort out your…problem?" Magdalena was trying to be tactful. Jet had told her a concocted story about a violent ex-boyfriend who was threatening their safety.

"Yes, I did. I don't think there's any more danger."

"Well, that's wonderful news!" Magdalena's tone was excited and happy, but Jet could sense an undercurrent of unease.

Jet smiled in what she imagined was a comforting way. "I was hoping I could stay the night, and then I'll figure things out tomorrow. I don't think I want to stay in Uruguay after this scare, though…"

"I completely understand. Don't worry about anything. I have the apartment for as long as you need me to be here, and of course, what's mine is yours. Stay as long as you like. Hannah has already made friends, but at this age, she'll make new ones in a day. What's important is that you're fine, and safe, and the danger is past."

"That's sort of how I feel." Jet eyed Hannah, now completely transfixed by her toys. "I'm going to get my stuff out of the car. If I remember, there was a twin-size bed in Hannah's room. That should work for one night."

"Yes, there is, but if you want to switch, the master has a queen in it. It's up to you, *Señora*."

Jet walked down the hall, and when Hannah looked up, waved to her. "I'll be right back, honey."

"Okay, Mama. I be good."

Jet's heart melted at her daughter's assurance. She was so upbeat and sweet. Hannah deserved better than to be left alone with Magdalena. A pang of guilt stabbed through her, but she stifled it – she'd only done what she had to do, to keep everyone safe. If it could have been helped, she would have played it completely differently. But that was the past. It was the future that was important. A future that was both bright and bleak – and until yesterday, filled with new possibility, with Alan by her side. But like so much else in her life, that bright light had been abruptly extinguished.

She descended the stairs and nodded to the security guard, who returned the gesture as she drifted through the glass and steel front door. The sun was warm on her face as she made her way down the block to her car, and she inhaled the salty sea air with relish, invigorated by the reunion with her daughter. She stared at the suitcase in the back seat with a sense of melancholy – that was about everything she possessed in the whole world, in that bag. A few clothes. Some basic hygiene products. It didn't seem like much, but then her hand instinctively went to her neck, where the small leather satchel with three million dollars in diamonds still hung. Things could have been considerably worse.

She locked the vehicle and returned to the condo, lost in thought, and hoisted the bag over her shoulder as she stepped through the entrance door, her ribs still tender from her battle with the Russian only a few short days before.

Two blocks away, a black van eased from the curb, the men in it grim-faced as they pulled around the block, its position quickly replaced by an SUV with dark-tinted windows.

CHAPTER 7

An old pick-up truck, easily forty years past its prime, sputtered to a halt at a stoplight on one of the main boulevards leading into Maldonado. A man jumped out of the bed, waving to the driver in thanks as the old conveyance creaked forward, loaded with precariously balanced crates, on its way to the organic market. Alan stretched and looked around. The buildings to his left looked vaguely familiar – he thought he recognized them from the last time he'd been in town. If he was correct, the condo was closer to the ocean as he approached Punta del Este. Glancing up at the sun, he decided that there was only one way to know for sure. He began walking.

Alan had spent a rough night in a park in Montevideo, avoiding hotels because he didn't have any papers. That, and he was trying to conserve his money – he only had a few hundred slightly soggy dollars to his name now, his credit cards and ID having gone up in flames on the ferry, along with everything he owned besides the clothes on his back. It was a precarious situation, no doubt, but he'd been in worse, and after a cold night almost freezing on a park bench he'd hitch-hiked his way north.

Hopefully Jet had made it to Magdalena's – he didn't remember her cell number, having programmed it into his phone, also at the bottom of the bay now. Everything would become clear once they were reunited. She had plenty of money, and that would buy a new identity. The explosion was a loose end, though, and had troubled him since he'd dragged himself onto the beach in Montevideo. While it probably didn't have anything to do with him, he couldn't shake the sensation that the men at the terminal had been watching him.

The question that nagged at Alan was why anyone would blow up a ferry, killing everyone on board. Could it really have been to get him? But why? Who would want him dead? And an even more niggling doubt had crept in – how could anyone have known that he was planning to board it? Nobody knew where he was – except…the director of the Mossad. Not because Alan had told him, but because if he'd really wanted to, he could have searched all the travel records to see what itinerary Alan's operational ID had used to depart Los Angeles.

That brought Alan up short. There it was again – a scenario where the director might have been involved in something nefarious. He considered Jet's distrust of all things Mossad-related, but shrugged it off. It was inconceivable that the director might have been involved in trying to have him killed – especially murdering almost a thousand innocents in the attempt. Alan was under no illusions about the world he lived in, but even in the shadowy clandestine no man's land he inhabited, you didn't slaughter a boatload in order to get one man.

He turned the corner. The street he was on looked like the right one. The condo would be around the bend, up three or four blocks. He was sure of it.

His thoughts returned to the ferry attack, and then went in an ugly direction. He remembered the Lockerbie bombing, where an entire planeload of people had been killed – the bombing ultimately pinned on a Libyan, who throughout his trial and imprisonment had maintained his innocence. The word in the intelligence community was that there had been four CIA agents on the flight who were flying back to Langley to spill the beans on a heroin smuggling operation involving a faction of the agency that was trafficking the drug, and that the flight had been taken down to silence them forever. The official reports glossed over smoking guns like embassy staff and family members of high-ranking politicians deciding at the last moment not to get on the plane, preferring to focus on the evil Libyan terrorist – but nobody ever contrived a believable explanation for why a Libyan would have wanted to blow up the flight. At the time, it was accepted by the mainstream that the terrorist mind was unknowable, and just wanted to cause maximum civilian damage.

Alan was no virgin, no innocent, and he had participated in myriad covert operations that were not what they seemed. But it was still hard for him to conceive of a conscience that would give the go-ahead to butchering a boatload of bystanders to get him.

A breeze blew off the ocean, chilling him in spite of the balmy day. As he headed toward the condo he mulled over his next step. He had no idea whether he was in danger or not, but if the ferry bombing had targeted him, then he was dead as far as the world was concerned. Perhaps that wasn't such a terrible position to be in – not that it had helped Jet much.

Jet.

The one bright spot in his life. Another broken soul, trying to find her way to something better and put the past behind her. Could they make it work? The two of them? Did he even dare hope? She definitely had a boxcar of her own baggage, but didn't they all? It was impossible to live in the world they had and not carry scars from wounds that would never fully heal. Maybe it was foolishness to imagine a future with her, or with anyone. But he knew that when he thought about her dancing green eyes and her impish grin, he felt something…real. At this point, he would take real. After a lifetime living in the shadows, real seemed good.

He could make out the condo now, little more than a block up on his right. His pace increased, and then some sixth sense sounded a warning as he neared it. Something was off, but he didn't know what. Then he saw it: a black van, parked ten feet ahead, but with the engine running. It could have been nothing, but he didn't think so. As he passed it he glanced inside, and as he suspected, the driver was watching the condo, talking to someone in the back. And he had a wireless headset on.

Alan continued on, keeping his rhythm, giving nothing away, and moved beyond the condo without looking at it, then turned the corner at the end of the block and made a right.

Whatever this was, it wasn't good. His operational instincts, bred of a decade of surveillance and clandestine work, told him everything he needed to know. Someone was watching the building. Which meant that Jet had a big problem – one that she probably didn't know about.

Alan continued strolling down the street, then made a left at the next block and continued on his way, doing a low-key grid search of the neighborhood. He needed to understand what he was up against, and the first step was to see who else was watching. Once he knew that, he could formulate a plan. For now, all he could do was wait for them to make a move. That they would went without saying. The question was when. Assuming that Jet was in the building, if it was him, he'd wait until it got dark – there was too much traffic on the street at this hour, but once the sun had set, it would be deserted as the inhabitants settled in for the evening.

Circling back to the street where the van was parked, he studied the other vehicles but saw nothing suspicious. So for now, it was just the van.

Once the night arrived, Jet wasn't the only one who was vulnerable. The watchers probably assumed that she was alone – and they would have been right, except for the fluke that had put him in her proximity. That critical piece of information could prove to be all the advantage he would need. They had no idea he was in the mix.

Which would likely be the last mistake of their lives.

❧

Just after dusk, as the street emptied of the few residents returning home, an SUV pulled past the front entrance of the building, and four hard-looking men in black windbreakers climbed out, their gazes sweeping the street in a practiced manner as they moved towards the condo doors.

The lobby security man looked up from his magazine with a puzzled smile when he saw the four men enter, and then the expression turned to a gasp when the lead man slammed the side of his head with the butt of a pistol. He fumbled for the telephone and then slumped over unconscious, falling to the floor with a crash, his swivel chair giving way. His skull smacked the tile floor with an audible crack, and the men exchanged glances – he wouldn't be coming to anytime soon. Two small flat-screened monitors displayed security feeds of the entrance, and the lead man walked over to the computer and switched it off, then turned to the other gunmen.

"Remember to grab that piece of crap on the way out. We don't need our smiling faces all over the news tonight," he instructed in a low voice.

The men nodded in response.

He tapped his ear bud and spoke softly. "Terry. This is Tango. Over. What have you got?"

"Nothing. The street's empty. I'd say you're game on," a voice murmured from the stakeout van. "Let's get this over with. You're clear to engage."

"All right. You two, take the back stairs. We'll go up the front. The target is the third door from the main stairs, on the street side. Be quiet as you approach. Remember who we're dealing with. I'll give you three minutes to get into position, and then we'll come up the main stairs. If anyone spots you, take them out," the leader cautioned, then pulled a silenced pistol from his shoulder holster and gestured at the long hall that led to the rear of the building. Two of the men moved stealthily down the passageway, also pulling weapons from beneath their jackets, and disappeared behind the heavy steel door that led to the service stairs.

Pausing at the ground floor landing, they were surprised at how dark it was – the bulb had burned out, leaving the area pitch black, with no windows to admit any glimmer of exterior light.

"Shit. It's dark in he—"

The lead man never got to finish. A figure dropped from the landing above as he brought his pistol to bear on the shadow, and then a paralyzing kick slammed into his chest, knocking the breath out of him and sending his weapon tumbling to the ground. He fell back into his partner, whose reactions were only a split-second too late to save them both, and then a warm gush of blood sprayed the second gunman's face as he raised his pistol to fire. The lead man crumpled to the hard concrete floor, his throat slit ear to ear, and his partner dropped his weapon, a streak of pain spearing through him, the blinding shock of his abdomen being sliced open ending any impulse to fight. His mouth contorted in agony as his intestines spilled onto his shoes, and he pitched forward, his dimming awareness grappling to process what had just killed them both.

Jet stood over the two bodies, her eyes fully adjusted to the gloom, and then leaned down and wiped the blood off the long serrated bread knife, using the first man's jacket to clean the blade and then her hands. She slipped the knife into her belt, then reached over and picked up the nearest gun before moving to the second man and scooping his up as well. Both were Ruger 9mm pistols with custom silencers, she noted, and both had one in the chamber.

She did a cursory search of the dead men and found nothing. Neither had any identification or money. They were obviously professional, judging from their weapons and com gear. And American. The few words the first man had uttered in English were enough to place them.

Listening intently, she pulled his ear bud out, cleaned off the blood, and inserted it into her own ear, then tucked one of the pistols into her pants at the small of her back before ascending the stairs to the second level.

The entire engagement had taken less than thirty seconds.

She cracked the second floor door open and verified that the hall was empty, and then calculating quickly, eased it shut and took the stairs to the third floor two at a time.

CHAPTER 8

"All right. Show time," the team leader said, checking his watch as he eyed the steps from his position at the base of the main stairs. It had been exactly three minutes. The lobby was empty, and he had taken a moment to lock the deadbolt on the entry doors so they wouldn't be disturbed.

Both men crept up the wide stairway, their crepe-soled shoes silent on the marble steps. When they reached the second floor, they nodded to each other before turning the corner and stepping into the hall.

The team leader's face registered a moment of annoyance. He tapped his ear bud.

"Where the hell are you? We're in position," he whispered angrily.

The first subsonic silenced slug tore through his clavicle, and the next two blew his skull apart, splattering the wall. A fourth round slammed into the second gunman's shoulder, causing him to drop his weapon. He grabbed for the wound and spun, and found himself facing Alan, who was calmly studying him from the landing.

Alan held a finger to his lips and then pointed to the wounded gunman's ear bud. The man's eyes went wide as he considered activating it and saying something that would warn the men in the van, but the unwavering silencer pointed at his forehead gave him pause – whoever this was knew what he was doing. He looked down at the dead team leader and held up a bloody hand, fingers open, before reaching to his ear and pulling out the ear bud, carefully avoiding tapping it to life. Alan gestured with the gun, and he leaned down and placed the ear bud on the team leader's chest.

"Very good. Now here's what we're going to do. You walk fifteen feet down the hall, and I'm going to retrieve your weapons. Then I want you to drag his corpse to the rear stairs, where we'll leave him, and then you and I are going to have a chat. If you don't lie to me and answer all my questions, you'll live. Otherwise you'll die, just like the other three. There's no third choice, so don't waste your breath." Alan considered the man's wound.

"That won't kill you, but I will. Do you understand what we're going to do?"

The man nodded.

"Okay. Walk down the hall, and stop when I tell you to."

The man did as instructed.

Jet appeared behind Alan but remained silent, allowing Alan to deal with his captive. He moved to the dead man, retrieved the ear bud, and wedged it in his ear.

"That's far enough," Alan called out to the gunman. He leaned down and gathered the guns, then tossed one to Jet before stepping back and nodding.

"Drag him. Now," he ordered.

The wounded man did so with effort, grunting from exertion, droplets of his blood mingling with the smear the dead man's corpse left as it slid on the marble.

Once they reached the rear stairwell door, Alan gestured again, and the wounded man twisted the steel knob and pushed it open, then pulled the corpse onto the blackened landing.

"Very good indeed. Now let's return to the main stairs. I don't want you getting any cute ideas in the dark." He turned and looked at Jet. "Let's get ready to leave. I'll deal with this and be back in a few minutes." Jet nodded and returned to the condo, moving silently.

When they reached the main stairs, both men stopped. The wounded man turned to Alan, panting, blood seeping down his jacket and soaking his shirt.

"Up. We're going to the roof. I want privacy. It would be a shame for us to be interrupted by your friends in the van," Alan said. The wounded man's eyes narrowed – his assailant knew about the surveillance team, which further reduced his odds of surviving the interrogation.

They climbed the stairs, the bleeding gunman clutching the railing for support, until they arrived at the roof door, which was unlocked, Alan having jimmied the lock earlier and left a small piece of wood wedged at the base to keep it open.

"Go on. Push it, but don't bother trying anything. There's nowhere to go."

Once outside, Alan motioned with the gun. "Sit. You'll need to get attention for that soon, so let's make this quick. Who are you?"

The man shook his head. "You know I can't tell you that."

"I know that if you don't, you'll die the most painful death you can imagine. You're a young guy. Do you really want to go out like this, on the roof of some shithole in South America? Come on. Think. I know you're American from your accent. So, last time. Who are you with?"

The man shook his head.

Four minutes later, Alan descended the stairs, calculating the amount of time he would have before the men in the van got really worried.

The ear bud crackled as he arrived at the lobby.

"What's going on?" a worried voice demanded in a whisper.

"A complication. Five more minutes," Alan hissed in unaccented English, and then tapped the ear bud off and made for the condo rear exit.

With any luck, this would be over before it had started.

And he felt lucky.

~~~

The man in the rear of the van cleared his throat.

"I don't like it. This is taking too long."

"He said they ran into a complication. Probably a neighbor. Relax. They're as good as it gets," the driver said.

"Look, we're at twelve minutes since they went in. This should have been over by now. You know it and I…oh, shit…"

The driver swung his attention back to the windshield, having turned to his partner, and found himself facing a disheveled man holding a silenced pistol. The com channel crackled.

"Both of you put your hands where I can see them, or I'll empty this into the van, and nobody will get out alive," Alan said in a quiet, calm tone, his voice slightly distorted coming out of the speakers mounted in the rear.

The surveillance man in the back dived for a shotgun, and Alan fired six shots through the windshield, spraying the cargo area with slugs. The man jerked as three found home in his torso. He slumped to the floor, blood pooling around him. The driver sat frozen, staring at Alan.

"Your friend didn't listen very well. That's a shame. You seem a little smarter. Do as I say – take your gun out of the holster using two fingers, and then toss it in the back," Alan ordered.

"I…I don't have a gun."

Alan's eyebrows raised slightly. "Really? If you're lying, I'll leave pieces of you all over the street."

"I don't have one. Just the shotgun in the back."

"Fine. Step out from behind the wheel. Slowly."

The driver's door opened and the driver did as he was told, fragments of safety-glass dropping onto the road from his shaking form. Alan could see he was in his mid-twenties but with a baby face.

Alan patted him down with his free hand, then jabbed him with the silencer.

"Come on. We're going for a walk. By the end of it, you'll have either told me what I want to know, or you'll be dead like the rest of your crew."

The driver didn't say anything.

"Move."

"Whe...where are we going?" he stammered.

"To the building you've been staking out."

"Are you going to kill me?"

"I don't want to. But I will." Alan prodded him again as they walked. "No gun. So you're really just the driver."

"That's right. I'm not an...operative. Only a tech."

"Like your dead wannabe hero buddy."

"He wasn't my buddy."

They reached the corner of the building and Alan slowed. "Turn down this alley," he instructed. "When we get to the parking area, stop and put your hands on your head. I'm going to ask a series of simple questions, and you will answer them. If you lie, I'll cut off a piece of you, starting with your fingers. I'm not joking. If you tell me what I want to know, you'll live. Do you understand?"

"Yes."

"Are you willing to die to be a hard-ass?"

"No. I'm not a hard-ass. No job is worth dying for." The driver looked like he meant it.

"Exactly. You know what? I have a feeling we're going to get along just fine."

CHAPTER 9

Jet gave Magdalena a brief rundown on what had happened: A group of killers, no doubt sent by her ex, had found them, and they were in extreme danger. Alan had dealt with them, but they needed to get away from the condo, with only a few minutes to gather their things.

Jet had been shocked to see Alan alive, but he'd explained what had happened and alerted her to the threat, and she'd instantly slipped into operational mode. In-depth explanations would come later. For now, a pro hit team was targeting them, and they had to take effective action or wind up dead.

Jet was rinsing the bloody traces from the bread knife in the sink, out of sight of the older woman. "Magdalena, I know this is scary, but don't worry. Alan is taking care of everything. He was in the army, so he knows how to handle something like this. In the meantime, he wanted us to pack our stuff and be ready to move when he comes for us. Can you do that? My bag is still packed. I can get Hannah ready if you can deal with yours." Jet had left out the part where she'd neutralized two gunmen with the bread knife. Better to not complicate things in Magdalena's eyes.

The older woman looked frightened, and for a moment Jet didn't know whether she would rally or not, but then she squared her shoulders and nodded.

"I'll be ready in three minutes."

"Grab your papers and any money you have. Don't spend a lot of time on clothes. Leave anything that will slow you down," Jet cautioned, and then softened her tone. "Thank you for not panicking, Magdalena. We'll get through this."

Magdalena gave her a skeptical look, and then spun and ducked into the master bedroom. Jet realized that she would need to be very, very careful with Magdalena until they were somewhere safe – not everyone was used to being attacked by armed killers and having to run at a moment's notice.

Soon afterwards, Alan's soft knock came from the front entry. Jet slipped the bread knife back into the drawer and then opened the door. Alan stepped inside and closed it gently behind him.

"It's dealt with. But we should make tracks. There could be another team here any second. If we're lucky we can get away before all hell breaks loose," he warned.

"What do you call what just happened?"

"Preamble."

Magdalena returned to the living room carrying her suitcase and her purse. Jet shouldered Hannah's backpack and her bag.

"Let's get this show on the road," Alan said, holding out a hand to help with Magdalena's things.

They slipped out of the condo and made their way down the main stairs. Alan stopped by the security desk and peered over it.

"Where's your car?" he asked.

"To the left, almost at the end of the block. A red Ford Mondeo."

"Warm it up. I'll be there in a minute."

Jet nodded and led Magdalena and Hannah out the entry doors and down the sidewalk. Alan rounded the counter and stooped, studying the computer, and then unplugged all the cables and stuck the box under his arm. He would deal with the hard disk later. With a final glance around the lobby, he nudged the security man with his foot and confirmed that he was breathing, took a last look at the driver, who was still lying unconscious where Alan had clocked him next to the desk, and then strode through the front door and over to the waiting car.

Jet pulled forward when she saw him, and the trunk popped open. He wedged the computer in next to the bags and slammed it shut, got into the passenger seat, and pulled the door closed after him.

"Where to?" Jet asked him in Hebrew.

"I have no idea. You know this country better than I do. Any suggestions?"

"Magdalena. Do you know anyone in San José de Mayo?" Jet asked, looking in the rearview mirror.

"No, *Señora*. I'm afraid not."

Jet exchanged a glance with Alan.

"Then that's perfect," she said to him, switching back to Hebrew so they could discuss their next moves in privacy. "Now tell me what's going on. Let's start with the ferry."

He gave her the two-minute rundown on his adventure, his face betraying nothing. Jet's expression also remained impassive as she processed the information.

"Who were the condo hitters?" Jet asked.

"American, as you gathered."

"CIA? Mercenaries?"

"Private. Nordhaver Industries. You ever hear of them?" Alan asked.

"Doesn't ring any bells."

"Me either."

"So why would employees of an American company appear in the middle of nowhere to take me out?" Jet asked.

"That's the question, isn't it?"

"And who blew up the ferry?"

"Another excellent question. I have no idea. Wish I did," Alan admitted.

"You think they were trying to get you?"

He told her about the two men he'd seen at the terminal as he was leaving.

She sighed. "You've been doing this long enough that your instincts are probably right."

They both stopped talking as she navigated through the light night traffic until they were on the outskirts of town.

"We need to dump that computer. It ties us to the condo. Right now, you were never there. Just Hannah and Mag, who won't answer the door when the police come knocking, and me. A group of women. Nobody will suspect us – we're the weaker sex, right? But if they set up roadblocks like last time…that computer is a go-directly-to-jail card," she said.

Alan gestured at a small market. "Stop here. I'll only need a few minutes."

She pulled to the side and shut off the lights, and while Magdalena went inside with Hannah to get some snacks Alan quickly got the PC out and undid the finger screws. A few minutes later he placed the box under the front tire.

"Drive forward."

The PC flattened from the weight of the tires rolling over it. Alan inspected the crushed computer and then got back into the car holding the hard drive.

"Stop when we're at the lake. I'll chuck this as far into the water as I can. End of story." He hefted the drive, and she nodded as Magdalena and her daughter returned to the car. Once they were buckled in, she edged back onto the empty road.

"How much money do you have?" Alan asked. "Cash?"

"I have about thirty-five grand in dollars left over from what I pulled out for Russia."

"I remember you were going to figure out a way to bounce your ten million all over the planet so it was sanitized…"

"Been kind of busy taking out Grigenko and keeping the world safe from terrorism."

"What were you planning to do? How were you going to get it off the radar, and how long will it take? Reason I ask is that thirty-five grand isn't going to get me a new passport and identity. Mine went down with the ship. Literally."

"I'll probably need a few hours. I have some other old operational accounts I can transfer the money to – account A in Luxembourg, account B in the Caymans. I'll close both after the wires have cleared, ending the trail, and then the money will wind up in account C. It should work," she said.

"I'd say the sooner you can get that done, the better," Alan said. "Whatever this is, we'll need a war chest to stay safe and have any chance at all."

"Agreed. In the meantime, we need to deal with Mag. I'm thinking she rents someplace in San José and lies low for a week or two. I'm sure if we nose around we can find a place where they aren't going to care about ID. I don't want her anywhere she can be found. The only thing I can think of is that they somehow linked her to me…and there's only one way that could have happened."

"The bank account?"

"Exactly. I used the account Matt provided to transfer the money to the trust. If somehow that one was flagged…"

"Then to find you, they would have needed to find where the trust was paying, and bingo."

"Which raises some disturbing wrinkles, but I can deal with those later. First things first. If necessary, we'll just put Mag up at a motel while we figure this out. Someplace that's happy with cash and won't ask any questions."

"Do you have anyplace specific in mind?" Alan asked.

"I actually do. I stayed in a motel that didn't even ask for my name. I liked it well enough. A lot more, now."

"How far away is San José de whatever?"

"We can be there by ten or so. I just need to concoct a plausible story for Mag so she doesn't freak out."

"She seemed pretty cool, even when she saw the blood in the hallway."

"I know. She's good people. But there's a limit to what ordinary folks will do, even for money," Jet said.

"How about I roughed the boyfriend up, but he didn't get the message, so he sent some goons to follow you, and I got to them before they could do any harm?"

"That's good, but she'll read about the killings in the paper."

"I had to kill them. Self-defense. These are mobbed-up murderers. It was me or them."

"Let me figure a way to soften that. I don't want her bolting."

"Agreed." Alan reached over and took her free hand. "You know you're probably going to have to leave Hannah for a little while longer while we figure this out."

"I know. I...it just seems like this never ends, Alan. We just finished neutralizing the Russian, and now I've got Americans gunning for me." Her shoulders sagged in resigned frustration. "I can't win. David was right when he said I would never be safe, no matter what I did." Her eyes moistened. "All I want is to be left alone and have my time with Hannah, and it seems like that's never going to happen."

"Nonsense. We'll find out who this is, deal with the threat, and that'll be it. Simple."

She squeezed his hand. "Big words for a guy who almost got blown up on the ferry." She hesitated. "Nothing in life is simple. Haven't you figured that out yet?"

Their headlights cut through the night as they worked their way down the rural road that would eventually lead them to San José de Mayo, Jet thinking through how to best position her request to Magdalena, Alan lost in his own thoughts, and Hannah dozing next to Magdalena, who was staring out the window, worry lines creasing her face as they raced from chaos towards uncertainty.

CHAPTER 10

Standish opened the front door and welcomed the stately gray-haired gentleman in a navy-blue blazer and gray slacks standing on the porch, and offered to take his worn, dark brown physician's bag. The man declined, and looked around at the art in the foyer before clearing his throat.

"How's he managing?"

"Not well. As you know, the last treatment did nothing. He's hopeful that this one might have at least some effect," Standish said.

"And the morphine?"

"He's going through it by the gallon, but is convinced it's impairing his cognitive functioning."

"Hmm. It's an uphill battle trying to manage his discomfort. How's he sleeping?"

"Terribly. He only gets an hour here and there, then the pain wakes him." Standish motioned for the doctor to follow him up the stairs – a trip the physician was more than familiar with. "What are the chances that this new batch does anything?"

"Frankly, not great. All of this is speculative. Stabs in the dark. I've never seen anything like this before, and neither have the chemists. It's like every nerve ending in his body is a pain receptor. Remarkable."

"Yes. Remarkable indeed," Standish said with a nod as he slowly ascended the steps.

"What about the rest of him? Any complaints?"

"He's completely healed, as you know. He has problems breathing, in bouts, and the sensitivity to light seems to be getting worse. It's not moving in a good direction."

"There's only so much we can do."

"*I* know. Tell *him* that."

They proceeded down the hallway to the bedroom door, and when they entered, the bed shifted as the occupant raised the upper section using the remote. The machines were pumping away, the humidity and warmth uncomfortable for both arrivals.

"There's the quack. What have you got for me today, you Philistine?" a shaky voice rasped out.

"Nice to see you too," the physician remarked, moving towards the bed.

"Have you decided to perform more science experiments on me? What's wrong – did all the guinea pigs die?"

"Yes, I'm here to try something else. But mostly, just to receive the warm welcome you always greet me with."

"It would be a hell of a lot warmer if you actually could do something for me."

The doctor ignored the barb and stood by the side of the bed. "How's the vision?"

"Awful. It's like someone's driving hot pokers into my eyes whenever there's more than this much light. Even so, it's agony. I wear these sunglasses all day just to manage."

"I need to do a physical examination. Ready?"

"You could at least give me a kiss or buy flowers first."

Two minutes later the inspection was concluded.

"How much morphine are you using?"

"I press the button and give myself a dose every hour. No more than that. But it makes me foggy. Which I can't afford."

"Yes, well, it's a known side effect. There are always trade-offs."

"Can't you use something else?"

"No. Morphine is, unfortunately, the best we have. As to the fogginess, I wouldn't worry about that too much – the pain management is more critical. And the truth is that your cognition shouldn't be impaired much, if at all. If you're experiencing lapses, believe it or not, it's unlikely that it's the morphine."

"So I can dose myself more often?"

"Yes. I'd say at this stage to do whatever is required to limit the pain."

"At least that's something."

"And what about constipation?" the doctor asked.

"About the same."

"A side-effect of the drug. Unavoidable. It reduces gut motility, so I'm afraid that the constipation is a necessary evil."

"For which I can take more morphine to kill the pain."

The doctor smiled wistfully. "There are tradeoffs to everything."

"I won't be eating a New York steak anytime soon. I think that's fair to say."

"No. And I'm a little concerned about the respiratory issues you're experiencing," the doctor said.

"That makes two of us."

"It could be a result of the injuries. We really need to monitor that carefully."

"Do whatever you have to do. Now what have you got for me?"

The doctor opened his bag and removed a syringe. "Something new to try. No guarantees, but the chemists felt it was an improvement over the last batch."

"Which did nothing but annoy me."

"Yes, well, I could see how it would be disappointing to have to endure this experimentation."

"Spare me the sympathy. Shoot me up. Let's get this over with. How long before I feel something?"

"Any positive effect will be nearly instantaneous." The doctor glanced at the patient's arm, where the veins near the catheter were reddish and slightly swollen. "You're still having a histamine reaction to the morphine. I would have hoped that would have settled down by now. I'll increase the effective dosage and add an antihistamine."

"Whatever. Get this over with."

The doctor decoupled the tube from the automated system and then deftly inserted the syringe, sans needle, into the catheter and emptied the contents into the line. For a few moments nothing happened.

"Shit. Hook up the morphine again," the patient gurgled as his fingers clenched.

"What's wrong?" the doctor asked, clearly alarmed as he hurriedly reconnected the machine.

"It's…it's not good. Argghhhh…"

The patient began writhing, so the doctor increased the dosage level of the painkiller and depressed the button. "It's not working."

"Give it a minute."

Slowly, the writhing decreased, and the patient's breathing normalized, the rasping gasps replaced by shallow breaths.

"I think it's safe to say that isn't a step in the right direction. I'm sorry," the physician said, shaking his head as he replaced the spent syringe into his bag. "That's a completely different reaction than what we saw in the test animals and the volunteers. Most unusual."

The patient didn't say anything, the morphine finally hitting his system with full force. The doctor turned to face Standish, who had been standing by impassively.

"Let's move out into the hall and let him rest," the doctor instructed.

Both men exited, leaving the patient to his private hell.

"Why didn't it work?" Standish asked once the door had closed behind them.

"The agent he was originally injected with obviously altered his neurophysiology. This is largely trial and error. In the lab, the volunteers reported a euphoric sense of wellness coupled with an almost complete deadening to pain. We induced severe discomfort and they couldn't feel it. Why he's not responding is anyone's guess."

"What's next?"

"I'll report back to the scientists in the lab and see what they come up with. This was obviously not as good a move as anticipated. Odd. I really thought this would deliver a marked improvement."

"Can you show yourself out? I'll need to talk him down. He's going to be furious. You don't want him acting out. When he gets angry and isn't thinking straight...you know he killed his dog?"

The doctor's face exuded shock. "Good lord. No. When?"

"Last week. At night it was in the room with him, as he preferred, and apparently something caught its attention – maybe one of the guards. Whatever. By the time I woke up, it had been barking for half an hour. When I made it to him, the animal was dead. He'd strangled it. He cried for days afterwards, but the noise was so painful he couldn't help himself – he said he tried everything to block out the sound, but when it came down to it, in his mind it was either him or the dog. He loved that animal. More than any human," Standish finished simply.

"I...I had no idea."

"No. You don't. But you don't want him staying angry. Ultimately, he pulls the strings, and his displeasure could be...significant."

"You'll talk him down, you say?"

"That's the idea. For everyone's sake."

The doctor descended the wide wooden stairway to the ground floor as Standish returned to the bedroom, aware that the next hour would be spent trying to reason with a human whose entire body was one raw nerve capable of manifesting only unspeakable agony.

He inched the door open and peeked in. The patient was still, the only sound in the gloom the rhythmic ticking of the machines and the hiss of the humidifier. Standish approached the bed, taking a moment to study the twisted flesh of the patient's face, disfigured by horrific burns, and then the gash that was his ruined mouth moved.

"Kill him," Arthur commanded, his voice barely a whisper.

"That's not going to solve anything. He's deeply regretful for his failure, but he's your best shot. He's got a staff of experts working on a solution. To kill him would be counter-productive."

"Your job is to follow my orders. If you won't, I'll find someone who will."

Standish was used to this. Since Arthur's near-death, Standish had received instructions to kill countless members of the staff for real or imagined indiscretions. None of which he'd followed through on. Thankfully, Arthur usually came back to earth once the rage subsided.

"You miserable bastard, if I could get out of this bed without going into shock, I'd tear your eyes out and make you eat them," Arthur fumed.

Standish nodded humbly in response. The threats were a good sign, as was the abuse. All part of the job as his personal assistant – one that paid very, very well. Arthur's fortune from the drug trade was unimaginably massive, which Standish had administered on his behalf since his near death. Arthur also relied on him to coordinate his affairs, some of which involved 'delicate' matters that required a great deal of diplomacy. Standish had been working for Arthur for nearly twenty-five years and was used to carrying out tasks that would have had lesser men questioning their sanity. Not Standish. He had gotten rich by being a trusted confidant to the great man – not hundreds of millions, but more than enough to live comfortably for the rest of his life, leaving the clandestine world far behind him. As he listened to Arthur rant and threaten, he wondered for the umpteenth time why he stayed, and then smiled to himself.

Power. Pure and simple.

As Arthur's mouthpiece, Standish moved mountains and commanded anything he could imagine. He shaped destiny, had the power of life and death – was a kind of minor deity.

"Are you listening to me, you shitbird?" Arthur hissed.

Standish nodded.

Ever since the night of the shooting, when Arthur had died three times on the table before stabilizing, he'd been completely dependent upon Standish for everything, and if Standish played his cards right, much of the man's fortune would wind up in Standish's account. Arthur had no relatives, no children, and had no time for charities or benevolence. Since the untimely demise of his dog, Standish was the only thing he had in the world; that, and a single-minded thirst for vengeance and a relentless drive to remain a vital player, in spite of his incapacity.

"Of course I am. I hear every word," Standish said obligingly, and allowed the toxic vitriol and recriminations to wash over him without soiling or affecting him in any way.

Every moment alive for Arthur was a worse punishment than any Standish could have imagined. And while Arthur could hurl invective all day, the truth was that he needed Standish, so he would settle down. That, and the increase in pain from each burst of his tirade would further bludgeon him with agony, so he'd eventually wear himself out.

Standish's phone vibrated in his pocket, and he turned to face the door as he viewed the small screen.

"You dare turn your back on me?" Arthur raged, working himself back into a lather.

"I'm sorry, sir. It's a message from our South American contact. I need to go make a call. It's about the woman."

"What did he say?" Arthur demanded, his fury forgotten in an instant now that his favorite topic was being discussed – kidnapping, torturing, and eventually murdering the person responsible for his purgatorial existence.

The woman.

Jet.

"I'll brief you once I know. All the message says is to call as soon as possible."

Standish ignored the growled rejoinder and moved to the door, anxious to be away from Arthur, at least for the moment.

"I'll be back shortly. Try to get some rest. It does you no good to put yourself through this."

Arthur sank back into the bed, his white hair sticking out in tufts, his scarred face contorted in a familiar expression of pain and fury, and then the door closed, leaving him to his silent ongoing punishment.

CHAPTER 11

Jet bypassed Montevideo by sticking to the less-traveled roads, and by eleven that night they were pulling into San José de Mayo. The small motel she had stayed at the prior night was no fuller than before, and she booked three rooms – one for Magdalena, one for Hannah and herself, and one for Alan.

Hannah had been a trouper all the way and had spent most of the trip dozing, as only toddlers can. Magdalena had politely inquired about their plans, and Jet had given her the abridged version – she was thinking that it would be best for everyone if Magdalena and Hannah stayed at a motel or a rental apartment for a week or so, while Jet and Alan dealt with the putative boyfriend once and for all.

Magdalena didn't ask what 'once and for all' meant, and Jet didn't elaborate, although the blood smears in the hallway had left little to the imagination. She had asked Jet repeatedly if Hannah would be safe with her, and Jet had reassured her that, yes, the boyfriend was after Jet, not her daughter. Perhaps a small white lie, but also one that could be true, given that they had no idea why the private security company from America was trying to kill her.

When they separated and went to their rooms, Jet pulled Magdalena aside and emphasized that she would be fine, and apologized for the continued chaos that seemed to follow her around. Magdalena was understanding, but Jet could tell that her patience would only go so far, money or not.

Which got Jet thinking. The only way that her assailants could have known about the condo was by following the money, and to do that, they would have needed to get information from the bank. Or, she thought, from the attorney who had handled the trust.

She prepared Hannah for bed and rinsed off in the shower, and then mother and daughter crawled under the covers and closed their eyes, the dull roar of an occasional car or truck their lullaby as they drifted off to sleep, exhausted after the long day. Hannah curled up with one of Jet's arms protectively encircling her, all well in her innocent world, while Jet fought to still the demons running amok in her head. Eventually, she won the battle, at least for a while.

༄༅

The streets of the Recoleta district in Buenos Aires were quiet at midnight, other than occasional couples hurrying down the empty sidewalks to a late dinner at one of the trendy restaurants near the Four Seasons hotel. A cold wind blew down the wide boulevards, rustling the trees that stood like stoic sentinels guarding the approach to the cemetery that was the final resting place of luminaries such as Eva Perón.

Music boomed from a Renault sedan rolling down a darkened street that fronted one of the countless second-floor nightclubs in the upscale buildings, where the city's privileged would dance and drink until dawn. Azul was the latest in a string of hot nightspots created and operated by a pair of young, hip entrepreneurs who ran successful discos in the ultra-trendy Palermo district only a few miles southwest.

The evening's festivities were just getting underway and wouldn't hit full speed until two to three A.M.; the custom among the party-goers was to dine at midnight, then hit the clubs until the sun came up. Those whose lives revolved around dancing to pumping beats didn't have to worry about mundanities like jobs or school – they were the offspring of the small percentage of the population where most of the nation's wealth was concentrated.

An already-drunken pair of young women in impossibly short skirts and towering heels giggled as they wobbled down the sidewalk towards Azul's entrance, and a smirking man in his mid-thirties with slicked-back hair and a two-hundred-dollar shirt greeted them from where he was lounging against one of the nearby buildings, savoring a cigarette, one of his blue suede Gucci loafers propped against the stone base of the French-inspired edifice. The girls smiled coquettishly at him, and the taller of the two waved, the promise of a night of sybaritic pleasure obvious from her body language.

He grinned as they teetered on their precarious pumps and greeted the club's doorman, who hugged them like they were long-lost relatives and then smacked one on the behind in a decidedly un-familial way as she moved past him, to titters from both. Taking another drag on his pungent smoke, he blew a haze of nicotine at the night sky and then flicked the butt into the gutter before peering both ways down the street.

It was a good night for unwinding. His pockets were full of cash from the latest gig, and he was looking forward to putting some of it to good use, perhaps buying drinks for the pair that had just gone into the club. He could do worse, he reasoned; he certainly had in the past. He checked the time on his new Panerai watch with quiet satisfaction, a purchase from earlier in the day when he'd been wandering the city's streets looking for something to blow money on – a way to treat himself after a big job well done. The watch had been a stupidly expensive acquisition from one of the most upscale jewelers in Buenos Aires, and he'd only decided to buy it after the clerk had looked at him with skepticism, clearly doubting that he could afford it. The look on the smug prick's face when he'd whipped out a wad big enough to choke a mule and peeled off the asking price without blinking had been reward enough, and he could still picture the man's shocked expression whenever he glanced at the glowing oversized dial.

César was street-smart, raised in one of the poorest neighborhoods in the unforgiving city. He'd been living by his wits since his mother disappeared when he was ten, going for cigarettes one night and leaving him and his twelve-year-old sister to fend for themselves. He had survived by picking pockets and selling drugs, working his way up until he'd made bigger money as an enforcer, his ruthless aggression and viciousness having caught the attention of the local organized crime gang who ran the shanty town that was his personal hell. He'd done his best to look out for his sister, but the reality of a life without hope had taken her early, dead of an overdose at fifteen, already a prostitute for three years, diagnosed with AIDS at fourteen.

The first man César had ever killed had been the pusher who'd sold her the heroin that was her chemical vacation from a grim nightmare existence. He still remembered the puzzled expression on the young tough's face when he'd fired a home-made zip gun point-blank through his right eye from five feet away and then urinated on him in front of his crew, daring them to retaliate. César's secret was that he honestly didn't care whether he lived one more day – a powerful advantage in the line of work he would eventually gravitate towards: executioner for the gangs that ruled the slums with brutal efficiency, above the reach of the law in areas the police didn't dare venture into. He became known for his brazen courage, and within a few years was commanding top dollar to kill – sometimes as much as twenty-five hundred pesos, the equivalent of almost eight hundred dollars.

Not much had changed, he mused, except for the price. He was a cold-blooded hit man who killed without remorse, and he'd learned to do so with anything at his disposal, ultimately leaning towards explosives – his patrons were willing to pay more for a car bomb than an attempt with a gun or a knife, and César always followed the trend that would pay the most.

He wished he could tell someone about his crowning achievement – the bomb on the ferry that the entire town was buzzing about – but he never, ever discussed work with anyone. It was part of the set of rules he'd been living by for years, and they had served him well. That he'd made it to the ripe age of thirty-three was proof enough that he was smarter and better than most – almost all his peers were dead by their late teens, killed by rivals or the police, or so addled by drugs that they'd fallen prey to other predators in the urban jungle.

He liked Azul better than most clubs – the clientele was upscale, and it made him feel superior when he was able to charm a local socialite out of her panties after a few lines of coke in the wee hours. That he, an autodidactic wonder from the wrong side of the tracks, could violate the city's princesses and then leave them used and humiliated when he was finished empowered him like nothing else…besides the power of life and death he controlled with his skilled hands. Murder was the ultimate rush, but when he was between jobs the clubs were the next best thing. His natural targets were the daughters of the rich, out for a thrill with a dangerous, brooding stranger, and he played to their fantasies with conviction, giving them just enough of what they wanted to get them to his nearby apartment, where things would inevitably take an ugly turn for the worse once the evening had gone too far.

A skulking figure stood in the shadows thirty yards away, and when César caught the man's eye, he knew he'd found what he was looking for – the perfect complement to the night's hunting, as he thought of it. He wanted to score some cocaine, and the streets around the clubs were inevitably prowled by dealers who catered to the convenience crowd that wanted to avoid having to buy in the dangerous barrios where drugs were ubiquitous.

The dealer nodded and then turned the corner, slinking into the gloom at the alley's mouth, and César sauntered after him, anticipating the night's possibilities. Maybe he would be able to get both of the girls to go home with him – they'd had a look that hinted they were up for anything. A look he knew all too well, and appreciated like no other.

The white hot jolt of pain stabbed through Cesar's ribcage a split second after he stepped into the narrow walkway. He stared in surprise at the handle of the ice-pick protruding from his sternum, where an unusually strong arm had jammed it through his heart. Blood dribbled from the edge of the puncture as he fumbled for the handle, and then he fell forward, his heart stopped from the shock, his eyes glassy, consciousness fading even as he hit the cobblestones with a smack.

His attacker peered out of the alley, and confirming that he was unwatched, methodically stripped César of the heavy gold chain he wore around his neck – Jesus on a crucifix suspended in hand-wrought fourteen-carat glory from its intricate links – and then pocketed the wad of cash. The new watch was the final item the killer took, and when he strapped it on, admiring its heft on his wrist, he grinned a reptilian smirk before moving away from the body and walking down the quiet street, quickly rounding the corner at the end of the block and disappearing.

෴

Jorge-Antonio's heavy work boots clumped unsteadily against the pavement outside his flat as he staggered home after a long night of celebratory dancing and anonymous sex in one of the gay clubs in San Justo, an area where he was a regular, his angry dark good looks and practiced sneer a magnet for young twinks looking for someone dangerous for a few minutes of fun and games.

His condo was modern, with all the latest creature comforts, decorated in contemporary glory by an old flame who had favored Bauhaus and had an eye for symmetry. Jorge-Antonio could have cared less about his surroundings most of the time, having spent years all over the globe hired out as a mercenary, earning top dollar for doing work nobody else wanted to be a part of. He'd killed child soldiers in Africa, tribal chieftains in

Afghanistan, union agitators in Colombia and Central America, and nuns in Brazil. He wasn't discriminating, and there was nothing he wouldn't do – for a price.

Posing as a truck driver had been easy, and slipping off the Montevideo ferry had been child's play, his soiled clothing swapped for a maintenance worker's in a quiet corner of the big boat. He'd never been told exactly why he was driving the truck onboard, but he'd learned not to ask too many questions, and when a job came along that paid for six months of high living, his curiosity went on permanent vacation.

When news of the explosion had shrieked from the news programs he'd been unsurprised, and he'd felt nothing at hearing that his efforts had murdered close to a thousand people. He'd long ago stopped counting the number dead in his wake; it was just a number, an abstract that had no meaning for him. Life came into being and flickered out every day. It was a natural cycle. With seven billion people on the planet, a thousand more or less wouldn't affect anything; but fifty thousand dollars in a slimline briefcase would, and that's what mattered to him, nothing more.

The client in this case was a group he'd done work for before, and they were reliable payers and completely discreet. With the cash, he'd lie low for a few months, go to Rio and hang out on the beach, sample the jungle rhythms, do the Copacabana right. Money was an incredible lubricant, and he could live in high style with the kind of loot he was toting. He'd been paid half in advance, and the other half would be his tomorrow, at which point he would be on the first plane to Brazil to enjoy that city's warm sun and hot-skinned young boys – a pleasure he'd indulged in before when he'd been there two years ago, and which never got old, even if he did.

Jorge-Antonio was fumbling with his keys on the front steps of his five-story building when a single round slammed into his skull, the mushroomed slug tumbling through his brain, instantly scrambling it and ending his life before he had a chance to register his blood sprayed on the green-tinted glass of the entry door.

Across the street, the shooter watched through the scope as the target tumbled to the sidewalk, inanimate before he hit the ground. Satisfied that there was nothing more to see, he carefully packed the custom-made rifle into a guitar case and made for the exit of the vacant apartment he'd broken into. By the time anyone discovered the target's body, he would be asleep at his hotel, and tomorrow he'd be on the first flight back to his native Peru, his latest assignment completed without complication.

～⁂～

"Ha! Come on, sweetheart. You know how daddy likes it!"

Tomás threw another hundred peso bill onto the table and motioned for the nubile young stripper to come closer. Eager to close the deal, Sylvie complied, a professional smile frozen in place on her face, the dim lighting of the club unnecessarily kind to her – even in broad daylight she was flawless, a beauty of German/Argentine heritage, her father a young carpenter who had emigrated in the late Eighties with her grandparents, her mother a barrio blossom who'd caught his eye soon after arrival. Sylvie was the only fruit of that brief and turbulent union, and she'd learned young to leverage her assets while she could; her mother had driven into her countless times that she had a very narrow window of opportunity in which to make her money, and that men would come and go, but if she were able to amass a nest egg she would be in control of her destiny when time moved on and others were favored for their transitory charms.

"What do you want, eh? You seem like a bad, dirty dog. Are you a dirty dog?" she purred, having sized up the loud blond man who was waving money around like he'd just printed it in his back room.

"You know it. They don't come any dirtier or badder. What do you want to drink? What's the most expensive stuff in this dump? Cognac? Brandy? Scotch?" He roared at a cocktail waitress. "Hey, honey, get over here and bring us a drink, would you? There's a tip in it if you're quick about it. What's it going to be…" he motioned with his hand for Sylvie to tell him her name.

"Summer."

"Summer! Perfect. What would you like?"

"Honestly? A bottle of champagne!" Sylvie rapidly did the math. Her slice of the proceeds from the bottle would easily be the equivalent of fifty dollars.

"You heard the lady. A bottle of your best bubbly. Two glasses. Make it fast."

Tomás threw a fistful of pesos at the hostess when she returned with a bottle of expensive French champagne, paying three hundred dollars for it without blinking. Within twenty minutes they had finished the bottle, Sylvie hanging off him, coaxing him to leave the club with her and pay the bar fine for her to take the rest of the night off – a charge to compensate the establishment for the money it presumably would have made had she stayed drinking with customers till her stint was over at five A.M.

Tomás didn't take much convincing, and in a few minutes the transaction was done and they were swaying down the sidewalk towards his car. She had agreed to spend the night with him for the equivalent of two hundred and fifty dollars, almost double what she normally could expect to get on a weeknight in the tough fiscal environment. She didn't speak English, so she was relegated to the second-tier establishments that catered to locals, where the pay was half the going rate of the tourist spots; but she could still earn twenty times what she could as a shop clerk, so she wasn't complaining.

And Tomás wasn't too bad-looking, for a slightly out-of-shape high roller in his early forties, she guessed, although she'd told him she figured him for thirty-five when he'd asked. The trick was to guess low, but not so low it was obvious she was lying, and she'd become an expert at calculating age during her three years out of high school working the clubs.

They fell into his Peugeot, laughing at some remark he'd made about her anatomy and his dishonorable intentions, and she snuggled against him as he slid the key into the ignition and cranked the engine.

A fireball tore into the sky as the small car disintegrated in a blinding flash. The passenger door blew against the brick façade of the nearest building, distorted beyond all recognition by the force of the blast. A car alarm clamored from down the block, the shock of the explosion having jarred it to life, and lights switched on in the darkened windows around the tiny vehicle as it burned to its frame, its two occupants vaporized instantly by the powerful detonation.

CHAPTER 12

Jet was up early the next morning, and let Hannah sleep as she turned on the TV at a low volume and watched the news. The killings were the second topic of the day, with the ferry dominating the broadcast due to the sheer numbers involved. An earnest anchorman with a bad hairpiece eventually shifted from the boat to the carnage at the condo, describing the slaying in graphic detail, with the *aviso* that the authorities were questioning everyone they could locate in the building. No suspects had been named, and speculation was leaning towards some sort of an organized crime or drug-related execution gone awry. No mention was made of the team member Alan had left alive; either the police had him in deep interrogation, or he had managed to convince the authorities he was an innocent bystander – highly unlikely, but this was Uruguay, after all.

There was also no mention of the nationality or identities of the dead men, which figured, Jet reasoned. They probably weren't in any Interpol or South American databases, so they might remain an enigma.

Even in the clarity of the morning light, Jet couldn't make the puzzle pieces fit together. Why would an American company that specialized in private security and military support – a euphemism for mercenaries – want her dead? Someone had clearly hired them, but who? Whatever the reason, she would need to get to the bottom of it. As with the Russian, the only way she knew to guarantee that she would be safe was to eradicate the threat, wherever it sprang from.

Today's first challenge would be explaining to Magdalena the ramifications of her being located through the bank records. She conjured up a simplified explanation and made a mental note to give her a big slug of cash – enough to last her at least another month or two. That way she wouldn't need the trust fund money, which was probably tainted.

Hannah rolled over and cracked open an eye at Jet as she sat on the edge of the bed listening to the barely audible drone of the television. Once Jet saw her daughter was awake, she turned off the TV and stood.

"Rise and shine. Time for a bath, and then breakfast. Did you sleep well?"

Hannah had a dazed look on her face as she became fully awake.

"Yes, Mama."

"Come on, then. Let's get you cleaned up. Nobody wants a stinky kid."

Hannah reluctantly pulled the covers off and plopped down to the tile floor, then padded around the bed to the bathroom. Jet watched her toddler's waddle and felt a pang of regret that she would have to leave her, yet again, if only for a little while.

Hopefully.

The truth was Jet had no idea what she was getting into, which added to her frustration. It seemed impossible to her that the ferry bombing and the attack on the condo were related, but could she really dismiss the idea out of hand? It seemed unlikely; but uncertainty was the enemy of intelligent planning, and right now all she had were doubts and questions.

Hannah showered with Jet, following her lead on using soap and shampoo with a little help from Mom, and soon they were standing in front of the mirror, Jet brushing Hannah's long hair, a child version of Jet staring back innocently at her reflection, the same intelligent eyes studying herself in the morning light. Jet was again struck at what a miracle her daughter was: She could see David's contribution in her features, but mostly it was her genes that had shaped Hannah, right down to the piercing green eyes.

"So have you learned not to touch cell phones? That they don't float?" Jet asked.

Hannah looked sheepishly at the floor. "Yes, Mama." When she mumbled she pronounced it 'yeth.'

"This is going to be really important, sweetie. Because I have to finish up my trip before I come back for good, which means you'll be with Magdalena alone, and my only way of talking to her will be with the new phone I get her. So that means hands off."

Hannah looked up at her. "You go again?"

Jet sighed and finished brushing the tangles out of Hannah's mop. "Yes, sweetie, but only for a little while. I don't want to, but I have to. It's for…for work."

Hannah nodded gravely, as though she too was familiar with the burdens of earning a living.

"But I'll bring you back a bunch of new toys…"

Hannah brightened.

"As long as you're good."

"I be good," Hannah assured her.

"Then you'll be a lucky girl when I return."

Hannah's face beamed at the idea, and then she trotted out into the main room and waited for Jet to select her new clothes for the day.

Jet watched her pull on her top, struggling with the sleeves, and then moved to help her, showing her the tag at the back of the shirt and explaining that was how she would know which side was the front. Once they were both dressed, Jet checked the time, and then they exited the room and walked two doors down to Magdalena's. Hannah knocked at the door at Jet's urging, and when Magdalena answered her face lit up with a smile at the little child standing in the doorway like she was trick-or-treating.

"Good morning, *Señora*."

"Good morning, Magdalena. Are you hungry?"

"*Sí, Señora*. Breakfast would be wonderful."

"Excellent. Let me go get Alan and we'll find someplace close. We have a lot to do today, so better to get an early start. Can you watch Hannah for a minute?"

"Of course. Come on, Hannah. Inside."

Jet knocked on Alan's door and he answered, freshly showered, his face smoothly shaven, looking much better for a decent night's rest. Jet studied him.

"We need to get you some clothes."

"Yes. Apparently sleeping in them for two days after being immersed in salt water for an hour or three isn't part of the recommended care instructions."

"Who knew. You ready to eat?"

"Lead the way."

At a small family-style restaurant two blocks from the motel, they feasted on farm fresh eggs and potatoes and discussed their plan with Magdalena, who had seen the news on television and was shaken by the killings, eyeing Alan warily, as though he would slit her throat over coffee. Eventually she calmed down, but Jet could tell the situation was tentative, and she did everything she could to reassure her.

After a lengthy discussion, they agreed that Magdalena would stay at the motel for a week with Hannah while they attended to the phantom boyfriend, and Jet insisted she take another ten thousand dollars in cash, even though she still had six thousand from the prior slug. Jet explained that she could not under any circumstances access the trust fund money until they had dealt with their problem – somehow, it had been tainted, so it was dangerous. Magdalena took the cash in the car, and nodded her understanding – she could easily convert it to Uruguayan pesos in small increments as needed, and that would be enough to last four to six months, no problem. She seemed to relax once the money had changed hands.

Back at the motel, Jet said her goodbyes to Magdalena and Hannah as Alan went and paid for a week's stay.

Jet got down on one knee and smoothed Hannah's hair with her hand as she gazed directly into her eyes.

"My love, I'll be back very soon. Mommy loves you, but I have to go finish some business. You need to be as good as you possibly can be, and listen to Aunt Magdalena like it was me. Do you understand?"

Hannah's attention was already wandering, the prospect of exploring the small park across the street pulling her out of the moment, and she returned her gaze to Jet with an effort.

"Yes, Mama. I be good," she recited earnestly.

"That's all I can ask for. I'm very proud of you. You've been great so far."

"Can I play?" she asked, pointing at the park hopefully.

"That's a great idea." Jet looked up at Magdalena. "I'm going to find a store and get you a phone. Can you take her to the park? She's so bored she looks like her head is ready to explode."

"Of course, *Señora*. I'll wait for you there."

"Take Magdalena's hand, Hannah, and watch out while you're crossing the street. And don't put anything into your mouth," Jet cautioned, but Hannah was already looking at the pigeons across the way, transfixed by their strutting to and fro, on the hunt for stray morsels under the spreading tree branches.

Alan approached as Magdalena and Hannah were walking across the road, and took Jet's hand – an easy intimacy that spoke volumes. Jet looked at him with a sad expression, troubled and conflicted. He squeezed her fingers and smiled reassuringly.

"Don't worry. They'll be fine."

"I know. It's the safest option. But it still sucks."

"Yes, it does."

She shook her head, then gestured at the car. "Come on. Let's get you some clothes, and Mag a phone."

"Fair enough. And then what?"

"After that, we're going to Montevideo."

Alan nodded. "Mind if I ask why?"

"The only way they could have traced Magdalena to the condo was to follow the money from the trust fund, which would mean getting an address from the local bank's records in Maldonado. Those would be simple, but getting the info needed to make the leap from Matt's account to the trust fund wouldn't be. That means either someone at the bank talked, or the attorney did. I need to know which before I can do anything about the trust fund."

"So we're going to the bank?"

"We'll start there."

"And what will you do once you know something?"

She gave him a dark look. "Depends on what I discover."

"Not a lot of ways to end the trail, are there?"

"Not really. I'm not worried about the trust. Once we figure out why the Americans are after me, it will take care of itself. Either I'll handle the problem on that end, or if I fail…"

"…then Magdalena withdrawing money in three months won't matter," Alan finished for her.

"Obviously, I hope it's the former. But I need to understand how much damage has been done. And if it's the attorney, I might have to worry about moving around all my assets."

"Sounds like a car ride, then."

"We can figure out our next move on the way."

"Nice day for it."

She led him to the car and pushed the button that unlocked the doors. "I'll drive. Let's get you some clothes."

"Something pretty," Alan said with a straight face.

"I'll get you whatever you want, big boy."

He studied her as he swung his door open. "Anything?"

Her eyes softened and a hint of a smile played at the edges of her mouth. "Be careful what you wish for."

CHAPTER 13

The sun peeked through the scattered clouds as the morning wore on, the turgid water of the Potomac rushing past the Fletcher's Cove marina, only a few short minutes from the hubbub of Washington D.C.'s urban sprawl. Red rowboats rocked gently from the surge, pulling at their lines, their hulls protesting the occasional soft bumping with muted squeaks and groans.

A solitary figure stood at the point, fishing rod in hand, casting a bass lure under the trees at promising eddies rippling the river's surface alongside the shore. A floppy hat and sunglasses protected the old man's skin from the worst of the glare off the water as he reeled in the plug, pulling the rod tip periodically to simulate a live bait fish for any watching bass.

Another man carrying a fishing pole made his way along the trail that led from the parking area to the unspoiled river banks, and when he reached the fisherman he watched him cast with a practiced eye before leaning his rod against a nearby tree. He crouched down and reached into the small cooler he'd brought and pulled out a cold soda, brushing the light film of ice from the sides of the can before popping the top and taking a satisfied sip.

"You want one?" he asked.

"No, thanks. They give me heartburn," the fisherman responded with a slight frown. "And they leach calcium from your bones."

"I like to live dangerously."

The fisherman glanced at his watch. "You're late."

"I got hung up in traffic."

The two men listened to the sound of the river, and the rumble of cars in the distant background, and then the fisherman exhaled noisily.

"What the fuck, Peter. A whole ferry? There wasn't a less…dramatic way to take care of our problem?"

"You read the dossier on him, right?" Peter replied. "Mossad execution squad, undercover operative, responsible for at least two dozen confirmed kills in nearly impossible situations. A target with that skill set would have made mincemeat of anyone trying to get close enough to take him out."

"But nine hundred and fifty people? With global headlines involved? Whatever happened to a good old sniper round, or maybe a poisoned omelet?" the fisherman groused.

"It worked, didn't it?" Peter took another strong pull on his soda, then belched. "Party over, just like that. No more loose ends. And may I remind you that if we had been more surgical, then the Mossad would have been curious as to why one of their top agents was offed."

"But we still don't know who else he might have told. Assuming that he knew anything."

"Oh, he knew. Ryker did the interview, and he's the best. When he smelled a rat he called in two more to confirm — and they all agreed. They were sure of it. The only question is how much the Arab told the Israeli before eating a bullet sandwich." Peter spat his disgust onto the riverbank. "Frigging raghead idiot," he lamented. "You sure you don't want one of these?"

"Quite sure."

"Anyway, it's too late to second guess this. We had to move fast. Frankly, it was a kind of small miracle that we were able to line it all up in time. You should be saying congratulations. Besides which, what if we'd tried for him and failed? Ever think of that? Then we'd have an even bigger problem — one of the more dangerous operatives I've heard of, on the loose, gone to ground, and wondering why someone is trying to end his stay on the planet. It wouldn't take him long to figure it out, and then...well, suffice to say we already have our hands full with the botched bio-attack. Which, may I remind you, I had argued for handling differently."

"I couldn't involve you. Nobody domestic. That was essential."

"I know. I'm just saying that you now have a big fat nothing on that," Peter said.

"Not completely. We got a huge PR win with a terrorist getting that close."

"Have you seen the internet coverage? There are at least a dozen sites openly questioning whether or not Iran is a set-up, à la Iraq. Like it or not, a lot has changed in the last decade, and people aren't sucking up whatever CNN preaches as gospel anymore. There are too many groups openly questioning whether Iran actually has any nukes. Personally, I think that's an uphill battle."

"Noted. And while I appreciate your scintillating wit and charming company, that's not your problem. What about the contractors who blew up the boat? Any liabilities there?"

"No. There are no loose ends. Nothing leads back to us."

The older man shook his head and cast his lure again. It hit the water with a pop, and he started reeling.

"You're sure? The ferry was far too high-profile to take chances with."

Peter finished the soda and crushed it on the ground, flattening it, and then tossed it back into the cooler. "And you say I'm cold-blooded?" he asked.

"You got it from your mom."

"I don't know about that, Dad."

"My concerns are valid. I want your assurance nothing's left to chance."

"I told you. I handled it. They've all been neutralized. At considerable expense."

"Fair enough." The older man looked at his watch again. "Dinner is still on for seven. Don't be late. And next time, be on time when we have one of our meetings."

"I told you – traffic sucked."

"You should have planned for that," the older man said with clear menace, steel in his voice. He looked about to continue with his scolding when his rod arched and the reel screamed as he hooked a fish. He grinned, his annoyance at his son momentarily forgotten.

"Looks like you've got your hands full," Peter said, then retrieved his cooler and tackle and made his way back up to the parking area. The old man distrusted phones for his more sensitive affairs, and Peter had inherited his caution in that regard. These were high stakes they played for, and even though he liked sticking it to the grumpy old bastard now and then, he wasn't foolhardy – if anything, he was even more calculating and clinical than his father.

He popped the trunk of his BMW sedan and collapsed the fishing rod, then tossed it in the back before sliding behind the wheel, taking care to wedge the cooler under the glove compartment on the passenger side, where it wouldn't slide around.

As the engine purred into action, he checked his reflection in the mirror. His close-cropped hair was a remnant of his early military days, but other than that, he looked like an innocuous manager – which is how his import-export company card described him: CEO of an obscure firm nobody had ever heard of. His true career was less socially acceptable but paid extremely well. His father saw to that. The last ten years had been a goldmine for him, handling special projects in Afghanistan, Iraq, Libya, Egypt…

He slipped the car into gear and gave the powerful motor some gas. It leapt forward obediently. For all of his faults, the old man had clout in some amazing circles, and Peter had long ago learned to follow his orders to the letter, even if he resented his iron-fisted approach. His father could no more change his style than he could, he mused. And rule number one was, never screw with something that was working. Regardless of what anyone thought, Peter was highly effective at his chosen profession – a fixer, like his dad, roaming the corridors of power without standing out, and yet capable of changing the world if it suited his purpose to do so.

Peter passed his father's parked car, the driver engrossed in his newspaper, studiously avoided noticing him, and pulled onto Canal Road heading south. Accelerating, he stabbed a button on the car stereo and a wailing guitar blasted from the speakers. He tapped his fingers on the steering wheel as he gave the car yet more throttle, enjoying the satisfying feel of power at his disposal as he contemplated the rest of his day, which included a lunch meeting with a contact at the Department of Defense – but he could easily fit in a few hours with one of his favorite girls that afternoon. Maybe two. After all, he had cause for celebration – another problem had been solved, another pawn removed from the board.

He twisted the volume knob and cranked the music, then opened the sunroof so the warming rays could soothe away any residual stress.

Indian summer was on its way.

And it was turning out to be a beautiful day.

Might as well enjoy it.

CHAPTER 14

Clothes shopping for Alan took no time at all; they were in and out of the shop in ten minutes, with several pairs of jeans, a hygiene kit, underwear, and three shirts stuffed into an airline carry-on bag. The phone purchase took only a few minutes longer, and they were back at the park across from the motel in short order saying their goodbyes.

Hannah and Jet hugged for a long time, as both tried to make their special, elemental connection as indelible as possible. Jet assured her that she would be back in just a little while – a fanciful notion she hoped was more truth than fiction. Magdalena watched as they separated, both of their eyes brimming, and then took Hannah's hand and held her as she watched her mother and Alan head to the car.

Jet's throat was tight as they pulled away, her tiny daughter waving at them as they rounded the bend and pulled onto the road leading to Montevideo, and neither she nor Alan spoke for a long time, the dull rumble of the uneven pavement beneath the Ford's wheels a rhythmic monotone.

She had to slow as they came upon a group of the local cowboys riding their horses down the two-lane blacktop. A short honk of the horn alerted them to pull over and allow her to pass. The scene reminded her that they were in farm country, a region where agriculture was the predominant way the locals made a living. Nobody would be looking for Mag and Hannah there – it was about as far off the beaten path as one could get. Their safety was her overriding concern, and the sight of the gauchos trotting down the rural road reassured her.

Alan shifted in his seat and cleared his throat as they breezed past the last pony.

"Time to figure out where we go from here," he began.

"Yeah. I'm thinking we hit the bank and find out what sort of security they have in place, and then I drop in and pay a visit to my trusted attorney.

I've mulled this over, and the leak had to have come from one of them. There's no other way a hitter could have tracked her to Maldonado."

Alan opened her purse and pulled out one of the pistols they'd acquired from their attackers, inspecting the silencer before ejecting the magazine and eyeing the rounds.

"The shells were hand-loaded. You can tell. And the silencers are custom. This American company obviously had no trouble getting weapons here on relatively short notice. That speaks to considerable resources."

"The borders with both Argentina and Brazil are pretty porous. And there are lots of guns in both countries. Same with Uruguay."

"My hunch is that these were brought in from the States."

"You could be right."

"Have you given any more thought to accessing your money? Doing your account bouncing thing?" Alan asked, watching as an ancient farm truck stacked at least two stories high with bales of hay crawled in the oncoming lane, black exhaust belching from the makeshift pipes on either side of the cab.

"Sure. Since I'm going to be in the bank, and since I know that account is compromised, I'm going to get a hundred grand out while I'm there. They should have that many dollars – they're the largest bank in Uruguay. That will buy us some breathing room. And I have three million in diamonds with me. Once we're out of Uruguay, I can convert some or all to cash."

"That's right. I keep forgetting that most of your riches are in diamonds."

"The point is we have resources. I'll take care of the account bouncing later, and just won't worry about the account Matt gave me until I understand who's behind this."

"Maybe we'll get a lead from the bank or the attorney," Alan offered hopefully, but his tone sounded glum.

"It's really the obvious place to start. I don't have any better ideas. Do you?"

He shook his head, then put the pistol back into her purse. "Not really. And don't forget that we have the niggling little problem of my passports being at the bottom of the bay."

"I haven't. We can always buy you something in Argentina or Brazil."

"That will take a while. And there are no guarantees that the quality will be good enough to travel on. I can't afford to have a diligent immigration clerk flag me."

They rode another few miles in silence, then Alan rubbed his face and sat up, more alert. "I can get another ID. I left an emergency kit with an attorney in Jerusalem that has two passports in it, along with a couple of credit cards. They're unused. But it will take a few days for them to get to South America."

"How much do you trust him?"

"Implicitly. He's had the package for almost four years, and he's done me other favors. He'll send it wherever I tell him to. No questions asked. But that doesn't solve one of our problems — we'll need to be somewhere for a few days for us to get the package, and I can't cross any borders without documents."

"Not necessarily true. But one problem at a time. If you have a kit you can have sent, that simplifies matters. In the interim, getting you into either Brazil or Argentina should be straightforward."

She had told him earlier that the borders weren't heavily patrolled, so a motivated, skilled operative would easily be able to slip across.

"And then what?"

"Let's see what comes up in Montevideo."

꙰

Alan entered the bank first and approached a window to change some dollars into pesos — a routine transaction that wouldn't require ID in the small quantities he was converting. His eyes roved over the tellers and the interior, and he noted the security cameras mounted in the corners of the room, as well as the tell-tale mirrored half globes strategically positioned all over the ceiling. There was no chance of evading the cameras, but the possible exposure was a necessary evil, which is why he was separate from Jet. There would be no linkage — the bank had at least thirty people in it as he claimed his pesos and exited.

When he got back to the car, parked around the corner, Jet eyed him as he slipped into the passenger seat.

"I didn't see anything. Nobody obvious watching the bank. Nobody inside but the staff and customers. A few security guards. But there was nothing suspicious," he reported.

"Okay, then. I'm going in. This will probably take a little while, so relax. I'll leave one of the guns, with an extra magazine." She extracted a pistol from her purse, popped the glove compartment open, and handed him a fully loaded magazine. "Let's hope you don't need to use it."

"My middle name is hope."

He smiled, and she felt a sudden surge of emotion. She leaned over and kissed him softly on his cheek, his freshly scrubbed skin smelling of soap and masculinity. A nice combination. He turned his head and his lips brushed hers; and then they were consuming one another, the dam burst, the cumulative tension of the last days coming to a head.

When she finally pulled away she was flushed, her breathing accelerated. It had been too long since she'd felt that way.

"I'm glad you didn't blow into a million pieces on the boat," she said, her voice husky.

"Me too. I'm glad the Russian didn't carve you like a turkey."

She smiled, her jade eyes glittering in the afternoon sun. "We both have something to be happy about, then."

The moment slipped from them, and after another, briefer kiss, she opened the driver's door and stepped out, narrowly avoiding being clipped by a bus roaring by.

"I left the keys in the ignition. If you want to get a cup of coffee, just lock it. Like I said…this could be a while."

"I'll stay put. Good luck in there."

Alan watched her stride to the corner and admired the fit of her jeans as she disappeared into the sparse early-lunchtime crowd. They broke the mold when they made her, he mused, and then punched the radio on to hunt for a news station.

Jet entered the bank and made straight for the manager, a different man from the one she'd dealt with the last time to arrange for the trust account. Short, paunchy, almost completely bald, with a feeble comb-over of oily black hair that matched his bushy moustache, he was nonetheless professional and courteous, and motioned for her to take a seat in his cherry wood paneled office. She did, and he closed the door and rounded the desk, pausing to catch his breath before beginning.

"How may I help you today?" he purred.

"I will be making a cash withdrawal, in dollars."

"Very well. That doesn't require anything special from me. We can just go to one of the tellers…"

"For a hundred and fifty thousand dollars," Jet finished, having decided to up the amount she withdrew while she had the chance.

The manager's eyes narrowed for a nano-second, and then he smiled, his eyes unreadable. "Of course. I'll have to get it from the vault and counted. That will take a few minutes. I hope you're not in a hurry."

"Not at all."

"I'll need your passport and account information."

"Certainly. I transferred over a million dollars a few weeks ago."

She slid a slim blue plastic card to him along with her Thai diplomatic passport. He dutifully recorded the information, then swiveled and placed her passport on a small scanner sitting on his credenza, making a copy before studying the image on the flat screen monitor at the edge of his desk.

"Ah, perfect. Here is your document back. I'll have some forms for you to sign, and if you'll excuse me for a moment…" He gestured at the telephone.

"No problem."

He dialed a three-digit extension and spoke in rapid-fire Spanish, then hung up. "It will take no more than half an hour. May I offer you some coffee? Soda? Water? A snack?"

"A bottle of water would be good. Thank you."

He pushed a button on his intercom and requested two bottles, and a secretary came in with them a few moments later.

Jet glanced at the nameplate on the desk. "Well, *Señor*…Garmindo. Where's the other manager I met the last time I was here? I think his name was…"

"Tamarez. Ah, a sad story. He passed away recently. Only a few days ago, actually."

"But he was so young!"

"Yes. It was a great shock to us all. A car accident. He was struck by a hit-and-run driver as he left the bank at night. Probably a drunk. Dead on arrival. Tragic."

"You say probably a drunk. Did they ever catch the driver?"

"No, alas. But they're still looking, I'm sure. Then again, you know how that is. They can only do so much."

"What a shame. Did he have a family?"

"*Sí*. Two young daughters."

They sat in silence.

"Let me ask you a hypothetical question about your security. How could someone find out account information? Things like where withdrawals are being made from a specific account, or other transactional details?"

"It's impossible. And against the law to reveal. That, and the screens the employees use limit the amount of information they can access. Even a vice president would not be able to discover all the details. Things are compartmentalized to keep the information secure. We are very serious about our bank secrecy here. We have to be. Uruguay has the reputation as the Switzerland…"

"…of South America. Yes, I know. I was just wondering. With identity theft, and pre-texting. I mean, it's theoretically possible that someone could buy the information, someone like a private detective, isn't it?" Jet asked.

He sat back and studied her more carefully.

"No. What you describe would never happen. There are too many safeguards." His tone was firm – if there was a way, he didn't know it, or wasn't talking.

"I was hoping that was the answer. It's just with different countries, it's so hard to know how the banks handle their affairs," Jet back-pedaled.

"I can assure you that Uruguay has among the most stringent standards in the world. Probably better than most other countries."

"That's good to know. I still can't get over the hit and run…the poor wife. And the children," Jet said, moving the subject to something less charged.

"One never knows when one's number is up, *eh*? It is a tragedy."

They made small talk, and then a few minutes later, the phone buzzed. He picked it up, listened, then replaced the handset and rose, gesturing with an open hand.

"The money is awaiting us in the vault. Would you be so kind?"

"Of course. Lead the way."

The officious little man waddled to the door and opened it. They made their way together into the back of the bank, where a security guard stood by the stainless steel outer vault door. After Garmindo held his hand to the scanner, the door released and they walked through. The main vault door stood closed. A woman was seated in an adjacent room with an automatic bill counter on a table next to a canvas bag with inch-thick stacks of hundred dollar bills lying on top of it. Garmindo motioned for Jet to take the other seat across from the woman, and stood in the corner and watched as she fed each stack through the machine – a hundred bills per bundle.

The counting was completed in a few minutes. Garmindo offered to 'lend' Jet the canvas bag, but she declined, extracting an empty black nylon satchel she'd bought while clothes shopping with Alan. The bills fit inside without difficulty, and she slid the strap over her shoulder like a laptop bag, with her purse on the same arm.

Garmindo eyed Jet, and doing his best to not appear judgmental, nodded at her. "May I offer you the services of one of our armed guards to escort you to your car?"

"Thank you so much. No, I have someone waiting for me. But I appreciate it. You've been more than gracious. May I have your card?"

He beamed and fished in his jacket, then pulled an embossed rectangle out of his pocket and handed it to her with a small bow. "I'm at your service."

Jet couldn't get out of the bank fast enough. Her eyes scanned the street from behind her sunglasses once she was on the sidewalk, and seeing nothing threatening, she walked quickly to where Alan was waiting and pulled the passenger door wide, then tossed him the bag. He caught it and looked at her with a neutral expression, and raised an eyebrow inquisitively.

"Everything okay?"

"Not really. Apparently, the bank manager was mowed down by a hit-and-run since I last visited with him," she said, standing with the door open.

"Dangerous town."

"I can't help but wonder whether being my banker made it more so."

"No way of knowing for sure, is there?"

"Not really." She swung the door shut, and he lowered the window.

"What now?"

"Time to chat with my attorney."

CHAPTER 15

Papua, Indonesia

Rain pelted the muddy road leading to the small town of Keppi Mappi Papua, and a brown stream flowed down the shoulder as the cloudburst dropped two inches of water in as many minutes. An Indonesian military jeep, its tires straining for purchase on the slippery surface, crawled its way to one of the checkpoints that had been set up throughout the region since the rebel insurgency had destroyed the mine. The motor groaned as the vehicle lurched past a car broken down at the side of the road. Several islanders were gathered around the motor, the hood open, their heads clustered like they were performing open heart surgery on the sad vehicle's innards.

The days following the attack on the mine had been tense, with the military rounding up hundreds of suspected rebel sympathizers in a brutal crackdown widely ignored by the international press, which preferred to focus on the devastation caused by the sabotage. Operations had ground to a halt following the blasts, and the damage and repair estimates were ugly at best. The pipelines had been ruined in several places, and worse, the crushing systems had been completely destroyed. Replacement would take months.

A few isolated additional incidences of sabotage had followed, but they had been largely ineffective, mounted against targets of little consequence using materials that inflicted only minor damage. But the ongoing attempts to destabilize the Indonesian regime had increased friction between the military and the locals, who were now largely prisoners in their homeland, with soldiers prowling the larger towns, stationed at virtually every street corner, machine guns brandished menacingly. Peaceful protests had degraded into conflicts with riot police and armed troops, and the largest had ended with six dead, shot at point-blank range by troops with hair triggers and little accountability.

The Jeep pulled to a stop twenty yards from the broken-down car and the three soldiers dismounted, their boots squishing in the mud as they trudged towards the islanders, the Jeep's driver remaining under the protective cover of the fabric top while the others rousted the natives.

"Hey. Get that piece of shit out of here. You can't stay here. It's not allowed," one of the soldiers, a corporal, shouted at the four men.

"If we could move it, do you think we'd be standing in the rain?" one of the natives yelled back, not bothering to turn to address the soldiers. "Dumb bastard," he muttered, but a little too audibly.

Two of the soldiers snickered as the corporal's features contorted with rage.

"All of you. Turn around. Now. You call me a dumb bastard? I'll show you who the dumb bastard is. You're all under arrest," the corporal sputtered, his voice climbing a half octave from anger.

"Arrested? For what? Fixing our car? Get out of here. Go make trouble somewhere else," the tallest of the islanders jeered over his shoulder.

"You heard me. You're under arrest. Now turn around!"

The islanders looked at each other and then the tallest shrugged and put down the wrench he was holding.

The soldiers never saw the attack coming. The islanders turned, holding pistols and a submachine gun, and emptied their weapons into the uniformed bodies. The driver panicked at the sound of the shooting and ground the transmission as he tried to put the Jeep in gear – and almost stalled the motor when he popped the clutch and bounced back onto the road, water and mud flying from the wheels.

The tallest man jogged easily to the fallen soldiers and scooped up one of their rifles, shaking the brown rain from it before chambering a round and training the weapon at the departing Jeep.

"How much you want to bet I can nail him in one shot?" he asked the men, but no one was willing to take the bet. "Going once….going twice…"

The rifle bucked and the Jeep windshield went red, and then the vehicle slowed before rolling off the road and colliding with a tree. One of the men ran to it and sprayed the initials TPN across the back with black spray paint before returning to their own car. The tallest man loped to the driver's side door as another islander dropped the hood, and then all four climbed into the decrepit conveyance as the driver started the motor.

Half a mile away, at the checkpoint, six more soldiers lounged around under a tarp held up by four poles, playing cards as the rain pelted the covering with drops the size of walnuts. Thunder sounded in the distance, a low rumble that seemed to shake the nearby mountains, and the seventh man, a lieutenant, shook his head and muttered a curse.

"Filthy shithole, isn't it? All it does is rain and smell like a dung heap," he said to nobody in particular.

The men were used to his regular condemnations of the place, the weather, and the people, and they continued their game without glancing up. He mechanically flicked an old stainless steel Zippo lighter open, closed, open, closed, a nervous habit that secretly annoyed the men under his command, and then finally withdrew a cigarette from his breast pocket and lit it, closing the lighter with an especially loud snap before inhaling the rich, strong smoke. He smiled to himself in satisfaction and inspected the bottom of the Zippo, engraved with his name and a few congratulatory words, a gift from his parents when he'd earned his commission.

Shots rang out from the surrounding jungle – the rapid-fire chatter of Kalashnikovs. A hail of white-hot death cut the soldiers down, dropping them before they could return fire. The lieutenant tumbled to the ground and groped for his service pistol, fumbling it free from his hip holster and firing indiscriminately at the bushes; a weak defense, but the only one available to him. When his ammo was exhausted a single burst from the nearby foliage slammed into him, and then the area fell silent, the report of the assault rifles quieted. The only sound was the rain as a group of six figures in camouflage emerged from the dense underbrush and moved to the checkpoint, weapons ready for any unexpected resistance.

At the tarp, the leader barked a terse command and his subordinates hurriedly gathered up the dead men's guns and ammunition, securing everything in a rucksack sitting near the radio, which had been ruined by a few stray rounds. One of the men pulled the pistol loose from the dead lieutenant's hand, and then his eye caught something shiny in the red water that ran from the bodies down the gentle slope to the road. He knelt and retrieved the Zippo and held it aloft, allowing the rain to rinse the mud from it before slipping it into his pocket with a grin, his few yellowed teeth gleaming in the rainstorm's half light. Another peal of thunder shook the ground, as if signaling that time was running short, and the attackers did a final policing of the area to ensure they hadn't missed anything that could be of future use.

Two minutes later, the islanders melted back into the jungle like silent ghosts, unfazed by the deluge. When the massacre at the checkpoint was reported by an outraged Indonesian press, the TPN painted on the front shirt of the dead officer would receive front-page treatment, further solidifying Indonesian anger at the Liberation Army of Free Papua, whose initials from the local language, TPN, had become a symbol of hope for the natives and a pretense for butchery for the military.

Over the next few days, another attack would take place at a remote military outpost sixteen miles away, and another atrocity would be recorded for posterity. The only unusual aspect of the entire sad episode was that both massacres received extensive coverage by the international press, further embarrassing the Indonesian regime and escalating tensions. More natives were rounded up and bodies were found floating in the rivers, the swollen corpses marred by evidence of torture and brutality, duly publicized by media outlets thousands of miles from the carnage – brief sound bites to fill the spaces between fast food ads and fitness commercials – unspeakable viciousness taking place in unpronounceable locales, covered by bouncy blond anchorpersons with serious demeanors and preternatural, cosmetically enhanced smiles.

CHAPTER 16

Jet paused in the lobby of the attorney's building and looked up at the clock. Lunchtime – which explained why the place seemed empty. Uruguayans, like their Argentine brethren, liked to take long lunches, often two to three hours, and businesses routinely closed during those hours so the proprietors could enjoy a relaxed meal and a siesta. The lawyer was near the top of the stairs, she remembered, with the law offices occupying most of the fourth floor of the small building. She ascended the stairs quickly, hopeful that the attorney hadn't left for lunch yet.

When she arrived, the receptionist was just getting ready to leave, and she looked annoyed when Jet entered and approached her. The young woman set her purse down with a sigh and fixed Jet with a frigid gaze.

"May I help you?"

"Yes. I'm here to see Alfredo. I'm a client," Jet explained.

"Ah, well, he's with another client right now, I'm afraid," the receptionist said, clearly not sorry at all, and hoping that would end the interaction.

"Will he be long?"

"Mmm, no way of knowing. Perhaps you could make an appointment? After lunch?" she suggested.

"That doesn't work for me. I'll just sit here and wait for him," Jet announced, and moved to the brown leather and chrome couch, a matching coffee table sitting in front of it with a pile of travel and leisure magazines strewn haphazardly across its top.

"Oh, well, I'm afraid you might have a long wait, then. And I'm getting ready to leave…"

"I really need to see him as soon as possible," Jet stressed.

"I…let me ring him and tell him you're waiting."

"Please."

Jet sat staring at the far wall, an impressionist oil rendering of sorry flowers lending a burst of color to the otherwise conservative surroundings, and listened as the woman murmured into the phone. When she hung up, Jet regarded her expectantly.

"Now he knows you're out here. He said it would be ten minutes, no more. Can I get you something before I leave? A drink?"

"No, I'm fine. Go ahead and take your lunch. I'll just wait for him. That doesn't seem like very long, does it?" Jet asked, smiling sweetly.

"If you're sure."

She motioned to the magazines. "No problem. With this library, I have plenty to occupy my time."

The woman looked unsure, and then hunger won out and she gathered her things and left with a final glance at Jet.

Once she was gone, the suite was still. The two other attorneys were not in – Jet could just make out their offices at the far end of the long hall and they were empty, as was the conference room. Apparently, practicing law in Uruguay was a relaxed affair, as far as hours went. Like everything else, she supposed.

Five minutes crawled by, and then another ten. Jet was getting fidgety, tired of reading about the lifestyles of the rich and aimless and their preferred resort destinations. She tossed her magazine back onto the table and stood, promising herself she wouldn't pace, and then did so anyway.

A muffled noise echoed from the back of the building where the attorney's office was located, like a door shutting or something falling on the hardwood floor; and then she heard a muted cry. A man.

Her operational conditioning kicked in, and she inched past the reception desk and down the hall, listening for anything further. Another thud, and then silence.

She debated pulling the pistol out of her purse, and then hesitated. Probably wasn't a great idea to be waving a silenced weapon around law offices. Jet moved the final steps to the closed door and paused outside. She didn't hear anything. Waiting a few more moments, she finally knocked.

"*Hola.* Alfredo?"

No response.

"Alfredo. Is everything all right?"

Still nothing.

"I'm coming in," Jet warned, and then cracked the door open and peered inside.

Alfredo was sitting, his chair back facing her, apparently gazing through the window at the buildings on the plaza across the boulevard. She stepped cautiously inside the office, and then smelled the distinctive metallic odor of fresh blood – a smell she was more than familiar with. She reached into her purse and jerked the pistol out as she approached the chair and, with a glance, confirmed her assessment. The bullet wound was centered between his eyes, shot at close range. Her eyes flitted to his hands, and she saw the fingers of his left cocked at unnatural angles, confirming that he'd been tortured. A dirty rag on the floor told her the rest – it had been stuffed in his mouth to keep him from screaming, and the killer had pulled it out so his victim could respond to questions.

She pressed herself against the wall, peered outside, and saw a dark-clothed figure at the edge of the far roof of the building next door. She pushed the window open and climbed out onto the ledge, then leapt to the roof a story below as the man momentarily dropped out of sight at the far end.

A bullet ricocheted off the wall behind her and she barely had time to register that the shooter was using a silenced weapon before she was rolling and bringing the pistol to bear at the silhouette of his head.

Which disappeared just as she squeezed the trigger.

Her shot went wide, the distance too great for any real accuracy, and it tore a divot out of the tar surface. Wasting no time, she dashed for the gunman's last position. She peered over the edge and saw him dropping to the ground in the dank alley three stories below, the fire escape clattering as he released it.

She fired a pattern around him, hoping to wound him with a lucky shot, but he was already running in a zigzagging line for the alley mouth a hundred yards away. One of the shots struck him in the upper torso, but he kept going; wherever he was wounded, it wasn't a mortal blow. He turned as he ran and fired a few rounds at her, but they didn't come close. She waited until he was at the end of the alley and, after stuffing the pistol in the waist of her jeans, threw herself over the edge, descending the fire escape ladder in a blur. Her hands burned from the friction but she ignored the pain. When she was twelve feet off the pavement she dropped, bouncing in a crouch, and then bolted after her quarry, dropping the gun into her purse so it wouldn't panic any passers-by.

When she reached the street she paused, scanning the throng, and then spotted a crimson drop of blood on the sidewalk ten yards away, to her right. She pushed past an annoyed businessman and picked up her pace to a trot, then saw another ruby drop. An exclamation of fright from a woman near the next corner drove Jet forward, but by the time she reached the intersection, she'd lost the trail. Her eyes roved over the rushing pedestrians, but she didn't spot any anomalies…and then she saw it. More blood leading down the block.

A car honked from the street thirty yards up as a VW Polo darted from the curb and cut it off, the little car burning rubber as it tore away. Without hesitating, Jet ran into the lunchtime traffic. A white BMW 325is locked up its brakes and screeched to a stop, narrowly avoiding flattening her, and she whipped her gun out and pointed it at the startled driver.

"Out of the car!" she screamed.

The driver raised his hands and fumbled with his seatbelt as the cars behind him honked in outrage at his vehicle blocking the street. He practically fell out of the seat, and Jet pushed him away and swung behind the wheel.

"Sorry. I'll try not to hurt it," she called to him, then roared off, leaving the driver standing in shock in the middle of the street, arms still held above his head as his car disappeared into traffic.

Jet tossed the pistol onto the passenger seat and concentrated on her driving, speed-shifting through the gears as she veered past slower-moving cars. The VW was several hundred yards up, but the BMW's superior horsepower quickly cut the distance by two thirds.

The gunman seemed to sense her pursuit, and at the next street he abruptly twisted the wheel, sending his car careening down a one-way three-lane boulevard into oncoming traffic. A symphony of horns greeted his maneuver, and he narrowly missed running headlong into a delivery truck double-parked in front of a restaurant.

Jet followed the Volkswagen, the heel of her hand jabbing the BMW horn, and redlined the RPMs as she gained on the killer. She shifted into third and felt on the seat for the gun, eyes locked on the shooter, and when her fingers felt the familiar grip of the pistol her features settled into a determined frown. It would be almost impossible to hit him from a moving car going the wrong direction down a one-way street, but she was going to try. She took the weapon in her left hand and held it out the window, slowing momentarily as she loosed three shots. Jet had years of practice shooting with both hands so she was deadly accurate with either – a requisite for all team members, should they be wounded and forced to use their less-favored limb.

Two of the three slugs slammed into the rear of the car, one shattering the rear window, but neither hit the driver, and the breaking glass seemed to urge him on rather than slow him. He stood on his brakes and simultaneously spun the steering wheel, putting the car into a skid that finished with him facing Jet. She did the same, but by the time her heavier car was under control and pursuing the VW, the latter had pulled sixty yards away and was headed for a busy intersection.

She watched as the little car bolted through a red light, missing being flattened by a bus by only a matter of inches, and then the gunman was speeding away, leaving pandemonium and near-collisions in his wake.

Jet cursed and stomped on the accelerator, committed to staying with the Polo at all costs. As she flew through the intersection a motorcycle swerved to avoid her, but too late, and its front tire clipped the BMW's rear fender. The bike flew into the air, flipping end over end, as the rider tumbled to the asphalt and rolled, his helmet saving his skull. Jet's last vision before she was through the light was the motorcycle slamming into another car coming the opposite direction, causing it to ram a truck, the car's airbags deploying as it bounced off the larger vehicle and ground to a halt.

Up ahead, she watched as the Polo glanced off a taxi, sending a shower of sparks into the air, and then missed a jaywalker by inches, who leapt back, throwing himself against a parked car. Downshifting to increase the engine revs she screamed past the cab, gaining steadily on the VW. She was preparing to shoot at it again when it began weaving back and forth to create a more difficult target. *Obviously professional*, she thought, as she followed the gunman onto a larger thoroughfare leading to a highway onramp.

The Polo stomped on its brakes and skidded to a near halt when it was confronted with two stopped cars waiting as a large truck backed into a driveway, and then it darted into oncoming traffic again, swerving around the blockage. Jet followed suit, but had to pull back into her lane to avoid an Opal, crushing her passenger side door against one of the two waiting cars before straightening out and accelerating after the escaping killer.

She hung her gun out the window again, and the pistol bucked as she fired four more shots. One of them hit the rear tire, which exploded instantly, sending shredded rubber skyward in a smoking cloud, and the little car lost control and slowed before the driver manhandled the wheel and it corrected. Another red light blocked its path, a line of cars idling as they waited for it to change, but it bumped up onto the sidewalk and edged past them, turning the corner before dropping back into the street and rabbiting for the onramp despite one of the rear wheels running on the rim. Jet followed suit, the BMW groaning in protest as its low-profile tires struck the curb, and then she was roaring down the sidewalk, one hand gripping the wheel as the other cradled the gun, her knuckles white from the strain of keeping the car steady.

She launched off the steep curb and landed with a bounce on the street behind the Polo, and was preparing to fire at it again when a garbage truck pulled into traffic just ahead of it, crashing into the passenger side and flipping the VW. It tumbled once, twice, and then slammed into a light pole as Jet locked up the brakes to avoid both vehicles.

After skidding to a stop, Jet threw her door open and grabbed her purse, sliding the gun into it as she ran to the ruined car. The telltale smell of short-circuiting wiring accompanied a wisp of smoke that curled into the air from where the ruptured gas tank was leaking fuel onto the ground.

A blinding flash seared her face for a split second as the tank ignited, and she shielded her eyes with her arm. When she opened them the car was burning, and she inched closer to see if she could save the driver – she needed him alive so she could find out who he was working for.

By the time she reached the driver's door, it was too late. She watched as his charred arm pulled weakly at the seatbelt and then dropped, the skin of his face bubbling from the flames and then peeling away as he succumbed to the blaze, what remained of his head lolling to the side as he burned.

Footsteps ran towards her from the garbage truck as well as several cars that had stopped, and she took a final look at the burning man before she backed away and took off at a full run, hoping to vanish before the distant sirens brought the police.

Two blocks away she slowed and flagged down a taxi on a cross street. She dropped gratefully into the back seat and gave the driver the bank address, and then rolled down the window and gulped air.

Ten minutes later she rapped on the Ford's windshield. Alan was in the driver's seat. He looked up, startled, and unlocked the passenger door for her.

"Took you long enough. Must have been a hell of a meeting," he said.

Jet's face was a blank, betraying nothing. "I thought I'd take my time," she replied as he started the engine.

He turned to her and studied her profile. "No big deal. I caught up on the news while you were gone. The killings are all over the radio."

"Not surprising."

"True. Hey, you want to drive, since you know where we're going?" he asked.

She considered a dozen replies, then shook her head. "No, you can, at least until we're out of town. I'm tired of driving."

He nodded, then dropped the transmission into gear. "Put your seatbelt on," he reminded her, then slid into an opening between two cars and pulled away. She gave him a neutral stare and then snapped the end into the buckle.

"Can't be too careful, right?" she agreed.

"So, how did it go? Did you learn anything from the attorney?"

She was silent for a few seconds, and then sighed.

"No. It was a dead end."

CHAPTER 17

Alan stopped for gas on the outskirts of Montevideo and switched places with Jet, concerned that if they got pulled over for any reason he didn't have identification; and not only was he driving without a license, but worse, he was in the country illegally. Typically in possession of at least two identities, to now be without any was clearly troubling him, and Jet could understand why. Passports meant the flexibility to easily move from country to country, and at this point he had nothing.

"Tell me how you're planning to get me into Argentina. It's still a bit fuzzy, other than the idea that the border isn't well manned," Alan said.

"The border is the Uruguay river. The good news is that a motivated boater could easily slip across at night in multiple areas."

"How do you know this?"

"I researched escape routes into Brazil and Argentina, just in case, when I was looking at moving here. There aren't a lot of people trying to slip from Uruguay into Argentina. Any smuggling usually goes the other direction."

"Fine. Assuming I make it across with no issues, then what?"

She slipped behind the wheel and started the car.

"We head to Buenos Aires, where there are many, many millions of people, and lie low until you get your travel documents. At which point we get out of Argentina and head to the United States. The answer to who is trying to kill me is there. The security firm is located there, and the men who came for me are from there. So we go there, and do whatever needs to be done to end this," Jet said.

"Not a bad idea. But getting into the U.S. won't be easy with the terrorist threat so fresh."

"Nonsense. There are any number of ways in that are either under-patrolled or not patrolled at all. By boat from Mexico. Or from the Bahamas. By land, from Canada or Mexico. I'm not so worried about that. There's a whole business devoted to smuggling people into the U.S., and if

102

you have serious money, like everything else, you can go first class. I checked around and have a contact who can make it happen."

"You've been busy."

"The last time I had to go to the States, I wasn't sure whether I'd be able to use one of my passports or not, so I leveraged some of Matt's contacts, which I still have. I can get into the country for twenty grand, no questions asked, and so can you, so relax. That will be the least of our worries. It's what we'll do once we're inside that will be harder. Although one bright spot is that the last time I was there, I discovered it's a gun enthusiast's dream. You can get literally anything, and all the parts and tools to modify civilian weapons to full-auto military spec can be bought off the internet. Same for everything else – you name it, it's available. One of the benefits of being the largest consumer society in the world," she explained.

"Hmm. Then the real hurdle is getting across the river. You have any ideas?"

"There's a stretch south of a town called Paysandú, where the river is only three quarters of a mile wide, and the current is predictable because of the dam upstream. My vote is for either stealing a boat or buying a plastic kayak, and you row across. I drop you off south of Paysandú, I'll do the legit crossing upriver at the bridge, and then I'll swing down and pick you up on the Argentine side. It's simple and effective. I'd rather get a kayak somewhere because it's even lower radar-detectable than a rowboat, but that will depend on what we come across on the way up. If we find a store, great. Otherwise we'll be looking for opportunistic targets."

Alan nodded. "How far is it?"

"About three hundred kilometers, but the roads are probably lousy, so it's going to take the rest of the day. But in the meantime, if you can remember the number, you can call your friend in Israel and get your papers shipped out." She looked at her watch. "Depending on how late he works, he's four hours ahead of us. Or five. I can't remember."

"Next internet café you come to, pull over. I can use their web phone, so we don't compromise your cell in any way."

"They have them about every four blocks in these neighborhoods, so it won't be long."

Sure enough, ten minutes later they were strolling through the doors of a small store with a dozen computers lined up on one wall and a makeshift phone booth in a corner for privacy.

Alan turned to Jet. "Where should I have it sent?"

"The Four Seasons. In Buenos Aires. The address shouldn't be too hard to get." She gave him the name on her current passport. "Have it delivered to the front desk."

Alan disappeared into the booth and returned five minutes later. "It'll go out tomorrow. The bad news is that it will take three days to make it. So we'll be in BA for that long, at least."

"That's actually not so bad. It'll give us more flexibility in getting you across the river and arranging to get into the U.S. We can take our time getting to Paysandú, scout out the place tomorrow, and do the crossing tomorrow night."

"Sounds like a plan. Sorry you have to drive all the way."

"No problem. Oh, speaking of driving, a funny thing happened earlier today in town…"

❦

The drive to Paysandú was excruciatingly slow, and saw them winding their way on rural two-lane roads that they had to share with horses, snail-paced tractors, massive semi-rigs on their last legs, and every variety of dilapidated automobile imaginable. By the time they arrived it was dark. After finding a decent hotel near the central park, they took the clerk's recommendation for dinner and walked to a restaurant a few blocks away. The air was humid and surprisingly warm, and the restaurant had tables outside in a courtyard.

Dinner was pleasant enough, but Jet was preoccupied, the weight of having to leave Hannah again wearing on her, and Alan gave her space to mull over events in silence. He knew it had to be difficult for her to try to adjust to being a mother, then a field operative, then back and forth again, and he didn't envy her the battle going on in her head. They kept what conversation they had light, skirting the larger issues they both had to contend with, and after a slow walk back to the hotel, they fell into bed exhausted and were asleep within minutes.

The following morning Jet awoke early and decided to go for a run. She sprinted flat out for ten blocks, taking in the ancient homes, which reminded her of Italy, and then turned and circled along the banks of the river before making her way back into town. At a park along the way she found some promising-looking walls and statues, and did twenty minutes of parkour jumps, somersaults, flips, and vaults before returning to the town center, running steadily in the cool morning breeze until she was spent. Checking her watch, she saw that she'd been at it for an hour and a half, so she set a course for the hotel.

Alan was up and showered by the time she burst through the door, watching the television coverage of the ferry explosion and the condo killings.

"Anything new?" she panted, then grabbed a bottle of water and drained it.

"No. Usual stuff. Terrorists hit the boat, and drug gangs killed the shooters."

"And nobody's questioning that?"

"Not that I can tell. And on the international front, the bio-agent attack in L.A. is getting some coverage, as is U.S. agitation to stop Iran from developing nukes. But the spin here is much more cynical about America's claims that it has credible evidence. Interesting how it differs from what I saw in Los Angeles."

"Not really. I saw an article the other day where a former reporter for one of the major news channels admitted that the network gets paid by the American government to kill certain stories and report inventions on others. And not just by the Americans – they apparently also take cash from places like Bahrain to do the same thing – to spin their nasty little domestic disturbances as anything but what they are. So all the best news money can buy…"

"I wonder how long it's been like this?" Alan mused.

"Longer than we've been alive. Some things never change." She watched the TV for a few more seconds, then walked to the bathroom. "I'm going to rinse off. You hungry?"

"Absolutely. You see anything promising on your run?"

"Yup. I'll tell you all about it over breakfast."

"It's a deal."

Half an hour later they were seated downstairs in the hotel restaurant, the only ones in the place, sipping strong, steaming cups of coffee, waiting for their eggs. Jet told him about the marina filled with boats, as well as the rowing club near it. She'd also seen any number of kayaks in the back yards of the local houses, so things looked promising for a night crossing in a bought – or stolen – craft.

"I also saw a couple of Uruguayan naval patrol boats docked by the port, but they don't look very modern. Besides, it won't be the Uruguay patrols you'll need to worry about. Argentina will be the problem."

"How fast did the current seem?"

"It's moving, but it was hard to be sure. I figure we can go down later to the public beach and check it out. You should be able to get into the water there, and that will tell you everything you'll need to know. It didn't look too bad."

"That's positive."

After breakfast they packed the car and checked out, then walked the mile to the river and strolled along the waterfront street, watching the occasional small craft plying its way downstream. They saw a group of kayakers paddling in the gentle water from the nearby beach, and Alan chuckled after tracking their progress for a few minutes.

"This won't be a problem," he said, estimating the current speed.

"And it's all downstream from here. That's the bridge I'll be taking to go across." She pointed at the structure in the distance, shielding her eyes from the glare. "Come on. Let's go check out the beach and the marina."

Their first stop was the clubhouse by the marina, which had a sign out trumpeting its kayak rental business. Jet and Alan approached the owner, who was busy watching a small portable television set up on the counter, and asked him whether he sold kayaks. He shook his head – he bought them in Montevideo and had them trucked here. Alan asked whether anyone in Paysandú sold them, and the man's eyes flickered with annoyance.

"No, look around you. Not a big business, selling kayaks in a population-nothing place."

"How about we pay you double whatever you paid for one of yours?" Alan countered.

The man's expression changed to one of suspicion, and he refused. Jet pulled Alan's arm, wanting to get out of there. This wasn't going anywhere good. They'd have to steal one.

They spent the day walking the town. At a little internet café, they checked out satellite images of the area for an hour, looking for a good place to rendezvous on the Argentine side.

Jet pointed at the screen. "Look. That's perfect. A campground four miles south. It's out of the way and likely to be deserted this time of year. And there are plenty of roads. Let's get you a throwaway cell phone so we can communicate, and then find some good prospects for kayak theft."

That evening, as they sat at a restaurant near the river, they agreed that Alan would liberate a kayak from one of the four nearby houses they'd seen and depart at midnight. Jet would drive across earlier and find a road that would get her near the shore, and then wait for him to arrive.

"With any luck we should be in Buenos Aires tomorrow by mid-day. I already made reservations at the Four Seasons," she said. "But we'll be staying down the street, at the Alvear Palace. Just in case, somehow, someone is tracking the delivery. I'd rather pay for a room at the Four Seasons so we can get the package, but stay elsewhere, in the event that someone wants to put some bullets through us when we're in the room. The whole ferry exploding thing isn't to be underestimated, and if you were the target…"

Alan nodded, and took it in a lighter direction. "The Alvear Palace. Pretty fancy, huh? Palatial…"

"Nothing but the best. That's my new motto."

"Really? What was your old one?"

She smiled sweetly and took a sip of her soda. "Kill 'em all and let God sort 'em out."

He nodded. "I've used that one myself."

She held up her drink for a toast.

"To midnight running."

"Hear, hear."

CHAPTER 18

The dusty streets near the river were empty at eleven-thirty, Paysandú being a quiet town where the city rolled up the sidewalks once it got dark. Slim illumination glimmered from sparsely spaced streetlamps and an occasional porch light, and Alan was the only person to be seen.

Jet had left for the border earlier, and Alan set out from the center square on foot, taking his time, in no particular hurry. He didn't want to attract attention of any sort, so he stuck to the smaller roads, all of which led to the banks of the Uruguay River. From off in the distance, from a street at least four blocks away, he heard the slow drone of a vehicle meandering through town, its questionable exhaust rattling windows as it crept down the deserted thoroughfare.

The temperature had cooled once the sun had set, and a low-hanging blanket of clouds filled the sky, blocking any light from the moon and stars, which would work in his favor. He had his new cell phone in his breast pocket, set to vibrate so it wouldn't ring at the worst possible moment, and his black zip-up light jacket effectively shielded him from the evening chill. He just hoped it wouldn't rain. That would make the crossing miserable, although ultimately, it wouldn't matter. He still needed to get across, weather notwithstanding.

As he neared the water, the distinctive smell of the river permeated everything, and the sound of it rushing past the banks echoed off the surrounding buildings. A solitary small dog barked from the open window of a two-story home on his left, yapping its shrill lament to an uncaring world. Alan didn't need anyone peering out at him and getting suspicious, so he shrank into the shadows and moved away from the building.

When he arrived at the street that ran parallel to the river frontage road, he stopped to get his bearings. His casing of the neighborhood earlier that day had yielded several promising opportunities, and the first was on this street, a block and a half north. It was a single-story affair with a large, unkempt back yard, and one of the items strewn about the premises was a lightweight red kayak, perfect for his purposes. He edged to the rusting iron fence that protected the yard from the street and stopped, listening for any animals or indications anyone was awake. The lights were off, a thirty-year-old Chrysler K-car slowly corroding in the driveway, weeds pushing through the cracked concrete slab growing around it. He placed a hand on the hood. It was cool to the touch. The residents hadn't been out for a drive in hours, possibly days.

The gate latch squeaked when he slid it free, and he froze. After a few moments, the area still quiet, he pushed it open, the hinges creaking alarmingly. There were no signs of life, though, nothing moving, so he crept along the side of the house, ducking below the scraggly hedge that ran along the perimeter so as not to be seen from the adjacent windows.

Once he was in the yard, he squinted, trying to make out the shapes, and almost fell face first when his shoe caught on an old rake lying hidden in the grass. He swore silently and peered around, then spotted the outline of the boat at the far edge of the property, near the wall separating the lot from the rear neighbor's. Alan stepped gingerly through the weeds, anxious to avoid another trip and fall hazard, and when he reached the boat he exhaled a muted sigh of relief. The paddle was lying next to it, where it had been dropped by an unconcerned owner.

His eyes took in the back of the house, and then he moved to the kayak and lifted it, careful not to bump anything with the hull. It only weighed forty-five or so pounds, and he easily carried it on his shoulder as he took a few steps and knelt down to grab the paddle.

Which was broken.

Shit.

That was a problem, but one he would deal with once he was off the property. He considered taking the useless paddle and then discarded the idea, choosing instead to inch back to the street, senses alert for any signs of life. Alan retraced his steps and, once he was back on the sidewalk, trotted with the boat so as to minimize the chances of anyone spotting him on his way to the shore.

The river was dark, an inky flood snaking from beneath the brightly illuminated bridge in the near distance. Alan knew the rowing club was next to the marina, up a few blocks from his current position. While the hard part of securing a boat was over, he would need to get a paddle or the kayak was all but useless to him.

He came to the main frontage road, and seeing nothing in either direction, crossed it and sprinted across the open field to the river. Once there, he wheeled around, searching for a convenient place to hide his newly acquired treasure, and settled on a clump of sparse bushes a dozen feet from the water near a large tree that he couldn't miss on his return. Satisfied that nobody would be able to spot the red hull in the dark, he set out for the marina, jogging so that if anyone came upon him they might think him an exercise nut out for some late exertion.

In the little protected harbor, rows of boats creaked against the dock, the surge from the river tugging gently at their hulls, straining the mooring lines. Alan passed the pier and slowed, taking in the darkened marina just beyond. It was deserted at the late hour, but even so, he was cautious as he entered the grounds. He knew that the building where the kayaks were rented was at the far end of the complex, the hulking main building situated near the drive that led to the public park and beach just north.

When he reached the doors of the yacht club he paused, checking his watch. He would need to get moving, and couldn't waste a lot of time with stealthy entries. He didn't have any picks, so he settled for the next best thing – a nearby chunk of brick. Alan took a deep breath and then shattered the tall window next to the door, wincing at the crash as the glass shattered out of the frame. He half expected to hear alarms go off, and was relieved when silence returned to the area, his crude entry approach unnoticed.

At the far end of the main room, wooden shutters were pulled across the window of the equipment rental concession, barring entry to the storage room beyond. He tried the door, but it was locked. Keenly aware that every moment inside exposed him to risk, he kicked it, and the second blow shattered the doorjamb. The door swung open and he entered the room, and to his relief quickly found a kayak paddle hanging with dozens of kindreds on the nearest wall.

In a large bin by the far counter, Alan noted a heap of spray skirts. True, the water was pretty flat; the likelihood that he'd flip and need to roll was small. Still, was there any reason to be unprepared? The answer came as he took the first step towards the bin: the unmistakable sound of a car engine sounded from the frontage. Glancing at the paddle in his hand, he weighed his options. If he was caught in the building he was dead meat – there was no innocent explanation for breaking and entering. He'd have to forgo a spray skirt and get the hell out of there. Headlights now played on the far side of the building at the front, and he quickly ducked through the broken window and pushed his way out into the night, hoping that the darkness would cloak him long enough to reach the kayak.

Two car doors slammed in the parking lot as he bolted for the dirt slope that formed the sides of the marina. The going was slippery from moisture and grass, but he managed to get sixty yards from the building before he heard anything more.

A blast of static from a radio reverberated across the water, and then a high-pitched man's voice cut through the night from a distorting radio, confirming a report of a B&E. He continued to work his way to the southern edge of the marina, and then dared a peek over the edge of the slope to see what was happening at the building.

The officers must have gone inside, affording him the opportunity he needed. He sprinted up the incline and onto the path leading back to the pier, and increased his speed as he distanced himself from the scene of his petty larceny, his running shoes slapping against the pavement, his breathing measured, as was his gait.

A shout from behind him sounded at the building and he poured on the steam, willing his muscles to greater speed. A flickering flashlight beam roamed over him as he rounded the bend at the pier, and then he was out of sight, temporarily safe. Anyone working the graveyard shift on a small town Uruguayan police force wouldn't be a practiced marathon runner – by the looks of the two uniformed men he'd seen that afternoon, nobody was skipping any meals, and the treadmill at the station had been out of order since the Second World War.

Another shout trailed him from farther away, and he slowed as he approached the kayak's hiding place. Wasting no time, he dragged it from behind the bushes and ran to the water, setting it into the river before slipping into the narrow cockpit and pushing off from the bank.

He glided away from shore and began paddling, hoping that his pursuers would confine their attention to the path and ignore the river. He wasn't too worried – he had enough lead so it would be almost impossible to see him in another few minutes. The kayak sliced through the water as he propelled it with powerful strokes, and then the current caught him and he felt himself moving south.

A beam of light played across the water to his right, and then it was joined by a second from the shore. The damned cops were tenacious, he'd give them that, but they were too late – he was gone, and they'd have to solve the case of the missing paddle without his assistance.

His rowing had now hit a steady rhythm, with the current carrying him downstream in addition to his efforts, and he was congratulating himself on his speedy progress when he heard a motor start somewhere behind him. Sound was deceptive on the water, he knew, and what might appear to be a hundred yards back could easily be a mile or two. Whatever the case, he couldn't afford to lose his concentration. If the authorities were so bent on catching him that they were willing to send a patrol craft after him, he couldn't change that – he could only keep slogging towards his destination and hope that they wouldn't be able to make him out in the night.

The rumble of the engine changed tone, signaling to Alan that the boat was now under way, and he redoubled his efforts, his arms and shoulders burning from the intensity of his pace. A spotlight flared into life and moved across the channel, focusing on the center, and he steered closer to the next island, driving himself to go faster. The beam moved from the water to the Uruguay side of the river bank, inching along, looking for any evidence of him pulling to shore and making a run for it. He understood the logic – to the Uruguay police he was a thief, and it was inconceivable that a petty criminal would try to escape to Argentina. The complications of trying to get back into Uruguay would be far greater than pulling to shore and vanishing into the brush.

Up ahead the expected sand buildup materialized, and he edged nearer as the sound of the patrol boat diminished behind him. Another minute went by and then he was rowing into the channel, veering right, where he would be out of sight within seconds.

Once on the Argentine side of the island, he stopped paddling and retrieved the cell phone from his pocket. He speed dialed Jet's number and she answered on the first ring.

"Where are you?"

"I just cut through the channel. I should be there soon. Where are you?"

"Near one of the campgrounds. Call me back when you think you're closer and I'll turn my headlights on for a few seconds. You should be able to see them from the river, and you can head to shore directly below. I'm about a hundred yards from the bank."

"Okay."

He resumed paddling, and then five minutes later dialed her again. "Hit the lights."

Up ahead to his right, a pair of headlights came on for a brief second, then extinguished.

"Got it. I'll be there in two."

When Alan pulled to shore, Jet was standing, waiting for him.

"How did it go?" she asked as he stood, then slipped, falling into the river with a splash. He looked at her as he sat in a foot of water and laughed softly.

"About like this. The only thing that didn't happen was a dog bite," he said, standing up.

"The night's still young. Come on. Let's get out of here. We have a long way to go before morning."

He nodded, and then followed her up the hill, the sound of the patrol boat now far in the distance on the other side of the river.

CHAPTER 19

Standish opened the front door of the house with a flourish, his suit impeccable, as usual, his shoes gleaming so brightly from their shine that they nearly blinded Sloan, who had actually proposed today's meeting, rather than the customary other way around. The security guards stood at a discreet distance on either side of the house, eyeing him without expression. Sloan nodded to Standish, who stepped back, leaving the door ajar.

"Right on time, I see," Standish commented, studying his Patek Philippe World Timer.

"I do strive to be punctual."

"Yes, well, he's waiting. But I should warn you. He's not in a particularly good mood today."

"I sort of figured. Did you give him the news?"

"No. I told him that you had some follow-up from the errand he'd entrusted you with, but I didn't want to infuriate him any more."

"You mean you wanted me to take the heat."

"It's yours to take," Standish reminded him. "I'm not going to put myself in the line of fire for anyone. Sorry."

"Whatever. I can handle it. Let's go see the big man, shall we?"

Standish nodded, then turned and led the way through the foyer. Sloan closed the door behind him and noticed a security guard in the living room, tapping at a laptop computer. That was the first time he had seen one of the men inside the house.

"How many bedrooms is this place, again?"

"Six, plus the separate service quarters."

"That's a lot of space."

"It's one of the largest homes in the area."

"Big grounds, too."

"It's a double lot. Almost two hundred yards of frontage. He told me once that he wanted a secluded wooded setting. You'll note that the park is across the road, which contributes to the sense of exclusivity."

"There's certainly a feeling of seclusion."

"He wanted something that could be well-protected after his experience with…the woman."

"Hmm."

They clumped up the stairs, and Sloan paid more attention to the art than he usually did. Expensive oil paintings, all originals, as far as his eye could tell.

Arthur had done well for himself with his little sideline.

Standish held the bedroom door open for him and they entered, the humid, warm air cloying, as usual. The ventilator and humidifier were humming away, and Sloan took his time approaching the bed, allowing his eyes to adjust.

Standish cleared his throat. An annoying affectation, Sloan thought in passing.

"You have an update for us on the woman?"

"Yes. Something went wrong. We lost the entire team."

Arthur clutched at his oxygen mask, groping to remove it. The low beeping of his heart monitor began increasing, and within seconds was over a hundred beats per minute.

"What! How? What happened?" Arthur croaked, pre-empting Standish.

Sloan shifted, uncomfortable now that the ugly news had been delivered.

"We were only able to have a short conversation with the lone survivor. The driver. He was arrested and is being held by the Uruguayan authorities. We were able to supply an attorney for him, who got as much information as he could, but they had to be cautious. He felt that the holding cell might have been bugged."

Arthur said nothing, and then lifted a solitary finger, indicating that Sloan should continue.

"The team was taken out by a man. Blond, younger, hard-looking. That was the only thing he could tell us."

Standish shook his head. "What about the woman? He didn't mention the woman?"

"He made no mention of her."

"So where does that leave us?" Standish asked.

"At square one, but covering our tracks. We took precautions with the banker and the attorney – they're no longer a concern. But the contractor we hired to take care of them was involved in a car accident and didn't survive. We're still trying to get information on that, but there isn't much. Apparently he was involved in some sort of a disturbance."

"Stop speaking in riddles. What happened?" Arthur hissed, the effort costing him a lot.

"The best our man can figure out, there was a car chase, a few accidents, some shooting, and then, well, the contractor didn't make it."

"Who is your man?"

"We have a seasoned operative who speaks fluent Spanish, has a law degree, the whole nine yards. He's been with us for a decade. He has contacts in Uruguay, and one of them made an introduction to a ranking member of the police force. So we're privy to whatever they come up with. That's how we know about the chase, and the driver."

"Kill him," Arthur whispered, then dropped the oxygen back into place over his nose and mouth.

"Who? The operative, or the driver?"

Arthur raised his hand at the mention of the driver.

"That might not be so easy. He's in police headquarters in Montevideo, being held without bail. It's not like we can waltz in there and–"

Arthur's voice grew stronger as he lifted the mask. "I. Said. Kill. Him." Arthur over-enunciating each syllable was as effective as rifle shots.

"Very well. It's likely to be quite expensive. Perhaps we should–"

"I don't care." Arthur fixed the mask back into place and then closed his eyes. The meeting was over.

Standish tried not to smirk.

"We're not price-sensitive on tying this up so nothing can be traced back. But it would appear that this is as much your problem as it is ours, so I would expect that you will share the burden, given that it's a direct result of your team's failure," Standish said softly.

Sloan glared at him but bit his tongue.

"I understand and agree. These were some of our best men. I'm still trying to understand how this happened. The woman had help. That's obvious. So the question is, who, and what's his role in all of this? As it is, the intelligence we got was incomplete – intelligence that was provided by your side. Before you start laying this entirely at my feet, I'd suggest that you think about how we learned about the attorney and banker in the first place, and consider any holes in the dossier you gave us. Because it completely missed a mystery man who could neutralize a whole team without breaking a sweat," Sloan finished.

Standish understood that Sloan was playing to an audience of one, and didn't argue. It wasn't his money anyway, so his interest was more in seeming to be attending to Arthur's best interests than anything. He'd dragged Sloan through the coals and done all that could be expected, so his role in the elaborately choreographed ritual was over. At least until Sloan left, when he could expect a multi-hour harangue from Arthur demanding he be exterminated.

"Very well. We will look at our sources and try to figure out what, if any, errors or omissions there were. But one final question. What is the plan moving forward about the woman? This 'Jet'?" Standish demanded.

"We're flying in a new group of specialists, and working on picking up her scent. But we have no promising leads at this point, other than the older woman and the child. While that may seem like a lot, in truth it isn't. Uruguay has three and a half million people. And it's a largely cash economy, so much of the commerce is done off the books. Much like Argentina. Which means we can't track her easily, if at all. Unlike the United States, many of the inhabitants don't use or have credit cards, so there's no transaction trail to follow. What I'm trying to say is that with only her name, it's a shot in the dark."

"But surely the child poses an opportunity."

"Yes and no. There are a lot of toddlers in that region of the world. And don't forget they've gone to ground with this Jet's help, and she knows the game. We have the condo staked out, and the police are looking for them, but there's only so much they can do – she's only wanted for routine questioning. The doorman wasn't sure who was in the building, so there's a low probability of the old woman being scooped up if she's hiding. Which I think it's safe to assume she is."

"What about the bank account?"

"There's been no further activity on it. And of course, the banker is dead, so our ability to gather more information is, er, limited."

"Did you have to kill him?" Standish asked.

"Yes. Don't second guess me. He was a loose end we couldn't have hanging out there," Sloan snapped. He was starting to get annoyed, answering to Standish with his insolent tone. He took a deep breath and exhaled evenly. "Now, if there isn't anything else…"

Standish looked over at Arthur, who raised his hand off the bed and then dropped it, indicating that the meeting was concluded. Standish moved to the door and opened it, gesturing to Sloan.

When they were back downstairs, Sloan turned to Standish. "It's going to cost a lot. And I mean a lot."

"Fortunately, he has a lot. You heard the nice man. Kill him," Standish said, then walked Sloan to the door. "Now, speaking of not wanting to take bullets for anyone, I'm going to have to go back upstairs into that oven and listen to him demand your head, and talk him down. It's going to be a very unpleasant few hours."

"I'll owe you one."

"You owe me more than one. He's degrading, slowly but surely, and his answer to everything lately is, 'Kill them.' Half the population of D.C. would be dead if I didn't talk him out of it."

"Well, that's not such a bad idea, but hey, I get it. I'll find a way to express my gratitude."

"Do that."

Sloan was pensive as he walked down the stairs to his car. Standish was getting too big for his britches. He'd become a liability at some point; but for now, he played a useful role in keeping Arthur in line.

Sloan slid into the back seat and adjusted the air-conditioning vent so that it was blowing on his face. The bedroom's warm humidity always put him in a lousy mood. Arthur was getting to a point where he was becoming too erratic to be a decent client. Sloan had made huge amounts of money working with the man, but everything ended eventually, and as Arthur's condition worsened, he was going to become more of a risk.

At some point soon, he would probably have to pull the plug on Arthur. Which, if it had been Sloan in Arthur's shoes, he would have thanked him for.

Sloan shuddered involuntarily at the thought of being sentenced to living the remainder of his life in agony. He would never understand why Arthur didn't just load up a syringe with too much morphine and drift off into oblivion. Anything would be better than what he was going through.

Perhaps there was something he was missing, but he didn't think so. Arthur seemed to be clinging to life with a tenacity that surprised everyone, even if it was torture. His obsession with rooting out his enemies and crushing them at any cost kept him alive, along with maintaining a position in the game he'd been playing his entire adult life.

Venom seemed to be keeping him going, waking up every day, continuing even though he was in unimaginable pain.

Maybe it wasn't that hard to figure out after all.

Arthur was probably just too damned mean to die.

CHAPTER 20

Dawn was breaking as Jet and Alan reached Buenos Aires, and the great city was stirring to life, its inhabitants rousing themselves in preparation for another grueling day. The streets were just beginning to see the traffic the metropolis was notorious for, and early delivery trucks jockeyed for position with taxis and partygoers just leaving the discos as morning light flooded the city.

The drive had been every bit as bad as Jet expected, with lousy roads and the occasional animal standing in the middle of the highway slowing their progress as they drove south. Alan had been silent most of the trip, and as they drew closer to Buenos Aires she'd caught him dozing.

Jet pulled up to the imposing façade of the Alvear Palace Hotel, and a valet ran down the steps to get their door, a second young man rushing to carry their bags up to the reception area as they entered the lobby – a reminder of bygone elegance, everything reeking of opulence, gold leaf and columns framing antique tapestries and elaborate artwork. The hotel was one of the stately edifices in a city known for its European architecture, and it took its job as a flagship of refined style seriously, catering to the well-heeled, a veritable who's who of diplomats, captains of industry, and the idle rich.

Jet and Alan gratefully followed the bellman to the bank of elevators, where gold doors glided open to whisk them skyward to their room. The suite itself was stunning, all French revival furniture that would have been at home in the most elegant residences in Paris. After tipping the bellman generously, Jet threw herself onto the embroidered cover of the king-sized bed with a happy sigh.

"Tell me this isn't a welcome change after the dumps we've been in for the last few days!" she exclaimed.

"Very nice. I just wish I was awake enough to be more impressed. I'm beat. Can we hit it for a few hours? Recharge the batteries?"

"You're singing my tune. I'm pretty worked."

"I'll bet. You want first dibs on the bathroom? I want to take a shower. Get the river water off me."

She slid her legs to the edge of the bed and stood up, then moved to her bag and unzipped it. "Would you put the cash in the room safe? It said online that they had oversized boxes."

"Sure. But you better hurry up, or I'll be asleep by the time you make it out."

She pulled some clothes out of the suitcase and disappeared into the bathroom as Alan secured the money and then turned on the television. The Argentine news stations were still featuring the ferry atrocity as their lead story, vying for prominence with coverage of an upcoming soccer match against their hated rival Brazil.

Jet was in and out within ten minutes, and emerged wearing a tank top and her running shorts. Alan grunted as he stood and handed her the remote, and then went into the bathroom to rinse off. When he came out, his wet hair standing on end, she smiled and shut off the television.

"Now that's a bathroom! I could move into this place," Alan announced.

"It's pretty nice, isn't it? But at five hundred dollars a night, it could add up quickly."

"Nonsense. Only the best for you, my dear," Alan said gallantly, and then plopped down next to where she was reclining against a couple of overstuffed pillows.

"At least you've got your priorities straight," she teased, and then switched off her bedside lamp. The heavy brocade curtains blocked all the light from outside as well as any noise from the street, and after Alan slipped under the covers he was snoring quietly within seconds of shutting off his lamp.

Four hours later, he stirred, and then rolled over and studied Jet's face in the gloom. She looked so serene and at peace. Young. It was impossible to believe all the hardship she'd been through, but he knew her story well. His heart went out to her. What his brother had done – the choice he'd made to keep Hannah a secret, even from her – was reprehensible, and he didn't see how she had gotten over the betrayal. But she had. She was resilient; one of the many qualities about her that captivated him.

Alan brushed a lock of her hair off her face, and her nose crinkled as she slumbered. He got up and padded to the bathroom, where he caught a glimpse of his reflection. Hesitating, he scowled at himself. It had been a hell of a week. From Yemen to Moscow to L.A. and then Uruguay. The terrorist bio-attack, the ferry explosion, the hit team, the river crossing. He'd survived worse, but it was still a record for him, and the worst wasn't over, he knew. He had no idea what they were going to be walking into in Washington, but he was pretty sure that whatever it was wouldn't be good.

Alan inspected his square jaw and confident eyes, and then turned on the tap and splashed cool water on his face. They had at least a few days to decompress before they left Buenos Aires, so perhaps they'd be able to relax a little. He was quite sure that Jet was torn inside over leaving Hannah, and God knows she could use a break – her week had been almost as bad as his.

He reached out and lifted one of the thick, heavy towels from the rack and dried his face, and then turned the light off and opened the door to the bedroom. Maybe he could get another couple of hours of rest, he thought, and then Jet's arms were around his neck and she was pressing herself against him, kissing him with her incredible mouth, her scent intoxicating. She moaned, a small sound of hunger, challenge, and surrender; they fell together on the bed, and all thoughts of the future faded as there was only her, her passion ablaze, her need as relentless as his.

∽∾

Jet dozed in Alan's arms, spent, dizzy from the intensity of their lovemaking. She snuggled against him and sighed contentedly, the tension that had been strangling her suddenly gone. He shifted at her touch but didn't wake up. She tried to fall back asleep, but her mind wouldn't let her. It had been so long since she'd been with anyone that she'd almost forgotten how good it could be, but another part of her felt…odd. Not bad or in any way guilty, but also not like she only wanted to melt into Alan's embrace. Perhaps that feeling would never happen again – the one she'd treasured with David.

Why did she have to complicate things with memories of his brother David now, of all times? He'd betrayed her, destroyed her faith in him. Part of her hated him. As well it should.

But it was undeniable that another part missed what they had shared. It had been special. She'd known it at the time, and knew it now.

It was unfair to compare the two. That wasn't what she was doing. But there was a core of her, deep inside, that wished, for only a split second, that David hadn't died and that they'd somehow figured their lives out, patched things up, and gone on to be a family – admittedly, a highly dysfunctional one, but a family nonetheless.

Jet stirred and pulled away from Alan, his soft breath still on her shoulder, and she opened her eyes and looked around the room. It was still dark as night inside, a tribute to the density of the curtains, and she had to check her watch to verify the time. It was five o'clock. They'd spent most of the day in the room, and she realized with a start that she hadn't spoken to Magdalena all day.

A stray tear ran down from the corner of her eye, and she rubbed it away on the pillow. Why was she getting so emotional? It was unlike her. Perhaps the memories of David had resurrected some conflicted feelings – feelings she could do without. Alan was a good man and an honest one, from what she knew. That she could allow his lying, controlling brother to intrude at a moment of happiness like this was probably proof of how screwed up she was, she thought grimly. A therapist could retire on what went on in her head. Of course, then she'd have to kill him, but still.

She slipped out of the bed and went to her purse, then collected her clothes from the floor before easing the bathroom door open and inching inside. Magdalena's new cell rang four times, and then her distinctive voice answered.

"*Hola.*"

"*Hola*, Magdalena. How is everything?"

"Good. Nothing earth-shattering to report. Hannah's bored out of her mind, but we found a playground three blocks away and she met some new friends, and we agreed to meet up tomorrow for some play time."

"That's great. I'm glad you're getting along well."

"No problems. And we've found a few more restaurants, so nobody's starving to death. All in all, everything's fine."

"I'm so glad. Is she there? Can I talk to her?"

"She's napping. Do you want me to wake her up?"

Jet felt a tug. Hannah, sleeping happily, oblivious to the drama surrounding her. "No, let her sleep. I'll call either later this evening, or tomorrow. Do you need anything?"

"Not that I can think of. Like I said. Everything is going well, and we're getting along fine."

"I hope to be back soon, Magdalena. I appreciate your helping me out and taking care of her."

"There's no chance of your…of this man who is after you finding us, is there?" Magdalena asked.

"None at all. You're safe. Just keep a low profile, and everything will sort itself out. I can't say anything more, but you can trust me on this. I won't let anything hurt either of you."

Magdalena sounded tentatively reassured, and after a few more minutes of small talk, Jet signed off. The decision to move them to the boonies had proved a good one. They were completely off the radar, and safe.

Her thoughts turned to their predicament. Alan's passport would be there in another day, and then they could sneak into the U.S. and find out who was trying to kill her and why. She'd done as much research as she could on the private security company while online, but there wasn't a lot of information available. The CEO, Jim Sloan, was reclusive and avoided the press, and because there were no public filings, her searches had shown up precious little other than that the company provided contractors in conflict areas, like Iraq, as well as handling private security matters domestically. Nordhaver had been founded two decades ago by Sloan, who had the reputation as a control freak – which went with the territory, she knew from David. Beyond that, the organization was a black box, and she had no visibility into it other than that its operatives had shown up at the condo with murder on their minds.

Jet peered at the phone screen and thumbed through the numbers until she found the one she was looking for, and then dialed it, waiting until a man's deep voice answered. She explained what she needed and he assured her that he could help, and then gave her brief instructions. She was to fly to Tijuana and contact him once there, and he would arrange for the trip into the United States. He named the price, which was higher than she had hoped, but she wasn't in the mood to negotiate. Fifty grand would get them both to California, and from there they'd be on their own.

Jet dropped the phone into her purse and turned on the shower, pausing to study herself in the mirror. She didn't look any different, but she didn't feel completely herself. Too many unknowns, she supposed, as she stepped under the warm spray and reached for the bar of herbal soap.

One way or another she would figure out what was going on and put an end to it. She'd had enough of being separated from her daughter, and she'd be damned if she would let anything keep them apart. Hannah deserved better than to have to hide in motel rooms, wondering where her mother was. Jet lathered her hair with some citrus shampoo and rinsed the excess off her face, enjoying the sensation of the stream of water on her taut skin as she thought about her daughter and what was to come. Hannah was innocent, and yet her life had been one of constant uprooting to evade danger. That had to end.

For both their sakes.

CHAPTER 21

"So, big boy, what do you want to do tonight?" Jet asked, swinging one leg as she reclined in a chair watching the news, her bronze skin shimmering in the soft light.

"Food sounds like a good option, don't you think?" Alan said from the bed.

Jet looked at him, his hair matted on one side and sticking up straight on the other, a two-day growth of beard darkening his jaw line.

"I was online earlier and checked out some restaurants. And also…a tango show."

Alan gave her a neutral look. "A tango show," he repeated.

"Yes. It's one of the must-see things in Buenos Aires. And since we're tourists for a few days…"

He considered her request and then smiled. "As long as you don't drag me to the ballet or opera, how bad could a tango show be?"

"That's very courageous of you. Being willing to try new things, and all."

He sat up and his eyes flitted over her long legs and smooth abdomen, her panties and tank top leaving little hidden.

"This has been one of my favorite new-thing-trying periods of my life. I mean that. Other than the midnight swimming, of course."

"Well, I'm glad you found something you like. All work makes Alan a dull boy. So I take it that's a yes on the show? I'll book it for tonight."

She reached over and lifted the telephone handset and turned down the television volume.

The concierge had recommendations for both the show and restaurants, even though by Argentine standards they were eating unreasonably early, having dinner at eight-thirty.

When they arrived at Rio Alba, in the Palermo district, the restaurant was only half full due to the early hour. They got a table near the rear of the restaurant, and a vested waiter with slicked-back hair approached them and took their order, suggesting a bottle of Argentine Malbec to accompany their steaks. Alan looked at Jet, shrugged, and took the man's suggestion – a La Flor Reserva.

"I know you aren't a big drinker," Alan started.

"I might just change my reputation tonight. When in BA, do as the locals do." She gestured at the other diners, all of whom had bottles of red wine on their tables. "Besides, this is the red meat capital of the world, and I've been warned that you can't have an Argentine steak without some vino."

"It smells delicious," Alan said, turning to the wood-fired grill, where the chefs were throwing huge strips of beef on the brander plates.

"And it's good for you. Did you know that all the beef in Argentina is grass fed – what they call free range?"

"Why does that matter?"

"Because the fat in the cows is different. Eating grass-fed beef is like eating salmon. All good fat, no bad. What makes red meat toxic in a lot of countries is the grain feeding. You feed a cow grain, it gets fat a lot faster, but it also converts into what they call bad fat. It's great if you're in the cow business, because you can get a cow to the point where it's ready for slaughter much sooner, especially if you throw in a bunch of hormones, but it's terrible for anyone eating it. The Argentines don't subscribe to that. They drink gallons of red wine, eat beef three times a day, and are generally healthier than people in the U.S., who are fed a diet of hormone-enhanced, corn-syrup-fortified crap while agonizing over every calorie."

The waiter arrived with their wine, and Alan nodded as he poured some for him to taste.

"Mmm. Delicious."

Once their glasses were filled, Alan held his aloft and toasted Jet, who clinked her goblet against his and took a sip.

"Wow. That's good. I don't drink a lot of wine, but if I stayed here, I might start," she said, then had another taste.

"You seem to know a lot about cows," Alan observed.

"I spend a lot of time on the web when I'm not flying all over the world to kill bad guys." She smiled sweetly. "Which is getting old, by the way."

"I can imagine. You must miss Hannah."

She nodded. "More than you know."

Their salads arrived with a flourish, and they dug in.

"So, tell me about this tango thing. What have I gotten myself into?" Alan asked between mouthfuls.

"We're going to the late show – normally it's a combination dinner and performance, but two nights a week they do just a cocktail show. This one is down in the San Telmo district, which is south of here, by the water. All the best shows are there, according to the concierge – and he hasn't lied to us yet."

"How long does it last?"

"About an hour and a half. Don't worry. They'll serve alcohol."

"As you know, I'm not a big boozer, either, but seeing as I'm newly retired, I could always learn. Especially if all the wines tastes like this one."

After a suitable wait, their steaks came: huge servings of mouth-watering meat cooked to perfection.

"This is enough for three meals," Jet commented, and took a bite. "Oh my God. I mean, really. You have to taste this." She cut a piece and handed her fork across the table to Alan.

He popped it into his mouth and chewed with relish. "Wow. What is that again?"

"*Entraña*. It says on the menu that it's a flank steak, but I've never had one like this, not even in Uruguay, which is also known for its beef."

"Here. Try a bite of mine. Filet."

They lingered over their meal, savoring the moment, and when the last of the wine splashed into their glasses Jet was feeling a little lightheaded – but in a good way. She looked at her watch and shook her head at the waiter's offering of dessert. As it was, she had left almost half her steak, although Alan found room for all of his and a few more bites of hers.

They paid the bill and took a taxi to the club, where they stood in line with a gathering of tourists from all over the world, the musical sounds of Italian mixing with English and German in the crisp night air. Ten minutes later the doors opened, the facility having been cleaned from the dinner show, and everyone filed into the large banquet room and took seats facing the stage.

Once everyone was inside and settled, the lights dimmed as a waitress brought carafes of wine to the tables. A couple moved into the spotlight, the man dressed in a 1930s-era black suit and his young female partner wearing a red velvet dress that clung to her like a second skin, with slits up either side that reached her hips.

Music followed a smattering of applause, and then the dancers began to move, slowly at first, he leading her in an intricate circle around the stage, their legs coming together and parting in an elaborate pattern known only to them. The swell of the tango pulsed as they meshed, she leaning into him, he maintaining an arrogant stance, chin up, the pomade in his severely-cut black hair glistening in the light. On and on it went, the steps increasing in complexity to the music's hypnotic throb until Jet felt dizzy just watching it, the dance unlike anything she'd ever seen – sultry, sexy, elaborate but effortless, the moves impossible to remember other than as a complex impression of the whole.

When the song ended, the audience burst into applause, and even Alan appeared transfixed by the performance, clapping heartily as the pair bowed and another couple took their place – this one an older man and a teenage girl, also in the garb of a bygone era.

An accordion started the next song, its plaintive stridency cutting off the last of the applause at the couple's appearance, and then a crooning male voice joined the pulse of the bass and the sweep of the piano and violin, crafting a melody that stopped Jet's breath in her throat at the tragic beauty of the heartbreaking ballad. The couple glided back and forth, a perfect expression of love lost and the futility of life's inevitable struggles, and when the song ended Jet felt on the verge of tears.

The applause this time was a roar, and when it died down, Jet took Alan's hand in hers. If there was such a thing as a perfect evening, this was shaping up to be one; and as they watched the endless parade of incredibly talented performers demonstrate the myriad different nuances of Argentina's famed dance, she felt a stirring and a closeness to him that had been fleeting earlier.

The wine disappeared and eventually the lights came back on, the performance finished, the magic of the mood broken as the tipsy tourists milled towards the exit. Jet waited until most had left before standing, and when she gazed up at Alan, her eyes were moist.

"Thank you for taking me to this, Alan. It means a lot to me. It was so...so beautiful."

He leaned down and kissed her softly on the mouth. "Maybe those Argentines know a thing or two about romance, eh? I've never seen anything like that," he conceded.

They held hands as they moved to the doors, and Jet had a comfortable feeling of closeness, of safety. Her doubts about Alan from earlier had vanished with the wine, and when they hailed a taxi she kissed him again.

"I could get used to Buenos Aires," he said when the car drew up.

"It does have its charm," she agreed.

They sat in silence while they returned to the hotel. She leaned against his shoulder as the cab swayed down the boulevards, her worries seemingly a million miles away, her awareness limited to the here and now, with Alan, and nowhere else.

CHAPTER 22

When Alan checked in at the Four Seasons the following day, he didn't go to the room, electing to just pay for two days before going up one elevator and down the other. He didn't detect anything suspicious in the lobby, but he was taking no chances, and he took the long way back to the Alvear Palace, watching for any telltale signs as he ambled along the streets of the Recoleta.

His attorney friend had emailed Alan the tracking number, and the next day at three, the website indicated the package had been delivered. Alan and Jet set out on foot to the hotel – the plan was to pick up the envelope and then leave, with Jet watching Alan's back to ensure he was still clean.

At the hotel, there was a small amount of confusion locating the package, but after a few minutes it materialized and he signed for it. As agreed, he sauntered to the restrooms off the lobby and opened the envelope in one of the stalls, disposing of the packaging in the wastepaper basket before exiting and meeting Jet outside.

"You're okay. Nothing obvious in the lobby. But I would suggest going over the documents with a fine-toothed comb to ensure there are no tracking chips hidden in one of them. As you know, nowadays—"

Alan finished the thought for her. "Yes, nowadays they can fit one almost anywhere."

She looked sheepish. "I'm sorry. You know as much about this as I do. I'm not trying to be patronizing."

"No worries. I don't take it as such. It's good to be reminded of the little things. Let's go get a cup of coffee somewhere and I'll go through both passports as well as the credit cards. There would have to be a power source, though, so the likelihood is pretty small. If there's one in either of the passports it would have to be in the cover. And the credit cards are even more unlikely – I signed them, so they're the originals I left with him. Both still have a year or so before they expire, by the way, so we have some more resources if we need them."

"I'd shy away from using anything that could be traced. Call me superstitious…"

"I know what you mean. Hey, let's stop in there. It looks as good as any."

He pointed to a café on the far corner, and they crossed the street and entered, taking a seat where they could see the sidewalk.

Jet ordered for both of them as Alan went to the bathroom, and when he returned five minutes later he sat down with a grin. "They're fine. Clean as a newborn."

"That's good. At least you can trust him."

"I never doubted it. Now, what's the plan from here?"

"There's an Aeromexico flight tonight at eleven-thirty," Jet said. "Gets in around six tomorrow morning in Mexico City, and then there's a flight a few hours later to Tijuana. I say we're on it, now that you have your passport."

"And then?"

"I call my contact once we're on the ground in TJ, and he gives me further instructions. But he guaranteed he could get us into the U.S., no problem, so my guess is that by tomorrow night we should be in California. From there, we can either rent a car, or buy or steal one, and hit the road. It should take us a couple of days, no more, to get to Washington, if we drive around the clock. The U.S. airport security is too tight to fly, and the trains and buses are also monitored. So it's a long haul cross-country, driving the speed limit."

"Can't we get in somewhere else closer to Washington? Canada? Florida?"

"I don't have anyone that can do that. I'm sure it's possible, but we'd waste more time trying to find someone than we would just driving. Besides which, Florida is a thousand miles from Washington, whereas California is about two. Basically, California adds a day of drive time to the schlep, but it's a lock that we make it in."

"Sounds good. What do they need to see if we rent a car?"

"Passport, driver's license, and credit card. I don't like that option as much as I do buying or stealing a car. Buying would be best."

"Maybe your contact can arrange for a vehicle?"

"I'll ask. I wouldn't imagine it would be too hard. And we don't need a Rolls. Just something dependable enough to get us to Washington. I'll give him another call and see if he can line something up."

"Any chance he would sell you out?"

"To who? We don't even know who's after me. If he could figure that out before we do, we should hire him." Jet tasted her coffee and sighed. "They do have great coffee here, don't they?"

"Too bad they don't give you a steak to munch on with the java."

"You can't be hungry again. We had a late breakfast."

"I'm a growing boy."

They laughed easily, Jet's eyes prowling the street out of habit. When they were finished, they paid and walked back to the hotel, arms around each other, a happy couple out for an afternoon stroll.

Back in the room, Jet went to work, first booking the flights and then talking to her contact. He assured her that he could get them a car by the following evening, and guessed that it would cost another fifteen grand for an older one, twenty for a newer – sanitized, with plates, a private party sale where she could put whatever name she liked on the pink slip once she was on her way. Jet was liking the man's professionalism more and more, and agreed to go for the newer option. When she hung up, she felt better about the next phase of their journey.

"What about guns?" Alan asked.

"Probably the easiest thing to do in the U.S. is get a gun – America is the most armed country in the world. We can get guns from private parties, gun shows…and if we need something specialized, there are a lot of criminals selling them. It's probably easier to get a submachine gun on the street than it is most places, other than maybe Yemen or Afghanistan."

"It sounds like you've done your research."

"No, I still need to check for gun shows in the vicinity once we're around Washington. And I need to map our route, and figure out where I can sell a few diamonds in case we need cash. I've actually got a decent amount to do before we leave for the airport."

Alan took the hint and went to clean up. "You want to grab dinner before we head out?" he called from the bathroom.

"Absolutely. We don't have to be there until around ten since we're only taking carry-ons, so we can go wherever you want."

He poked his head out of the door and eyed her. "How about that place down on the water we heard about? Puerto Madero?"

"You're on. Give me a few hours to get this stuff sewn up."

~~~

They were the only ones in the restaurant at eight o'clock, and they were in and out in an hour. Their experience at the airport was equally expedient, and they made their flight with forty-five minutes to spare, sitting around the departure lounge, the airport nearly empty at the late hour.

Unlike Alan's flight south from Mexico City, the trip north was smooth, and they were able to sleep most of the way. When the stewardess came by to offer them an early breakfast, Alan started awake, and Jet could see him stiffen for a few seconds until he registered where he was. She knew the feeling, and wondered if they would ever be able to put that survival instinct aside and become normal. She wanted to believe it could happen, but her gut said that wasn't possible, given their histories.

The Mexico City airport was quiet when they landed, and customs took a third of the time she would have expected, their passports waved through after barely a glance by a sleepy agent with a hound dog face and a Pancho Villa mustache, who looked like he had just woken up. They had more than a few hours to kill before their flight to Tijuana, so they found a restaurant and dallied over their coffee, Jet using her phone to connect to the wireless and surf the web.

"I got an email back from a jeweler in Washington who said he'd be very interested in looking at a couple of my stones, so it looks like we'll have some mad money if we need it," she reported, peering intently at the screen.

"Oh, good. Because after we're done with the smuggler and the car and the flights, we'll only have…sixty thousand U.S.?"

"A little more than that, but I figure it can't hurt to be loaded with cash. My experience is that it can get you out of a lot of jams."

"What will the stones bring?"

"Pretty close to a couple of hundred."

"Thousand?"

"Yup. They're nearly flawless, and at the top of the color class. There's tremendous variation in cost, but for a VVS1 stone with a B or C color in the three to four carat range – that's a very valuable diamond."

"And you have a bag of them around your neck. I want to party with you."

"I thought you were interested in more than my money."

He reached across the table and took her hand. "That's what I tell people who have a lot of money."

She swatted at him playfully, and then closed the browser.

"How long will it take to get to Tijuana?" he asked.

"About three and a half hours. We should be there just before three o'clock."

"It's a lot of flying."

"Followed by a whole lot of driving. Might as well get used to the idea. It's going to be a lousy couple of days no matter how we slice it," she said.

The flight north was also smooth, and Jet caught another few hours of sleep, reasoning that it might be the last she got for the foreseeable future. When the plane descended on final approach she roused herself and stared out the window at the sprawling city, with San Diego in the near distance, only a few hundred yards separating the seemingly boundless prosperity of the richest nation in the world from its struggling neighbor to the south.

Once they were in the main terminal, Jet called her contact and he told her to get a taxi from the airport and take it to the port city of Ensenada, an hour and a half south of the border, and to tell the driver to drop her off at the Hotel Coral marina. They quickly located a bank of waiting vehicles and within moments were racing through town to the coast road that ran from Tijuana to the tip of Baja.

At four-thirty they pulled up to a large hotel on the water, just north of Ensenada, with a prominent sign announcing it as the Coral. The cab pulled around to the side, and once past the security guard, sped down a drive to the marina offices. Jet and Alan exchanged a look, and Jet paid the driver as she withdrew her phone and dialed the contact again. He answered on the third ring, and when she announced that they had arrived, he told her to hang up and look to her left.

A man in colorful board shorts and a long-sleeved T-shirt waved at her, his baseball cap on backwards, sunglasses perched on his hawkish nose, a three-day growth of graying stubble adorning his face.

"Welcome to paradise. You got my cash?" he asked by way of greeting, carrying a six-pack of beer in one hand and a paper bag in the other.

"As agreed. How do you want to do this?"

"We go to one of the boats down in the marina. You pay me. I start the engines and point the bow north. In less than three hours you're in San Diego, free as birds, meeting my man Pancho, who has a car lined up for you," he responded.

"Just like that?" Alan asked skeptically.

The man eyed him, then looked back at Jet.

"We could make it more dramatic, and have you try to crawl through a tunnel in the worst section of TJ, hoping there's nobody with a gun waiting for you on the other end. But I was thinking maybe a nice boat ride in a sixty-five foot Ocean that will do an easy thirty-knot cruise might be more your speed. Up to you, but I'd opt for the boat ride," he said easily.

"I love boat rides. Let's go," Jet said, and without further discussion they followed him down to the docks, where he opened the security gate and motioned for them to walk onto the floating concrete slabs. Once they were on the water, he led them to the end of the dock, where a beautiful fishing yacht was docked. A Mexican deck hand lounged on the transom, a blue bandana on his head.

Jet inspected the back of the boat. "Pipe Dream?" she said, reading the name, noting it was flagged with Dana Point as its home port.

"That's right. It's a U.S. boat. I run it back and forth all the time. Two ways to do this: either you take the dinghy once we're in the harbor and head to the inspection dock, or we hook up with another boat out at the Coronado islands, you move to that boat, and it takes you in. If we do the dinghy, it's a little riskier – the customs guys are used to me, and I know their drill cold, but nothing's a hundred percent. Today, we'll just do a straightforward switch to one of my buddy's boats. He's out fishing, but the fleet will head back by dusk, so we'll have some privacy. You take that boat in, which doesn't have to clear customs, and meet my contact for the car. Simple."

"You can't be serious. There are no patrol boats to stop us?"

"Sure, there are harbor patrol boats, but they don't work for customs and immigration. They have to send a guy over from the airport to meet me and sign my forms. But it won't matter – you'll be coming into the harbor on a boat that's not being watched," he explained, and then grinned. "I've done this a few times. Don't sweat it. I've got it down to a science. We can make it really difficult, but it isn't. They aren't expecting illegals to be on luxury cruisers. Hell, they don't even inspect the boat. I could have a hundred kilos of coke in the bilge and they'd never notice. It's wild. But there it is."

"Shall we count your money?" Jet asked, convinced.

"My favorite part of the day. Watch your step as you board," he cautioned.

The deckhand reached out and helped her, taking her hand as she stepped onto the swim step. Alan followed, shrugging off the offer of assistance, and a few minutes later they were sitting in the expansive salon, the air conditioning humming, as the smuggler slurped at his beer and counted hundred dollar bills, the big diesel engines throbbing below them as they warmed up.

"All right. It's all there. Pleasure doing business with you. I don't want to know your names or anything about you. Stay down here, out of sight, in case they're tracking us on satellite, and when we get close I'll give you a holler." Jet gave him a troubled look. "Kidding about the satellite."

Jet and Alan exchanged a glance and then nodded.

The smuggler stood, dropped the money into the paper bag and rolled up one end before walking to the rear door and moving out onto the deck and up the stainless steel stairs to the fly-bridge. The deckhand untied the lines and stowed them inboard, and then they pulled out of the slip and putted the fifty yards to the harbor mouth. Once they had cleared the jetty, their anonymous captain opened the engines up and the bow rose out of the water. Soon they were well clear of land, and they were slicing through the five foot swells like the seas were flat.

Once they rounded the point, a pair of islands on their left, the seas got larger – six to seven footers with white water on top, but the big boat cut a clean swath through the blue waves, pounding until the captain backed off the throttles a little and they weren't flying off the top of each swell.

Jet settled into the leather sofa and closed her eyes, the drone of the diesels a constant, their low rumble and the motion of the boat lulling her into a drowsy state as they fought their way north against the prevailing winds.

Two hours later the engines dropped in volume and the boat slowed. The captain reappeared and pulled two fishing rods out of a storage locker and set them into rod holders on either side of the boat, then swung the salon door open.

"We're here. There are only a couple of boats out. A crap day for fishing – everyone pretty much got skunked. I talked to my buddy Carl on the boat you'll be taking into San Diego. He's going to meet up with us on the western side of the biggest island, out of sight of the mainland and the other boats, and we'll do the transfer. Should be about five minutes. I'll hang around for an hour so it looks like I'm fishing, then head into San Diego for the night. Anyone tracking me on radar will think I tried to get some hook time before I headed in." He looked off in the distance, where a huge Coast Guard cutter sat near the horizon. "He's looking for drug smugglers. Not respectable white fellahs out for a little south-of-the-border fun on their yachts."

"Who's driving the boat?" Alan asked.

"Auto-pilot. But I better get back up there. Won't be long now." The captain reeked of beer, and Jet cringed inwardly as he leaned towards her. "Lemme know if you need anything else. You got my number. Anything at all I can do for you."

"Thanks. I'll remember that."

The captain waved and then returned to his station up top, and they watched through the side windows as the big boat approached a smaller fishing boat, a thirty-five-foot Cabo bristling with fishing rods. *Cohiba* rocked as they approached, the captain of that craft using his engines to hold it stationary, and their boat slid alongside it, a bumper keeping the two hulls from scraping.

A bear-like man with Oakley sunglasses and a biker beard extended his hand from *Cohiba*. "Welcome aboard. Throw me your bags, and then the lady comes over first."

They did as instructed, and Jet leapt easily onto the deck of the other boat, followed by Alan. The big Ocean pulled nearer to the island, and the captain waved from the fly-bridge as the Cabo got underway.

"You want a beer?" the big man asked, the captain up top ignoring them, concentrating on piloting the boat.

"No, thanks. How long will it take to get into port?" Jet asked.

"About an hour. Just make yourselves at home in the salon. There's water, soda, and beer in the fridge. And a bag of corn chips. Go wild," he said, and then handed them their bags and ascended the ladder to the flybridge without another word.

The trip in was routine, as expected, nobody stopping them, and when they eased into a slip on Shelter Island, a wiry Vietnamese man approached and helped them off the boat.

"Pancho?" Jet asked, her face a blank.

"Yeah. That's the captain's idea of a funny. Name's Mike. Welcome to the land of the free and all that shit. You wanna see your new car?" he asked in rapid-fire English with a surfer-dude accent.

"Sure." Jet didn't see any point in elaborating.

They walked up the dock and onto land, and Mike led them to a newer Ford Focus. It was the perfect car for their needs: completely invisible, millions like it on the roads all over the country. He held out the keys to Alan.

"Plates are legal. Pink slip's in the glove compartment. Won't be listed as sold for a few weeks – I get forgetful sometimes. You've got another month on the tags. Full tank, runs like a charm, only forty-six thousand miles on it. This baby will take you to the moon and back, no problem," Mike assured them, looking every bit like a swindling used car salesman.

"Is this yours?" Alan asked.

"Sort of. I buy and sell them. A little sideline when I'm not doing charity work at the orphanage," Mike quipped with a grin.

"Nice. Anything we need to know?"

"Nah. It really is a good car. If you run into any trouble, my cell number is on the registration. Have whoever call me if there are any questions about the sale. I don't know you, you gave me cash, end of story. Work for you?"

"Perfect." Alan moved to the back seat and peered in through the windows, then opened the driver's door and popped the trunk before dropping his and Jet's bags in and slamming it closed. Without a word, Jet held her hand out for the keys, and he tossed them to her as he rounded the front fender and got into the passenger side.

The engine started with a purr, and soon they were pulling onto the freeway that ran just south of Los Angeles and then east across the U.S..

"At least it'll get good gas mileage," Alan said, trying to get comfortable in the seat.

"We trade off six-hour shifts. I'll take the first one. We should be able to make it to Las Vegas before we switch. We can get fast food on the way. A bathroom break every three hours or so. If you want, climb into the back seat and get some shut-eye. You're on the midnight shift," Jet said, hitting her turn signal to get over a lane.

"I'll wait until after our gourmet dinner at McCrap or whatever. You got a map?"

"Don't need one. It's all in my phone. But we can pick one up if you want."

"Any time. We're not in any rush. Probably be plenty of opportunities."

"Maybe in Colorado. It's pretty straightforward. Keep going east until we hit Washington. If we run into the Atlantic Ocean, we went too far."

The Ford's engine hummed reassuringly as the little car sped down the freeway. They were both silent, lost in their thoughts as the sun sank into the ocean, creating a kaleidoscope of color in the evening sky, the second phase of their long journey finally begun.

CHAPTER 23

"We have to kidnap him. It's the quickest way to learn the truth."

Jet was driving, dawn breaking as they crossed the Rocky Mountains, Grand Junction, Colorado just south of them. So far the trek had been smooth, no snow, Las Vegas come and gone in a blur, the road across Utah well-maintained and empty other than trucks carrying the nation's necessities across the mountains.

"You recognize that won't be as easy as it sounds, right? I mean, the man is the head of a powerful security force – his own private army," Alan countered.

"Doesn't matter. And what do you want to bet that the very last thing that ever occurred to him would be that someone would come after him? I researched him on the web. Very low profile guy. You could mention his name or his company to a thousand people and nobody would know either. And he's not a spook. He's a businessman."

"Whose main product is exporting death. I know. 'Security.'" Alan held up his hands.

"You got any better ideas?"

"Not really. But it just seems that's the most radical possible approach."

"Exactly. We take him, we extract the information, and then we pursue whoever he's working for."

"And what do we do with him once we're done?" Alan asked as he flipped the sun visor down to shield his eyes from the morning rays.

"I think you know the answer to that."

They rode in silence for another half hour, admiring the mountain scenery, and then they stopped at a convenience store in the tiny berg of Parachute and bought coffee and rolls.

"At least we have the element of surprise. That's a big advantage." Alan continued the conversation as though they'd only taken a pause. Jet was happy to see that as he thought about it, he was beginning to see the wisdom of her approach. "The question is what kind of safeguards he has in place."

"That's just logistics. All targets are vulnerable. We'll watch him until we see his weak spot. We may actually be overthinking this. It's entirely possible that he has minimal security, because he's just a simple businessman earning a living the American way. I mean, we know that he sends murderers to other countries to kill on contract, but I bet he doesn't advertise it. Probably goes to church, pets dogs, takes the kids to soccer on Saturdays."

"He doesn't have any kids. I checked," Alan observed. "No wife, either."

"Whatever. You know what I mean."

They left the store and Alan stretched by the car. "My back is already killing me from sitting in that seat," he complained.

"I told you – sleep on the back seat. Might be more comfortable."

"How do you manage to stay so perky? You slept in the damned thing, too."

"All my clean living. That, and I'm almost a foot shorter than you. I think they built this model for us smaller people, not you towering circus freaks."

He grinned at Jet. "I'm pretty average height."

"If you're on a basketball team, maybe."

The rest of the day was spent traversing the mountains and then descending into the flatland of the Great Plains, finally stopping in Omaha for dinner and to stretch their legs.

"You know the whole story about Omaha, right?" Jet asked once they were seated in the restaurant and had ordered.

"The CIA goon who helped David with Hannah wound up trying to kill you after you completed a mission he'd blackmailed you into doing. Hannah was hidden here," Alan confirmed.

"It's a little more complicated than that, but yes, that's the gist."

"Can't be a lot of fond memories of the place. You okay?"

"Truthfully, I was only here for a short time, so I have almost no memory of it. Just that it was flat, the people were big-boned, and all the houses look the same."

They plowed through their meal with relish, and then packed back into the car for the second night of cross-country driving. Much of the route was familiar to Jet from her adventure with Hannah in the motor home, but she was still amazed by how different the various areas were. The U.S. was a huge place, with incredible diversity, and everything she had seen so far was better maintained than most of the rest of the world. The roads were smooth and they had made good time, averaging sixty-five miles per hour since they'd started. The Ford was running like a top and sipping gas, extending their range, although they still filled up each time they changed drivers in case they ran across a dry patch.

The drive wore on, but by the following nightfall they were almost at their destination. When they were within fifty miles of Washington, Jet began looking for hotels.

"We're too late to do surveillance on Sloan tonight. Doubtful he'll be at work, and I couldn't find where he lives. We'll need to take this up tomorrow and put his offices under surveillance. For which we'll need at least one more car. Last time I was here, I bought one. I don't think it makes any sense to steal one – subjects us to unnecessary risk. So let's get a place to stay, look at car ads, and get a pair of disposable cell phones to stay in contact with each other. I don't want to use mine here," she said.

"Makes sense. You have any preferences for hotels?"

"Not really. I'd say let's find a business suites place somewhere near Sloan's building and then look for vehicles. Might as well get something done tonight."

Jet pulled over when she passed a superstore at a strip mall. They got two phones and two pairs of binoculars, as well as a couple of baseball caps and some cheap tops so they could easily change the color of their outfits on the fly, and then drove the rest of the way to Washington, choosing a motel near Lincolnia, Virginia, only two miles from the Nordhaver building.

Alan scoured the newspaper he'd bought while she checked in, and found a few good candidates for cars – several Fords and three Dodge sedans. He called the ads while Jet unpacked and took a fast shower. He made appointments for the following morning to see them – nobody wanted to show their car at night, and Alan wasn't in a mood to look at any after two days in a Focus. He rinsed off next, and then they went in search of a restaurant.

A nearby Italian eatery looked inviting, so they stopped and went in, and were pleasantly surprised by the rich odor of garlic and basil drifting through the dining room. They studied the menu and made their selections, and then the waiter brought bread and their drinks.

"Don't forget we have a gun show tomorrow, too. What time is our first car viewing?" Jet asked.

"Eight A.M. The guy wanted us to stop by before he has to go to work."

"Hopefully we can find something suitable. The gun show is about an hour drive from here."

"Don't worry. We'll get it all done."

"I know. But I don't want to lose an entire day. I'd really like to start watching the building tomorrow afternoon. Once we get the car, we can split up. You take the building, and I'll get weapons. I'm thinking a couple of Glocks or H&Ks. You have any preference?"

"Hard to go wrong with either. Any chance of finding silencers?"

"You know what? You never know. I was blown away by how many items at the last gun show I went to were pretty sketchy. I mean, one guy was selling full-auto conversion kits for AR-15s. So never say never."

That night, when they drifted off to sleep in each others' arms, Jet had a sensation of progress, now that they had their target within spitting distance. Her hope was that it would take only a day or two before she could get her hands on Sloan and find out why she'd had to fly halfway around the world. And when she did, it wouldn't be pretty.

She hadn't asked for this battle.

Or for any she'd been forced to fight since Trinidad, where her solitary safety had been shattered by the Russian's hit team. No, she hadn't invited any of this.

But she would definitely end it.

Once and for all.

CHAPTER 24

Montevideo, Uruguay

Water dripped down the gray walls from where a pipe seal had worked loose in the ceiling, the moisture leaching through the cement and blistered paint, gravity having exerted its powerful pull. A cockroach scuttled across the floor and paused at the small pool of dank fluid in the corner, then decided that it was too questionable for even its indiscriminate taste.

Hazy light filtered through a window nine feet above the floor, iron bars protecting the opaque glass from the inmates. The man lying on the steel bunk stirred, disturbed by a clank from the main jailhouse door at the end of the corridor. Unlike American jails, there was no rowdiness, no catcalls or hoots, just the desperate silence of the imprisoned awaiting whatever came their way.

The captive stood and moved to the steel toilet in the corner – no seat, no flushing mechanism, just a rank hole that led God knew where – and relieved himself, gagging at the noxious stink, his eyes watering as he struggled to hold his breath. One of the guards had told him that he was lucky to have even that – in the main jail, there was only a bucket, and when a drunk kicked it over in the middle of the night, the inmates got to swim in filth until someone came to hose down the cell the next day.

He felt his head with shaking fingers, the tips grazing over the scab from where he'd been struck, whether by his assailant or the guards during questioning he couldn't be sure. Bruises covered his face and upper torso, and he was certain that he had some sort of internal injuries from the more spirited inquisitions the day before. One guard in particular seemed to enjoy using him as a punching bag, and he had heard a distinct crack at one point, a rib fracturing from a particularly well-landed blow.

At least he wasn't peeing blood anymore. That had lasted twenty-four hours – several slams in the kidneys from a truncheon had gifted him with that bit of fun, but his body had apparently healed itself, at least to the point where he wasn't dribbling his vital fluids down a rat hole.

His demands, and then requests, and then pleas to see his attorney again had gone unheeded, and seemed to amuse his captors no end. The way they grinned at one another and exchanged looks of genuine merriment when he had begged to talk to him was ominous, as was their refusal to get him a doctor. Apparently the rules in Uruguay were slightly different than in the U.S., and he was not only presumed guilty but viewed as a nuisance now that they knew he wasn't going to tell them anything.

Not yet, anyway. He wasn't sure how much more of this he could take. The fat, tall guard on the night shift had threatened him with rape if he didn't talk tomorrow, and by his demeanor it wasn't an idle promise.

How the hell had he gotten to this point? He was just a lowly driver. He hadn't killed anyone – well, outside of his tour of duty in the infantry, but that had been from a distance, with a rifle, almost surrealistic. Just a few squeezes of the trigger, a couple of pops, and then a fighter a thousand feet away had collapsed. It had been over before he'd even had time to process what had happened, and he'd told himself countless times, when the memory came in the dead of night, that it was almost like a video game. It had seemed impossible that life could be snuffed out so easily, with such casual randomness, a few thimbles of lead streaking invisibly through the air and a man was dead, and he'd almost convinced himself that it was more akin to a dream than reality. A different place, a different time; he'd been frightened, confused, dropped into a desert hell with other young boys barely old enough to shave.

The bravado that was their operating norm had faded after that first gun battle with hostiles during an ambush, and the medal he'd received had seemed odd – like it belonged to someone else. Mostly, he'd just kept his head down, other than shooting that one gunman, and when it was over he'd vomited at the sight of his three dead friends, lying twisted next to him where other bits of lead had found a home in their bodies.

After he'd been discharged, one of his buddies had contacted him a month into his civilian life. His frustration with a job search that had yielded only minimum wage openings was palpable during their discussion, and the buddy had suggested he interview at the company where he was now working. He'd jumped at the chance, and when they'd told him the starting pay, it had floored him.

This was his third international assignment. The first two had been pieces of cake – surveillance gigs where he'd spent weeks doing nothing, the first in Iraq, the second in Colombia. This job was supposed to have been a simple one, too. Watch the condo; a team would go in and do whatever they were supposed to do; and then they'd all go home. They had their own vehicle, so all he had to do was keep his partner company and not fall asleep.

It hadn't turned out quite the way it had been described to him.

And now he was being treated like public enemy number one by a group of malevolent cops who didn't seem to have the faintest interest in due process or humane treatment.

The attorney the company had sent had told him that he'd be out in no time, that they were working on it, to be patient and brave and not say a word, but he didn't know whether he could keep up the charade much longer. He wasn't brave. He was just desperate for a decent job, and his only skills were the ones he'd learned, poorly, in the army. It actually surprised him that he'd held out as long as he had – the fear that the company wouldn't get him out if he talked had driven his false courage more than anything. A future in misery like this – or worse, being passed around for brutal sex like a pack of cigarettes at a rock concert – was an impossibility. Things like that didn't happen to people like him. He was basically decent. This was some sort of mistake. A nightmare from which he'd soon wake up, comfortable in his bed back in Virginia.

The main door at the end of the corridor groaned as it opened, and then two guards made their way down the long concrete passage until they came to his cell. They stopped, and he looked up fearfully, and then relaxed when one of them held up a food tray.

"Back away into the far corner," the larger of the two guards ordered.

He did as instructed, then watched as the big man unlocked the door and moved into the cell, pausing to stare at him blankly before setting the tray down on the bunk.

The driver was starving, having not been fed since the previous day, and began salivating at the sight of the hard bread roll and the unidentifiable gruel in a plastic dish next to it.

"Eat. You have five minutes," the guard said, and then retreated out of the cell and shut the door, locking it with a key from the ring he held. The second guard grunted as the big man sneered at the prisoner, and then they both had a chuckle before moving back down the hall.

He almost ran to the tray and tore into the food like a wild animal, stuffing huge pieces of bread dipped in the stew into his mouth, only hesitating to chew a few times before swallowing. The plate was empty in two minutes, and he finished by licking the bowl clean, disgusted by his desperation even as he sucked the last of the nourishment from the hard plastic surface.

When the spasms hit twenty minutes later he doubled over, racked by agony, his stomach muscles contracting spasmodically. He tried to get up from the bed and then collapsed on the floor, groaning, the pain unlike anything he'd ever felt.

Ten minutes later the large guard came back, alone, and stared down at the writhing prisoner with misery written across his face as his eyes begged for help. The guard unlocked the door and stepped into the cell, a look of concern on his face.

The first kick from the stiff black boot took the driver by surprise, knocking the wind out of him with an *oof*. He barely registered when the guard pulled a plastic bag over his head and cut off his air supply, and by the time he rallied what little strength he had left he was already blacking out.

The big man held the bag in place as the prisoner jerked, his arms and legs flailing, and then went limp, his pants soaking with the paltry contents of his bladder as life departed his tortured frame. Once the guard was sure the driver was dead, he removed the plastic from his face and carefully folded it, then slid the small square into his pants before reaching into his shirt pocket and retrieving a tennis ball-sized chunk of bread. After forcing the dead man's mouth open, he stuffed the bread as far down his throat as he could, then wiped his hands off on his shirt. He stood and regarded the driver with disgust and, careful to avoid the spreading puddle of urine, stepped around the corpse and left the cell, taking care to lock it behind him.

When the body was found the next morning, the death was quickly blamed on the prisoner choking on his meal, no doubt as a result of injuries sustained while he was trying to escape arrest as he was taken into custody.

No post mortem was performed – the system didn't coddle prisoners and didn't have the resources to waste on that sort of thing. What was done was done, and no investigation would bring the dead back to life.

It was just another in a string of mysteries in a land renowned for them. South America was a continent shrouded in a kind of magic, where nobody questioned anything too closely. There were better things to do than dwell on that which couldn't be changed, and a weary pragmatism greeted the terse announcement that one of the suspects in the condo slayings had died in prison of natural causes.

Nobody cared, and the body was cremated as quickly as a fire could be stoked.

CHAPTER 25

The following morning, Alan and Jet drove to inspect the first candidate car and spent fifteen minutes going over the vehicle – a relatively recent model Dodge Stratus with the wrong side of eighty thousand on the speedometer.

"All highway miles," the owner insisted proudly, an insurance salesman who had used it to travel his route on the northern seaboard. "I've got all the maintenance records. Had the oil changed every three thousand miles, and never had any problems with anything besides some minor bulbs burning out and stuff."

His sensibly cut thinning blond hair bobbed in the sun as he recited his best sincerity pitch, his eagerness to close the deal palpable. Buyers for high mileage domestic sedans were few and far between, and he was clearly not going to let them slip past him if he could help it.

Alan went through it carefully, being more mechanically inclined than Jet, and eventually gave the vehicle the nod after a perfunctory test drive. Jet handled the negotiation, and after a few minutes of haggling agreed to a cash price five hundred dollars less than the very reasonable asking price. The owner watched with hungry eyes as she counted out the hundred dollar bills, and was practically dancing back into the house to get the title as they stood in the driveway and waited.

"Seems pretty decent. We can have it checked over later, but there's nothing obvious. And we're not going to keep it forever, so it should do the trick," Alan told her.

"It looks more comfortable than the Focus, that's for sure, which is a good thing if you're going to be using it to stake out the building."

"My back still hasn't forgotten the last two days of design issues with that seat," Alan said as the owner returned with the pink slip and the second set of keys.

The man pumped Alan's hand as Jet examined the title. "You won't regret this. She's been a real jewel for the last three years. I hate to see her go," he enthused.

"Well, thanks. This is just what we were looking for. I'm sure it'll be fine. And the dealer here knows the car?" Alan asked, disengaging and stepping away from the man.

"Absolutely. As you can see from the service records, I always had the dealer take care of her. You don't want to be stranded in the rain or snow by the side of the road because you cheaped out on an independent mechanic," the insurance salesman assured him.

Alan drove the Dodge and Jet the Ford, and he followed her back to the hotel, then met her in the lobby for a second cup of free coffee.

"It actually drives nicely. I think we got a deal," he said to her as he came inside.

"Great. Let's hope I get as lucky with the gun show. The good news is it's a big one, so we should have no problems finding something interesting. Are you going to go over and start the surveillance now?" Jet asked, impatience obvious in her voice.

"Yes. Just let me use the bathroom and grab some more java and I'll get over there." They'd agreed that Jet would lead the way, and then he'd find somewhere discreet to park once they'd both eyeballed the property.

When they drove past the building, they saw a large, unremarkable two-story brick industrial building in a busy business park only five minutes from the hotel. From the outside it could have been anything; it gave no indication of being the headquarters of a killer-for-hire service. They pulled out of the area and stopped at a gas station. Jet slipped from behind the wheel of the Ford and walked to his driver's side window.

"You know what he looks like, right?" she asked, anxious.

"I've only looked at the images you got off the web about a million times. He won't get by me. When I see him, I'll know him instantly. I've got my new cell phone. Go do what you need to do, and don't worry. I've done this before," he said with an easy grin.

"I'm sorry. I'm just...I want to get this over with, so I'm feeling impatient."

"I know. So am I. But it'll take as long as it takes. You know how this works."

She did, and she appreciated his calm support.

"All right, then. I'm off to get us an arsenal." She leaned down and kissed him, and then returned to her car as he rolled off.

The drive south to Richmond took longer than she had planned, but the gun show was just getting underway when she strode into the large hall. Vendors were set up on tables in long rows, and she took her time roaming, looking for pistols. Eventually she narrowed it down to two newer-looking CZ-USA 75 9mm semi-automatics. She haggled with the vendors and eventually bought both of them, each with two extra magazines, and then rounded out her purchases with a pair of shoulder holsters and a stun gun.

On her way out, she spotted an old man with a white beard selling combat knives, and got two folding Blackhawk CQD Mark 1 Type E knives with razor-sharp blades.

Silencers would be a problem. She'd need to buy some machine tools to make them, as well as create threads on the barrel nubs of the pistols, as she'd had to do on her last trip to Washington. She recalled renting the storage space, and reconciled herself to running the same errands this time around. On the way out of the hall she asked a few of the vendors about ammo, and one of the men agreed to sell her two boxes of 9mm shells with no questions asked. They met at his car and he popped his trunk. He had easily twenty boxes of different caliber bullets, so it appeared that it was a popular sideline for him.

Fully outfitted, she quickly found a shop that had the requisite lathes and welders, and bought what she would need to fabricate the silencers. As she pulled away from the store, Jet checked the time and saw that the day was half over.

She called Alan after she'd rented a storage unit in an anonymous complex on the way back to the hotel and told him about her purchases and the silencers, and he assured her that he had everything under control. Sloan had appeared in a black sedan with a driver, and had stayed for two hours before leaving for lunch at an upscale restaurant near the river. He was now back at the building, and Alan was resolved to tail him and find out where he lived. He told her to get the silencers made and not to worry about him; he had things covered.

At seven that evening she was finishing cleaning up the stall when her cell phone vibrated, startling her. Alan's voice was hushed when she answered.

"Bingo. I'm outside his place. The driver dropped him off. No signs of security other than electronics. Alarm, some lights on the roof. Possibly motion detectors in the back, but nothing I can see in the front from here. How are you doing?"

"Good. I just got done."

Alan gave her the address, which she memorized. She would look it up on her phone later and plot directions to Sloan's lavish estate home on Lake Barcroft. Alan wanted to spend more time on surveillance, to get a good feel for the situation, and she agreed. They would only have one shot at this, and they didn't want to blow it by rushing anything.

~~

Alan had left his car at the lake's small beach, where a parking lot was open to the public, and after skirting the dense trees had found a spot where he was hidden from view but still had a good visual of the house. It was dark, the sun having set hours earlier, and the surrounding homes were lit up like floats in a holiday parade. Sloan's was one of the larger houses in the community, at least six thousand square feet of contemporary mansion – obviously expensive, perched on a prominent point surrounded by verdant grounds, with its own boat dock and pool.

"You see anything interesting?"

Alan jolted and nearly dropped his binoculars at the sound of Jet's whispered question. He took a deep breath before turning to her.

"Very nice. I didn't even hear you," he said.

"Good to know I still have the ability to surprise you," she whispered back.

He could hardly see her in the gloom, and when she crouched down beside where he was lying, he could more smell her than make her out.

"Here's a gun. Handy pieces. CZs. Nine mils. And here are two extra boxes," she said, handing him a silenced gun and the two loaded magazines.

"You made the silencers?"

"With loving care."

"Excellent."

"What's going on in there?"

"All's quiet. The house is wired. I watched him punch in a code when he opened the door. And then a woman came by an hour ago. She's still inside. Looked professional."

"Colleague?" Jet asked.

"Hooker. Just an impression, but a strong one."

"I won't ask how you know so much about hookers."

"All part of my training," Alan whispered.

"I missed that part."

"It was for extra credit."

"Ah." Jet kicked him as she lay next to him. "Sorry."

Alan ignored it. "Any ideas how we're going to get in there?"

"I was hoping you'd have come up with a plan by now."

"Not so much."

They stared at the house through field glasses, and after fifteen more minutes, a tall blonde woman exited, got into a Lexus coupe, and drove away.

"Could be a girlfriend," Jet said.

"Anything's possible. But did you see the schoolgirl skirt?"

"Was that what it was? I thought it was a kilt or something. I haven't been keeping up on pervert fashions."

"Let's assume she's a professional. Does that buy us anything in terms of strategy?"

"Not unless we can intercept a call to his favorite pimp and I show up dressed like a naughty nurse or something."

"I'd actually pay extra to see that."

"I bet you would."

They spent the next two hours watching the house, and then the lights switched off, leaving only the exterior lamps illuminated. Their quarry had gone to sleep for the night. They waited another half hour, then crept back to their cars and returned to the hotel, exhausted from the day's demands. As Jet brushed her teeth the germ of an idea began to form, and by the time she was in bed, it had blossomed into a full-fledged strategy. An unexpected one that would bypass any security measures Sloan had in place. It was perfect, assuming that the target didn't stop to think things through.

"So what's the plan for tomorrow?" Alan asked, yawning as he rolled towards her.

"We're going clothes shopping."

CHAPTER 26

Sloan was having another crappy day. On the plus side, he'd tied up the driver problem in Uruguay, but on the minus side his men on the ground there had found no new leads so far. The condo was deserted, according to his contact in the police, and while there was an APB out to bring this Magdalena woman in for questioning, she wasn't a suspect. There was nothing to link her to the killing of his men – she was just another resident of the building, who could have been on vacation, for all anyone knew.

They had tried tracking her via the banking records again, but there had been no activity – and now that the attorney had been dispatched, there wasn't much they could get on the trust side beyond what they already had. Perhaps terminating the man had been a miscalculation on his part. Things certainly hadn't progressed since then, and the daily calls he was getting from Standish asking whether there was any reason for a meeting weren't helping matters.

Fortunately, the Indonesian campaign was going much better than the South American one, and the island had been all but shut down following the civil unrest and rebel strikes – supervised by his men. The islanders were basically useless left to their own devices, so he had four seasoned operatives on the ground directing matters. He wasn't sure why Arthur wanted Papua plunged into chaos; but then again, his remuneration didn't depend on him knowing. For twenty-five million dollars, he would have shot the queen of England on national television – so destabilizing a backwater on the ass end of the planet was a no-brainer. And it seemed that the assignment was almost over. They had achieved all their objectives to date, and the mine was shut down for the foreseeable future. The Indonesians were flooding the island with troops, and human rights workers there were reporting savagery and indiscriminate killings on a wholesale basis, further poisoning the region for the duration.

His company was thriving, he was wealthy beyond any reasonable measure, had a stable of platinum-level call girls at his beck and call; and yet lately every day seemed to bring with it a new body slam. At fifty-one, Sloan had been through a lot. He'd crawled his way up from being a simple grunt marine corporal to a CIA advisor to the owner of one of the premier boutique security solutions businesses in the country. He was at the top of the heap, had well and truly arrived, and yet he had a sense of foreboding he couldn't put his finger on.

Perhaps it was just a latent reaction to having to deal with Arthur as he became increasingly erratic and demanding. Their relationship had always been good, with Sloan more than willing to provide support when, for whatever reasons, the CIA couldn't be linked to something, and Arthur had helped him grow his company at crucial junctures, providing lucrative contracts and whispered recommendations that had granted him entry into the Beltway's circles of power. He owed Arthur, but the debt was weighing heavy, and as Arthur's health degraded, doing business with him was becoming a liability. The Uruguay matter was a case in point. They'd had almost nothing to go on, had worked a near miracle finding the target, and then his team was wiped out by a mystery man – obviously an ally of the target that Arthur should have alerted them about. That was the kind of oversight that would have never happened in the old days.

But it wasn't the past, and he had to contend with the future. Uruguay was becoming a problem now, a money suck, dead bodies piled up like cordwood, and all to satisfy Arthur's bloodlust. Sloan had been told the story by Standish – the kidnapped daughter, the mission, the attack that nearly killed Arthur, the injection. But from his standpoint, Arthur had brought the woman's wrath down on himself by screwing with her family and then trying to double-cross her. What had he expected? Flowers?

No matter. It was the end of another eight hours of struggle and conflict, and he was looking forward to going home and relaxing with a nice bottle of Shiraz he had flown in from Australia by the case, and perhaps one of his young ladies. Debbie, last night's encounter, had worn him out, her young, athletic body insatiable, but perhaps he would rally after a little vino and some food. Appetite came with eating, and he wasn't getting any younger.

He punched a button on the intercom and told his secretary to have the car brought around. It would take five minutes, he knew, during which time he straightened up his desk and updated his calendar for tomorrow. More meetings, one with a potentially lucrative client from the Middle East who needed some help with a contentious offshoot of his mother's family. Business had never been better, and it seemed that demand for his specialized services would only increase as the world situation became more precarious. The financial system's near collapse had created boundless opportunity for him, as adversarial factions in faraway places battled for the hearts and minds of their populations – and Sloan could always be counted on to provide men and knowhow to decide the contests in the favor of his clients.

Sloan shut off his lights, said goodnight to his secretary, and departed through the towering glass doors of the main entrance, admiring the rich leather furniture in the lobby, tasteful art on the walls, and photos of himself with dignitaries and presidents, shaking hands, smiling, playing golf. It was quite an empire he'd built with his wits and sweat. Something to be proud of.

The drive home took twelve minutes, and when he exited the car he told the driver to be at his house at eight forty-five on the dot tomorrow. He wanted time to prepare for his ten o'clock meeting with the camel jockey from whatever the hell dustbowl he ruled.

He swung his front door open and stepped inside, taking care to punch in the sequence of four numbers required to disable the alarm. If someone broke in, the local cops would be there within five minutes, the silent alert an expensive feature that was worth it to him for peace of mind. In the seven years he'd had the house, he'd never had a problem; but there was always a first time, and he took no chances.

Sloan pulled his suit jacket off and tossed it over the back of one of the expensive contemporary sofas and moved to a room off the kitchen – a two-thousand-bottle wine cellar with a stone table and four seats inside, climate-controlled at precisely fifty-eight degrees, with just the right amount of humidity. His investment was protected with a backup generator that would kick on if he ever lost power, ensuring that the house and his cellar would always have its temperature within a two degree range, even if the storm to end all storms was ravaging the city.

He reached into a rack and removed a bottle of Elderton Command Shiraz, checking the year to ensure it was the newest arrival. Wine collecting was an expensive hobby, but one of his few luxuries, and he made plenty of money, so why not drink the best? At around ninety dollars a bottle it was rarefied grape juice for a weekday, but since he made that about every two minutes, the cost meant nothing to him. He knew what he liked, and that's all that mattered. Many in his collection were worth five to ten times that, but he reserved the really good stuff for the weekends – Penfolds Grange Shiraz, Screaming Eagle Cabernet, Cobos Malbec, and of course, all the French first growths, but only in exceptional years.

Returning to the kitchen, Sloan placed the bottle on the black granite counter and walked to the picture windows, sighing contentedly as he took in the lake only a few yards away. He had a good life, even if it had its rough patches. He watched as the sun set on the water, the sky all orange and red and yellow, and then he scooped up his jacket and walked upstairs to where his expansive bedroom suite awaited him.

The home had been an extravagance, at roughly five million after some remodeling, but it was an investment, as far as he was concerned. Even with the market in the doldrums, it had retained its value and he wasn't worried. It was one of four homes he'd acquired over the years, and he'd done well on all of them – a condo in Manhattan, a ski chalet in Vail, an oceanfront getaway in Florida.

The lights came on automatically as he stepped into the bedroom, and the blinds drew closed, computer controlled for privacy. He changed out of his suit, tossing it into the dry cleaning bin his housekeeper emptied twice a week, and pulled on a pair of gray sweat pants and an old Georgetown T-shirt, completing the ensemble with a pair of flip-flops. Finally comfortable, he debated calling one of his paid companions, and then decided against it. Just some vino, the dinner his housekeeper had made him before she'd gone home for the day, and some TV. Time to recharge the batteries. He could trip the light fantastic with his stable of hotties tomorrow.

Downstairs, he switched on the eighty-inch flat screen television and found the news, then turned the volume down and attended to the wine. He opened it, poured an oversized goblet half full of the inky black nectar, and took a deep sniff, enjoying the chocolate, eucalyptus, and currant notes.

He swirled the viscous liquid and watched as it coated the glass, then took a sip, swishing it around in his mouth so as to hit every taste bud.

"Brilliant," he muttered to himself, setting the glass down before he padded to the forty-eight inch Viking fridge and pulled out the container of pasta he'd requested – home-made lasagna with an Italian sausage sauce to die for.

Half an hour later Sloan was full and the bottle was empty. He was sitting in the living room, feet on the coffee table, the remainder of the wine in his Riedel goblet as he watched the constant coverage of the Iran debacle and the aborted terrorist bio-strike.

When the doorbell rang it took him by surprise. He scowled as he looked at his platinum Rolex Masterpiece watch and rose unsteadily to his feet. The wine was a high-alcohol punch, clocking in at fifteen percent, and he could definitely feel it as he walked to the front door and peered through the peephole.

A female police officer stood with her hands on her hips, her partner behind her, frowning. He noted in passing that she was hot, and a momentary erotic fantasy involving her wearing only her hat and her gun belt flittered through his brain as he tried to make sense of what he was seeing.

"Yes?" he called through the intercom, his finger holding down the button while he barked the question.

"Mr. Sloan? Mr. James Sloan?" the woman asked, checking her clipboard.

"That's me. What do you want?"

"Your alarm went off six minutes ago. Are you all right, sir?"

He stared at the alarm console, which was reading fine, and shook his head. "Must have been some kind of glitch. There's nothing wrong here."

"I see." She looked annoyed, which made her seem even hotter to Sloan, who realized as he thought it that he was a wee bit tipsy. It felt good. "I'm afraid I need to ask you to open the door so we can verify that you're okay. Do you have your ID handy?"

"What? Why do you need to come in?"

"I'm sorry, sir. It's for your own protection. To ensure that nobody is forcing you to tell us that you're fine."

"That's stupid."

"Maybe so, but it's the rules. That way we can make sure some crazy isn't holding a gun on you. Can we please get this over with? If this is a false alarm, we have other things we could be doing, sir."

He sighed, taking one last look at her before unlocking the deadbolt and cracking the door open. She had vaguely Asian features, breathtaking green eyes, and a face that matched her tight little body. Maybe he could get her interested in coming by in her off hours to play cops and robbers with him, he thought as the door swung wide.

"Okay, come in and verify that I'm fine, but be quick about it." Part of his awareness sounded an alarm as he registered that there was no police cruiser out front, and then the thought was swallowed up by pain as every nerve in his body seemed to fire at once, and he dropped to the floor, twitching, the agony blinding as he fought for breath.

Jet stepped into the foyer, her finger continuing to depress the stun gun button. Alan followed her in and closed the door behind him. She stopped shocking Sloan once they were both inside. Alan dragged him to the living room and left him on the floor as he moved to the dining room to get a chair.

Two minutes later Sloan was bound, his hands duct-taped behind him, straps of tape securing him to the hardwood seat, his feet taped together in front of him, and a dish towel stuffed in his mouth. Jet studied him with interest as Alan stepped in front of him and pulled the rag out.

"Please. I have money upstairs in my safe. Don't hurt me," Sloan began.

Alan backhanded him across the face. Blood trickled from the corner of his mouth, and his eyes watered in response to the surprise blow.

"Shut up. I don't want your money."

Sloan's eyes narrowed. "Then what do you want?"

"Information," Alan said.

Sloan noticed with alarm that both he and the female cop were wearing latex gloves. "About what?" he asked, puzzled.

"Uruguay," the woman said, speaking for the first time since they'd entered the house. "Your men came to kill me. They failed. Now I'm here to return the favor." She watched as his eyes got wide with the realization that he was in real jeopardy, and that his money wouldn't buy his freedom. "That's right. You must have read my dossier – you know what I specialize in. So let's cut to the chase. Why did you send a death squad to Uruguay, and who hired you? The sooner you tell me, the sooner this will be over."

"You're going to kill me, aren't you? Even if I tell you?" Sloan sputtered.

Alan stepped back, studying his face, a bead of sweat now working its way down Sloan's forehead and into his eye.

"There are worse things than death, my friend. Much worse things. We have all night, and in the end, everyone talks. Always. The question is how much damage will be inflicted before you figure it out. Personally, I couldn't care less whether you tell me now or in two hours, when you're begging me to kill you, praying for death. Doesn't matter in the least. It's really just how much suffering you want to endure," Alan said, matter-of-factly, his voice soft. He turned to Jet. "See what he has under the sink and in the garage. I'm sure I can improvise something that will convince our powerful friend here that I'm dead serious."

She nodded, then walked down the hardwood hall. Sloan eyed Alan with a combination of terror and hatred, but Alan seemed oblivious to it and stepped into the kitchen, returning in a moment with several Swiss gourmet knives.

"Whoa. These are nice. I mean, seriously nice cutlery going on, you know? The man knows his knives, I'll say that." Alan smiled, and Sloan's blood froze. "Did you know one of my specialties is skinning a man and making him eat his own flesh? Guess how you get really good at that? Three guesses."

Sloan didn't say anything.

"Do you want to test me? I killed the best you had in a matter of seconds. You want to see whether I'm serious about turning you into a circus freak before midnight?"

"I...I don't want to die," Sloan begged. "Please. I'll tell you what you want to know, but don't kill me."

"Well, that's progress. I'll leave your fate to the lady, but I'm afraid she's a little testy after you tried to erase her from the planet a few days ago. She can take those kinds of things personally. Moody, she is."

Jet returned with a smile on her face, holding a propane torch and a bag of pool chlorine.

"I'll check the kitchen next, but these should start the party on the right foot. Imagine what chlorine will feel like in his eyes. Or once you've skinned his face. Ew. I don't even want to think about that, much less the smell of his skin burning. You never get the stink out of your clothes from the burning." Jet set the items on the dining room table and moved to the kitchen, where she ferreted around noisily under the sink. When she stood, she held a can of bug killer and some ammonia. "I think we hit the jackpot. Get some of this in his eyes and he'll be begging for death, blubbering like a schoolgirl."

Alan regarded Sloan impassively.

"If you're getting the idea that she's going to enjoy this, you're on the right track. She's a psycho. Which you know if you've seen her file," Alan whispered.

"I can hear you, you know. And I don't appreciate the judgmental tone," Jet protested, her face struggling to contain a smirk.

"Oops. Sorry. Our boy here says he'll tell us everything, but he doesn't want to die."

Jet turned her attention to Sloan. "Really! That makes it all easy, then. Let's start with something simple. What's the combination to his safe, and where does he keep his guns? A macho fellah like this always has a bunch of guns. So where are they, and what's the combo?"

Alan and Jet watched as Sloan struggled with his internal compulsions, and then capitulated.

"It's thirty-seven left, nineteen right, sixty-four left. You have to turn it two full turns to the left before you begin the sequence. Safe's behind the built-in dresser in the closet. There's a button hidden next to it in the molding. And the guns are in their own safe in the study. Key's in the bedroom safe. Please. I'm telling you the truth. I'll tell you whatever you want to know. Just don't kill me."

"We'll see. I'll be right back," Jet said, and then ascended the stairs to the second floor.

The safe was where he said it was, but then Jet felt a flash of concern. It was too easy. He'd given it up too quickly.

She returned to the living room and was vindicated by the panic in his eyes.

"Be a shame if the safe was wired in to trigger a silent alarm somewhere if it was opened without turning the alarm off, wouldn't it?" she said.

Sloan's face froze as he did his best to affect a neutral expression.

She looked at Alan. "Looks like we should get started. This lying prick tried to set us up. Start with the eyes."

"No. Wait. No, I mean…okay, yes, I tried to set you up. You would do the same thing. Please. I'll tell you where the switch is. There's a lot of money in there. Gold. Over a half million worth of maple leaves. Cash. Whatever you want," he pleaded.

"See, that makes me not trust you, Jim," Alan said. "I can call you Jim, can't I? And if we don't have trust between us, what do we really have? Nothing." He looked over at Jet, who nodded, and he picked up the roach spray.

"That will blind you. Probably permanently. Maybe not. For your purposes, permanently isn't going to be that long, anyway," Jet said in an even tone. "Take a last look around at the world, because this is it for you."

"No. I...I swear, I won't try to trick you any more. The alarm switch is in the bathroom cabinet, under the left sink, in the back. Flip it to green. It's got a little light."

"Not good enough, big boy. You're losing your eyes. Then we'll see how you feel about telling me what I really want to know."

"No. I'll tell you everything. Really. The man who wants you dead. His name's Arthur. He's ex-CIA. You injected him with something. He wants revenge."

Jet's face changed. "Arthur? That's a lie. He's dead. I watched him die on the sidewalk."

"No. He didn't. He lived. Barely. He's bedridden."

Jet paced in front of the picture window, and then spun and glared at Sloan. "Why is he using you to do his dirty work? He's got a whole network of operatives he could send."

"His reach isn't what it used to be. He's not with the CIA anymore. Now he's...freelancing. So he needed someone operational to handle this. Please. It isn't personal with me. It's just a contract. Really. I have no beef with you."

"Not personal? You sent men to kill me, in front of my daughter. That's not personal? How much more personal could you get?"

Sloan didn't say anything. His eyes took on a cagey look. "If you kill me, I'll never tell you where he is. I can give you Arthur on a platter. But you have to agree to let me live."

Jet looked at Alan, and nodded. "I'm going to have a look at the safe. Get the information out of him."

Sloan's wily look changed to one of terror. "No. I'll tell you. Everything."

Alan stepped in front of him with the dish towel in one hand and the spray in the other. "Yes, you will. I'm absolutely, a hundred percent sure of it. And my job is to ensure that it's the full, complete truth."

The last thing Jet heard as she climbed the stairs was a muffled scream, as Sloan shrieked his agony into the towel, the bug spray hard at work.

CHAPTER 27

Jet got the safe open and rummaged through it, confirming that there was indeed a big pile of gold coins, as well as more than a hundred grand in hundred dollar bills. Four insurance policies sat on the bottom of the safe, along with two keys, what looked like a few grams of cocaine in a glass vial, and a USB flash drive.

She pulled the metal tray the gold was sitting in from the safe and lifted it. The coins weighed about twenty-five pounds but were surprisingly compact, the plastic storage tubes holding twenty ounces apiece. Jet evaluated her options and quickly decided to take the gold and the cash – what a robber would do. The drugs could remain. Give the police something more to think about, with Sloan's prints all over the vial.

She rooted around in the closet and found a gym bag and upended it, dumping the water bottle and towel it contained on the floor. She transferred the gold and cash and then moved down the hall to the study. The gun safe was a two-door model, easily five feet wide. She tried the two keys, and one slipped easily into the lock.

When she opened it, her eyes widened. Sloan had a serious gun love thing going. She studied the contents of the safe and selected several pieces from among them, including two gold-colored titanium Desert Eagle XIX .44 Magnum pistols and a box of shells, an M4 assault rifle with a spare magazine, and a Heckler and Koch MP7A1 with three thirty-round box magazines. At the bottom of the safe was a piece of paper – a permit to own fully automatic weapons. She supposed if you were a bigwig contractor who supplied mercenaries to the government, it was a piece of cake to get one. She put the pistols, MP7, and magazines into the bag, pulled the M4 out and set it next to the desk, and then left the safe open – more evidence of theft for the detectives to mull over.

She moved to the computer, shook the mouse, and the screen blinked and lit as the system came to life. She fished out the USB drive and plugged it into one of the open slots, then selected the icon that appeared on the desktop.

Ten minutes later she was done. She slipped the drive into her pocket, shouldered the M4, and returned to the living room where Alan was standing, staring at a motionless Sloan.

Alan looked at her, taking in the rifle without comment, and then raised an eyebrow. "I got everything out of him, but he didn't make it."

She stepped around Sloan and handed Alan the assault rifle, then turned to face the security tycoon, whose eyes were swollen shut, his face marred from where Alan had used the torch.

"What happened?"

"I think he had a stroke. The fat bastard probably ate his body weight in foie gras, so it's not surprising. His face sort of melted and sagged on one side, and then he started choking and convulsing."

"Is he alive?"

"He stopped breathing about three minutes ago."

"Shit."

"Don't worry. I have what we need."

"I wanted to ask him about some of the items I found," Jet said.

"Unless you can go into the afterlife, that's off the table."

"I got that. What do you want to do with him?"

"I think we carry him out to the water and toss him in. If we do it right, it'll be a day or two before anyone finds him."

"What about the housekeeper?"

"Sloan had a computer, right?"

She nodded.

"Printer?"

"Yup."

"Write a nice one sentence letter telling the housekeeper that he had to leave for an emergency and he'll be back in a few days. That will buy us enough time for him to start seriously decomposing. If there are any fish in the lake, by the time anyone pulls him out the better part of Sloan will be in their bellies."

"You need to weigh him down with something."

"I know. You take care of the stuff upstairs and I'll deal with Sloan."

Jet ran back up the stairs and composed the note, and then waited as it printed, closing the gun safe as the paper slid into the completed bin. She did a final scan of the bedroom, shut that safe as well, and returned to get the letter. By the time she made it back downstairs, Alan was standing in the kitchen, waiting for her.

"All done?" she asked.

"Affirmative."

"What did you use to weight him down?"

"He had a little gas-powered portable generator. That and about twenty meters of chain in the garage solved the problem. At least the nylon-backed rug I used to drag his fat ass to the lake saved my back. He didn't float, so we're good."

"Then let's get out of here."

"Ladies first." Alan gestured at the front door.

Jet carried the bag with the guns in it and Alan eased the door open. They inched into the gloom, their dark police uniforms making them almost invisible in the dark of the night.

When they reached the car, Jet tossed the weapons into the trunk, along with her hat. Alan did the same, and in sixty seconds they were pulling out of the community, making their way to the freeway.

"What did he say about Arthur? I still can't believe he survived, but it all makes sense now that I know he's alive. He's got to be in agony every moment. I'd be testy too, if it was me."

"He's got a compound someplace called Wolf Trap. Well over an acre of land, heavy security. That's all Sloan really knew. Gave me the address before he croaked, but beyond that, we're on our own."

"Feel like going for a drive?"

"Sure." She looked up the address on her phone, and gave Alan directions.

"What's in the bag?" he asked as they rolled onto the highway.

"Oh, this and that. An arsenal. Half a million bucks in gold. Hundred grand in C-notes. Maybe we should consider going into the home invasion business. Turns out it's pretty lucrative."

"I may have to. You don't, remember? You're rich."

"Hey, half of the take is yours. So you've got some game now, too."

"Only half?" Alan asked, eyebrows raised.

"Okay, you talked me out of it. You can have it all."

"Now that's more like it. I've got expensive tastes."

She considered him, driving the Dodge, a seventy-dollar watch on his wrist, and then they both laughed together.

"Maybe not that expensive. But still. I could learn," he suggested.

"That's good to know. That you're open to personal growth."

"Am I ever."

They arrived in Wolf Trap in fifteen minutes, and were surprised and relieved that it seemed like the country, abundant trees and vegetation creating a sense of secluded privacy as they wove through the empty streets. Densely populated areas could be problematic to mount operations in – there was always a kid chasing a ball or a nosy neighbor turning up at the worst possible moment. In a heavily wooded area like this, they'd have more options.

When they got to Arthur's street, they prowled down it at twenty miles per hour. On the right sat a huge white southern plantation-style mansion that would have been more at home in Georgia, with a white-suited fat man sipping a mint julep on the front porch, than just a few miles outside the nation's capital. Jet noted the guardhouse and the illuminated grounds, and thought she saw a guard patrolling the perimeter as they coasted past – this wouldn't be as easy as Sloan's place, that much was obvious. When they were several hundred yards past the house, they dead-ended in a cul-de-sac, requiring them to loop back around and go past the hulking edifice again. This time she was sure that she saw at least two men walking along the iron fencing on both sides of the grounds, as well as two lounging in the gatehouse.

"What do you think?" Alan asked as his eyes roved over the house, an easy seventy yards off the street at the end of an elaborately maintained drive.

"It's a palace. But it's also got a fairly alert security detail. What time is it?" she asked.

Alan glanced at his watch. "Eleven-forty."

"And there are at least four men on duty, and judging by the lights on downstairs, more inside. What are the chances we can get something on the house – plans? A layout?"

"Probably not great. If it isn't in the public domain, I can't get it. Unless I can somehow get into the Mossad servers…but even then, it's doubtful we'd have anything on it. I'd have to pull in some favors from the Embassy here."

"You're not going to get in touch with the director again, are you? After the ferry incident? Alan. You don't know who's after you. Right now you're dead. Don't you think it's better to stay that way?"

"I've been thinking about that. I have to let the director know I'm resigning. I don't have to tell him where I am, but after so many years devoted to the cause it just doesn't feel right to disappear with no explanation. I owe him that much. And there's no way that he blew up a ferry to try to get me — think about it. For what? He could have just called me back to Israel and put a bullet in my skull."

Jet shook her head. "I don't like it. At all. I think you're better off dead."

"I know, but it's not your decision to make. I would rather let him know that I'm okay but leaving the Mossad than have him wondering what happened to me, or whether I went over to the other side or something. It can't hurt, and it feels like the right thing to do. And again, I won't tell him where I am. So there's no possible harm that can come of it."

"Famous last words. You ever hear of the law of unintended consequences?"

"Not really."

He made the turn and they drove away from Arthur's house. There was nothing more to see.

"We should come back tomorrow and stake the place out."

"That'll be hard to do. It's deserted, and the few other homes around it are also mansions set well away from the street. There's no place to park and hang out."

"I know. So we'll have to hike in and find a spot. Not like we haven't done it before."

Their tail lights disappeared and the area was quiet again.

Across the road from the compound, several hundred yards inside the grounds of Lahey Lost Valley Park, a black-clad man lowered his binoculars and made a note of the Dodge's license plate in a small book he carried in his breast pocket, and then returned to watching the house from his perch in the branches of one of the trees.

CHAPTER 28

The morning meeting at the club was unusual, but these were unusual times. The older man stepped to the curb, his black-suited driver holding the door open for him, and he walked shakily to the front entrance, which opened as if by magic as he approached.

The group was convened in the usual room, and the heady smell of rich coffee and mouth-watering omelets pervaded the atmosphere. The older man took his place at the table, and after taking a sip of coffee from the steaming, waiting cup, he looked around the room at the gathered men.

"We're not getting traction. We need something more. There are too many questioning the data on Iran, even though all the sympathetic stations are playing our tune," he said perfunctorily.

"I've got every string pulled that can be pulled. The problem is that there's a credibility gap due to our past claims that they're trying to develop nukes. And Iraq screwed us on the idea that everyone would give us the benefit of the doubt." The speaker was one of the younger men in the ensemble, chartered with handling the media onslaught.

"Yes, I'm aware we're coming from behind. That's why the damned attack was supposed to kill everyone. Now we're standing around with limp dicks and bogus data, and our adversaries smell blood. I'm not here to bemoan how hard it is to make this happen. I want ideas on how to turn it around."

"There's already intel being fed to the Brits and the Canadians that would strongly suggest that there's a threat in Iran."

"Again, that card was played, and burned, with Iraq. The usual suspects all corroborated our position that Saddam had WMDs he could launch within forty-five minutes, and it was proved false after we invaded. You don't get two bites at that apple. Nobody's buying our spin," the older man seethed.

The younger man nodded. "And the Iranians are being pretty savvy about this. They know what we're up to, and they're ahead of it. They've got independent observers now who are all saying that there's zero evidence of anything but peaceful nuclear development. It's not helping."

"I want an honest assessment, and I need some new ideas, people. We need to recognize when what we're doing isn't working, and come up with something better."

"Well, sir, the polls all show that the public is behind us on a pre-emptive strike. So the American people have bought it."

"That doesn't really matter if the rest of the world is saying hands off, does it? Again, the whole media thing to get the sheep on board could only help us if the attack had been successful. Which it wasn't. And the bastards have opened the oil exchange and are trading now in non-dollars. The Chinese are their biggest customers, and they're paying in yuan. The Russians are paying in rubles. This is a disaster for the dollar if it continues. I trust I don't need to remind everyone of the stakes."

Nobody said anything.

"If we can't invade Iran, the dollar is doomed. The Germans are already pulling their gold back to Germany and putting the pork to all the EU countries, in preparation for a meltdown. They tightened credit on the lower productivity countries, which jacked their borrowing costs, and now the European central bank has stepped in and offered emergency loans. But countries like Greece and Spain and Portugal have to sign over their hard assets to collateralize the loans." The older man took another pull on the coffee and leaned back. "Russia is also calling its gold back and stockpiling it. China, the largest producer of gold in the world, hasn't exported an ounce. Everyone sees a paper currency disaster in the making, and they're all positioning to be in hard assets to the extent possible when the music stops.

"And we have another problem. The damned Germans are now demanding to audit the gold at the New York Fed. We've been able to get by with a 'trust us, it's all there' for decades, but now they actually want to see it, count it, and verify that it's real gold, and not tungsten cores with gold overlay. Do I need to tell you what will happen if the world discovers that…well, let's just say that nobody is taking our word for anything anymore. Getting Iran to tumble so we can get back to denominating oil in dollars, and nothing else, is critical to the survival of the currency. Other countries are watching this closely, and it's just a matter of time until the

Saudis or Nigeria also want to get paid in something other than dollars. And when that happens, we're screwed."

The group discussed possible options for an hour, with no resolution and no breakthroughs. Eventually, the older man sat back with a groan and stared at the ceiling.

"What's the latest on the Mossad agent that might know about this, sir? I know you said you would handle it, but could you give us anything more? Is it still an issue?" asked a fat, sweating man in a vested suit from across the table.

"It's been handled. He's no longer a threat. Met with an unexpected accident. It happens."

"Then at least that's one thing we can scratch off the list."

"Yes. But I want some new thinking here. Let's get together again next week and establish a more productive direction. What we're doing may be stirring up the hayseeds, but it's not swaying anyone that matters. Put on your thinking caps. Same time on Monday," the older man said, looking at his watch as he stood.

Outside, the driver pulled to the curb as the club door opened, and the older man fumed over the lack of progress they were making as he descended the steps. The entire house of cards could come down if they didn't do something. If things continued in the direction they were going, it would be time to start taking precautions for a dollar collapse. He could see it coming. It had always been planned, of course, but not for another decade or more. A default was the only way to clean the slate of the two hundred trillion dollars of unfunded liabilities the system was saddled with – Social Security, Medicare, Fannie Mae… When the dollar collapsed, the government could shrug and say, sorry, we're bankrupt, but let's focus on the future with a new currency which, this time, we'll administer responsibly. It was the ultimate land grab. All the mortgages in the country would be immediately accelerated, with demands for payment in whatever the new currency was, ignoring that most people would be wiped out because they hadn't had their wealth in tangible assets but rather in worthless stocks and bonds and ETFs. So he and his allies would wind up owning everything the middle class had accumulated since the Second World War, and the average Joe would be left out in the cold.

After all was said and done, nothing would change, except for the middle class – just like in the Great Depression, when the poor had still been poor, the filthy rich had stayed that way, and it was the middle class that went from having massive collective wealth to being destitute. It was amazing to him that people didn't learn; but then again, that was all by design.

The U.S. would become like Argentina, or Britain, where most of the hard assets of the country were owned by banks or foreign corporations, and the population was living in its own country with no ownership of the land or the riches. The apocalyptic view of everything grinding to a halt was overblown, he knew from watching those countries. There would be six months of adjusting to the new currency and the new austerity, and then life would go on, only without the prosperity of before. People would still buy burgers and go to work, but they would be paid in a new currency instead of dollars, and their dollar-denominated savings would be a distant memory, just as they were for most in the Great Depression. Things would continue. And he and his cohorts would have redistributed four generations of wealth, and nobody would know how it happened.

It was the perfect crime, but the timing was off. They still needed more time to convert all the dollars that were being printed into hard assets without causing a run on the system. Iran trading oil in non-dollars could seriously disrupt the long term plan.

One way or another, it had to go. And soon.

֎

Alan shook his head as he spoke on the internet phone to the director.

"No, sir, I'm not being disrespectful. I'm retiring. Effective immediately. I don't want to do this anymore. I've done my time. I'm out. I quit."

"You don't get to decide when you're out. I do," the director warned.

"All due respect, no, sir. It's my life, and I'm taking it back. I've done more for the country, and for you, than anyone. But it's time to go on without me."

"Where are you?" the director demanded.

"I'm not at liberty to say."

"Why not? Since when do you keep these things from me?" the director spat, outraged at his authority being questioned.

"Since I have reason to believe someone's trying to kill me." There. It was out in the open.

"What are you talking about? Speak plainly, damn it."

"I was on a ferry. In South America. It exploded. I believe that it was destroyed to take me out."

The director was silent, digesting the new information. "The Americans have been asking about you," he said quietly.

"What? Why? What Americans?"

"It's been very low key, but they expressed interest in interviewing you some more about the bio-attack."

Wheels meshed, and the light bulb went on in Alan's head. "They want to know where I am?"

"They haven't asked since a few days ago."

"Around the time the ferry exploded."

They were both quiet for a few moments.

"Who's looking for me?"

"Their homeland security. An agent named Ryker was mentioned. I believe he interrogated you before?"

"Yes. And you're sure he was trying to get to me again?" Alan asked.

"Do I strike you as muddled or confused?"

"No, sir."

The director sighed. "What did the terrorist tell you, exactly? Before he died?"

Alan repeated the story.

"Does anyone else know about this? Have you told anyone?"

Alan hesitated. "No. Only you."

The director breathed heavily into the phone, each man trying to read the other over the line. Eventually the director came to a decision.

"For your own good, and perhaps mine, this call never happened. I haven't heard from you. You're dead to me, and I have no knowledge of any of this. Do you understand?"

"Yes, sir. That's probably best."

"Of course, it could take a few weeks for me to cancel out your server access. I've got a lot on my plate. And Alan? I'd stay off the radar if I were you. Don't plan any trips to Disneyland, do you get my drift?"

Alan decided not to share that he was in the United States as they spoke. "Yes."

"This Ryker works out of Los Angeles. He left a number. An enterprising young man would be able to figure out exactly where his offices were located with that." The director rattled off a 310 area code number. "Not that it would be a good idea, mind you."

"I understand. It would be a bad idea."

"A very bad idea." The director paused. "Good luck, my friend. You're going to need it. God go with you," he finished, and then hung up.

Alan replaced the handset in the cradle and sat back, then rubbed his face and stood. He exited the booth, paid the young man at the internet café counter for his time, and walked out onto the sidewalk, foreigners like himself milling around him – the only place he'd been able to find an internet café had been downtown, where tourists abounded. Apparently, everyone and everywhere else was wired, so the cafés couldn't make a living. A sign of progress, he supposed.

He ambled to his car and handed the parking attendant a few bills, then got into the Dodge and started the engine. Jet would already be at Arthur's, keeping watch. He had agreed to meet her there later, whenever she called him. From all appearances the prior night, getting in might turn out to be harder than they had hoped.

But now he had another, perhaps bigger, problem.

A problem named Ryker.

CHAPTER 29

Jet strolled down the lane in the late morning sun, the weather balmy, heading into Indian summer soon. The gravel at the side of the road crunched under her track shoes, which completed her outfit, consisting of a flowing hippie skirt and a tie-dyed tank top with a ratty sweater pulled over it. The wig she had bought that morning fitted well, a light blonde job that completely hid her still-short natural cut.

Her backpack contained a water bottle, binoculars, and some energy bars, along with a book, a blanket, and few odds and ends that would seem innocuous if she was searched – unlikely, but she was taking no chances. Dark sunglasses shaded her eyes, and to the world she would appear to be a trippy college-age girl out for a day communing with nature.

Her steps led her into the park, across from Arthur's lair, and when she reached a spot where she was far enough into the woods that she wouldn't attract attention, she pulled out her blanket and spread it on the grass, and then plopped down with her book and the spyglasses. She watched as the morning guards went about their routine, patrolling the grounds with robot-like efficiency, their demeanor anything but the relaxed casualness she had hoped to see.

At one point a thin man in a black suit exited the front of the house and approached the front gate guardhouse, so she took a few photos with her high-resolution phone camera for later study. He lingered there for a few minutes, then strutted back to the house with an officious bearing. Clearly in charge – perhaps Arthur's second-in-command.

From watching the house itself she got no clue as to where the master suite might be. The windows afforded no visibility, the curtains tightly drawn in all but two of the rooms. Apparently, Arthur was taking no chances after his miraculous near-death experience. She didn't blame him.

A box van pulled up to the gates and the driver had a brief exchange with the guard, who stepped into the security area and depressed a button.

The gates swung slowly open and the van rolled down the drive, pausing inside the gate before easing to the front of the house and parking. Two uniformed men got out and went to the back of the vehicle, where they got toolboxes and some electronic testing gear and moved onto the grass near the fence. They stopped near one of the stone posts and knelt down, then began fiddling with something – a motion detector, Jet thought as she peered at them through the glasses.

With Author's knowledge of tradecraft, he would be able to command the absolute best security money could buy, and with his ill-gotten profits from his multi-decade drug trafficking scheme, he had piles of cash to spend. The house was easily ten or fifteen million dollars with all the land, maybe more. And the level of security he was paying for had to run six figures per month.

He had gone from having only cursory safeguards to overkill, which would make him much more difficult to get to this time. If he never left the house, which was likely based upon Sloan's description of his condition, he was effectively encapsulated within a protective cocoon. While she had penetrated many such facilities in the past, she had none of the supporting technology on this one she might have had if she were doing this for the Mossad – surveillance teams, blueprints, sat photos, deep research from an ongoing multi-month effort.

She was under no illusions that she would be able to waltz in, put a bullet between Arthur's eyes, and then saunter out undetected. As it looked right now, it would be messy and risky. They would need to get in, neutralize the security team, stop them or the hidden devices from alerting anyone off-site, and then kill Arthur. That he had a small army guarding him was bad enough, but that he had access to the very latest countermeasures made it even dicier.

At eleven-thirty her cell phone vibrated. Alan's disposable number popped up on the screen.

"How's it going?" he asked.

"Not bad. Just watching the watchers."

"Any revelations?"

"Not really. Just that they're pro, he's got at least a dozen men there, and serious electric countermeasures."

"Your specialty."

"Yeah, but I have a bad feeling about this, looking at it from here. We don't have a month to figure out the best way in. And we don't have intel support. Even on the Russian, we got to lean on the Mossad for blueprints. Without those, I'd still be sitting over there hoping for a break."

"Well, I might have some good news in that regard. I spoke with the director." Alan recounted his discussion.

"So what are you planning to do?" she asked when he was finished.

"I think I've got to put some of that Sloan money to use, charter a plane to Los Angeles, and have a serious one-on-one discussion with Ryker. I need to know what the score is and who's after me. Just like you did."

"The difference is that as far as they know, you're dead."

"All due respect, my confidence in that being the perfect way out of the maze isn't high after your experience. Being dead didn't really simplify your life like you thought it would, did it?"

"I'm not going to argue that. When are you going to leave?"

"Today. I'm at the hotel. I got fifty grand out of the safe and talked to a charter service that will fly me to Los Angeles for sixteen grand. I'll worry about the return trip once I've got things sorted on that end. I can use one of my passports for the private flight – they didn't ask for much in terms of ID other than either a domestic driver's license or a passport. Apparently, terrorists aren't winging around the sky in Lear jets."

"Then you'll be there by this afternoon? How many hours will it take?" Jet asked.

"About four and a half, and I leave in an hour. I've been online, on the servers, doing some checking. I think I have a handle on where he's working."

"Are you thinking about…"

"I don't see a lot of ways to get information quickly other than interrogating him, do you?"

She thought it through, then shook her head and closed her eyes. "Not really. But he's a…he's a high-profile target. That will increase the heat exponentially. When one of their own gets it…well, you know."

"I'm aware of the risk. I'll be careful."

"Please. And call me when you know you'll be returning."

"Do you have this covered?"

"For now. Although I'm going to ask that you, in all your spare time, access the servers for anything you can find about the compound." Jet paused, thinking. "You know, something just occurred to me. It's likely that Arthur was using Sloan's company for security, given their relationship and his paranoia level. If so, maybe there's something on the flash drive I found. Worst case, I can try hacking into their servers. Shouldn't be too hard, given my abilities."

"Modest, too," Alan teased, breaking the tension.

"Just be careful. There's a lot that can go wrong on a solo snatch. As you know."

"I'll do my best to not get caught. How's that?"

"I guess it'll have to do."

They spent another two minutes on logistical matters and then Jet disconnected, her attention returning to the van. She took a photo of the license plate, wishing that the vehicle had some sort of identifying markings. Then again, that would defeat the whole point of being a discreet security company. Sloan had the kind of business that he wouldn't be interested in advertising. Between the government contracts, his legitimate business, and Arthur's black ops errands, he'd made a fortune.

Not that any of it had done him any good in the end.

It was going to be a long afternoon, she knew, and she returned to pretending to read her book as she eyed the security men's comings and goings.

A hundred and fifty yards away, a man sat in a tall tree, on a small platform he'd constructed for that purpose, his focus split between the house and the hippie woman who looked to him as though she was also keeping an eye on the place. The binoculars gave her away. He'd bet a million bucks that if she was asked about them, the answer would be bird watching, and he had no doubt that the book she was reading was filled with photos of birds – he'd gotten a glimpse of the cover through his telephoto lens, his suspicions aroused by her choice of locations.

He shifted on the wooden slats, invisible in his green camouflage outfit and the netting he'd put up under the cover of darkness. Whatever was going on with the woman, it had nothing to do with a defensive play by the men on Arthur's grounds. They were going about their business by the book, as far as he could tell.

But the woman.

She bore further watching.

CHAPTER 30

Agent Ryker stretched his arms over his head and yawned, another stressful day of doing not much of anything finally over. Since the terrorist attack at the stadium, the Los Angeles office had been on full alert, which meant a lot of supervision of security details at public buildings and events – none of which had been targeted by anyone, and none of which showed any danger of being targeted. But orders were orders and it was a good paycheck, so he did what he had to do to get by.

He checked the clock on the wall of his office, walked over to the rack, and got his sports coat. It was quitting time and things were blessedly quiet, his colleagues all busy pushing paper around until they could reasonably leave. Ryker was one of the senior members of the Los Angeles staff, so he could cut out a little early on days like this one – one of the perks of management, among others.

"Nighty night, Camelia," he said to the receptionist as he breezed past the front office, intent on making it to his car before rush hour really got under way. Always a failed plan, but one he never gave up on. Bad as it was at four-thirty on the L.A. freeways, five-thirty put it to shame. The seven miles from his offices in downtown to his home in Pasadena could easily take an hour to traverse, and sometimes double that in heavy traffic. It was an insane way to live, but that was his norm, and many had it far worse.

His footsteps echoed in the underground parking lot, shared by City Hall and a host of city government offices, and when he pulled out of his stall with a squeal of tires he was relieved to be ahead of the crowd – the parking area was still packed, a good sign he'd gotten the jump on his fellow grunions. He pulled to the attendant and waved as the man pushed the button that lifted the barrier, failing to register the car behind him hurrying to pay in order to keep up with him.

The 110 freeway was already clogged with commuters inching their way angrily north, and as he settled into the drudgery of crawling towards home he turned on the radio, favoring a talk radio station that leaned heavily towards political topics. He listened as wholly uninformed callers dialed in to be abused by the show's abrasive and opinionated host.

Forty-five minutes later he signaled and took an off ramp leading to the quiet streets of South Pasadena, where he had a modest three-bedroom home he'd bought as an investment back in the heady days of property doubling in value every three years. Now he lived in it, his divorce final two years prior. He valued his solitude, bought at a horrendously high price from a harpy who had sucked the life out of him during their seven-year marriage.

Fortunately, he'd been clever about hiding his off-the-books income, so while she'd taken him to the cleaners, it could have been far worse. He was still reasonably wealthy, although he lived like a pauper, preferring to bank his secret income rather than waste it on frivolities.

The garage door opened automatically and he pulled inside, turning the radio off as the steel panels slid shut behind him. He killed the engine and grabbed his briefcase, wrinkling his nose at the stagnant atmosphere from the windows being closed all day, then moved to the rear door that led to his small back yard and opened it. He set his briefcase on the shabby kitchen table and shrugged out of his shoulder holster, placing it next to his valise before going into the kitchen to grab an icy cold beer.

His bedroom wasn't much fresher, so he slid a window open before going to the bathroom and taking off his work clothes, replacing them with a pair of running shorts and a Lakers jersey – his preferred attire for pizza and beer down at the corner Italian joint, where he spent three or four nights a week watching sports and trying to pick up waitresses with Stairmaster asses. One good thing about anywhere in Los Angeles was that the women were world class, and often clueless, there from the heartland to try to make it in show business, working two shifts to pay for a shared tiny apartment in a lousy area while waiting for the big break to announce itself. His favorite was Monica, a fiery brunette from Stockton, of Hispanic extraction, and the kind of girl who knew her way around the block.

When he walked back into the living room he was surprised by a man sitting in the shadows.

"Agent Ryker. Nice to see you again. Have a seat. I hear you were interested in seeing me?" Alan said, his tone steady, Ryker's Colt 1911 .45 caliber pistol held casually in his hand, the barrel trained on Ryker.

"What the — have you gone mad? What the hell are you doing here, in my house?"

"I'm here to have a talk. Man to man. About the bio-hazard, and why someone is trying to kill me."

Ryker's eyes narrowed to slits.

"Sit. I'm not going to tell you again." Alan eased out of the easy chair and motioned to the sofa.

Ryker sidled over to it and sat down. "I have no idea what the hell you're talking about. But I can tell you that, diplomatic immunity or not, breaking in here and holding a gun on me is the worst mistake of your life," Ryker seethed.

"Let's start at the beginning, shall we? Who were the two goons who showed up at the end of my interrogation?" Alan said, moving to the front window and closing the blinds.

"Who?"

"I'm going to start getting really annoyed if you don't start talking. Who were they?"

"I...FBI."

"Really. What were their names?"

"I don't remember."

Alan sighed, took three quick steps, and rammed the heavy pistol into Ryker's solar plexus, causing him to double up and pass out.

When he came to, it was completely dark, and he couldn't move. He opened his eyes wide, and saw that he was in the dining room, tied to a chair. Alan was sitting in Ryker's recliner, watching him, ominously silent, a peaceful expression on his face.

"I guess we're going to do this the hard way. A shame, but I have no real preference. I want to know everything you know about my interrogation, and who's after me."

"I don't know who's after you."

Alan's eyes shot to the side, then he stood. "You're lying. I know. I've done this often enough. So now we'll take this in an ugly direction, and find out what you're lying about. This is your last chance. We'll start with the two men. Who were they?"

"You realize that you're a dead man after this, don't you? There's nowhere you'll be able to hide, especially if you torture me. I know that's what you intend to do, and I'm telling you that you're wasting your time," Ryker growled.

"I must have been unclear. Maybe it's a language issue. I've interrogated countless men – far tougher cases than you, my friend. Men who believed in their causes. Men who thought God had instructed them to act as they had. Men of devout faith and firm resolve. Do you know what I discovered?"

Ryker sat silent.

"They all talk. All. One hundred percent. Even those who were convinced that a trailer-park full of virgins waited for them in the afterlife talked. Men who would have gladly blown themselves up to take some of their enemies with them. And do you know why, Agent Ryker? Because the flesh is weak. We're flawed creatures, molded from imperfect clay. And every one of us will talk, if not to live, to escape unbearable, unspeakable pain. I know this to be true. Because I don't come from the same world you do. How many men have you killed in your life, Agent Ryker? You're a tough guy. A badass. How many men have you looked in the eyes and sent to eternity?"

"Enough."

"My guess is a few in the army. But that's nothing. I've killed dozens. Maybe by now, over a hundred. I don't even bother to keep count anymore. I learned a secret a long time ago. Everything we see around us" – he waved his hand in an arc – "is temporary, including us, and there's none of us that's more important in the scheme of things than the ants we step on without realizing it when we walk down the street. We all think we're special, but we aren't. And when our time comes, we all die the same way. Once you realize that, you become comfortable doing a job nobody should have to do. I never enjoy torturing, inflicting pain. I'm not a sadist. I actually don't want it to go on any longer than it has to. I feel sorry for the victim. Just like I'm sure the guy in the slaughterhouse feels sorry for the cows he's going to butcher that day. But he does his job. And today, I'll do my job on you, to find out what you know. Look at me. Do I seem like I'm lying to you, Ryker?"

For the first time, Ryker seemed to understand what was going to take place. "I'll never tell you anything. I don't know anything. I can't tell you what I don't know."

Alan shook his head, and then moved into the kitchen, where he had a pot on the stove. "This is boiling oil. It will be only the first of many horrors you'll become acquainted with this evening. This is your last opportunity to talk. Then, I'll go with the tried and true methods that work every time. So again. Who were those men? What were their names?"

"You'll never get anything out of me, you sorry prick."

Alan turned the flame off and grabbed a dish towel, then approached Ryker with a frown.

In the end, Ryker told him everything. As Alan had known he would.

The fire spread quickly in the old house, the wooden studs and siding like dry kindling, forty-something years of sun having dried them to perfection for a fast ignition and hot blaze.

Alan watched as the flames consumed the structure, the gasoline he had drained from Ryker's car doing a passable job as an accelerant, and then started his rental vehicle and pulled away from the curb as sirens echoed in the distance, called by a vigilant neighbor who had been up late, unable to sleep. He looked at the console digital clock and did a quick calculation – he could call Jet in another few hours. She'd be just waking up, but would want to hear from him.

The little car rolled around the corner and towards the freeway, where Alan would drive to the airport and then call another charter company, his work in Los Angeles done.

CHAPTER 31

The next morning Jet was back at the park, this time sporting a backpack, an oversized dark green T-shirt, baggy jeans, and a flat-brimmed baseball hat on backwards, the embodiment of a slacker teen playing hooky. She cut into the park before she got to Arthur's street and moved stealthily through the trees until she had a vantage point on the opposite side from the prior day's.

Jet had returned after dark the previous night and circled the perimeter, taking her time, watching the guards and noting their shifts. She'd had a scare at around one A.M., when an unseen neighbor's dog had sensed her and begun barking, but fortunately she had been able to slink away unseen and take up a position a hundred yards away.

The good news was that the house's grounds were remote by American standards, with many of the surrounding properties also on huge lots, some easily commanding an acre or more. So whenever she and Alan made their move on the complex, they would have relative privacy. The negatives were far more plentiful. A crack team of professional guards. State-of-the-art technology. Super-paranoid procedures. And perhaps worst of all, an alert security detail. The men weren't complacent. They were taking their job seriously, which told her that there wouldn't be any mistakes or oversights she could exploit. This wasn't a provincial warlord in the Middle East or a shoddily run team of out-to-pasture commandos in Russia. These men looked fit and ready for anything.

Jet knew from experience that mental edge was often the difference between success and failure, and the guards looked hard and seasoned. Arthur had probably wanted the very best of the best, and he'd likely paid enough to get it.

Still, there was always a way. She just needed to find it.

At dawn she'd gone back to the hotel and caught two hours of sleep and then returned in her new garb, ready for another long day of tedium. She hated this part of the job, but it was unavoidable. Normally a surveillance team would have done the grunt work, and she'd have simply studied their report and then sprung into action, but she didn't have that luxury. It would be a big relief when Alan got back – at least that way they could do split shifts, which would make things easier on her.

He had called early that morning to tell her that he was flying back, but didn't want to discuss anything more over the phone. Hopefully he would get there by the end of the day, allowing for the time difference.

She found a suitable spot far enough away that she'd be unnoticed by the security team and began her stint near the ancient burial grounds, a vague sense of anxiety playing at her, which she attributed to the limited amount of sleep she had gotten. It was almost the same as the feeling she experienced when she was under surveillance, but different somehow. Besides which, nobody at the house was showing any interest in the park, which wasn't surprising. If something came inside the walls, it was fair game, but their job wasn't to police the park and all the surrounding land.

The huge walnut trees provided more than adequate shade as she pretended to read her new book, a puerile tome about vampire boyfriends and werewolf suitors that she'd picked up at a drugstore, peering over the cover periodically to take readings on the guards' positions.

The day wore on and she found herself nodding off, the duty as tedious as any she'd done, albeit not unpleasant in the wilds of nature. She reached into her backpack and retrieved a soda from its depths, hoping that the caffeine would give her a much-needed jolt and keep her alert. Lunch was a pre-wrapped sandwich from a convenience store made from slices of chicken and cheese-like product that she had to choke down, fighting her gag reflex with every mouthful.

When her phone vibrated at dusk she almost jumped. She brought it to her ear with a palpable sense of relief. "You're back?"

"Yes. You need any help?"

"No. I'm about to take off. I want to get a few hours of sleep before tonight, unless you can take the night shift. Hint, hint."

"I'd love to. When will you get to the hotel?"

She consulted her watch. "An hour?"

"Perfect. That will give me time to do a little research."

"Care to share?"

"When I see you."

She wasn't accustomed to him being so cloaked, so whatever Alan had discovered was probably big. He wasn't prone to melodrama, and if he was suddenly this cautious, it could only mean that whatever it was had him worried, if not scared.

Jet thought about Alan, his operational history and all he'd been through, and decided that if it was big enough to frighten him, then it was probably pretty scary. Pensive, wondering what it could be, she slowly packed her bag and stowed everything she'd brought, leaving no evidence that she'd been there – nothing to track or give her away.

From the trees in the distance, the watcher followed her passage through the park with his binoculars, taking note of her departure time before resuming his watch on Arthur's house.

※

Alan had gotten an early morning start, and the chartered jet had been in the air by five A.M., touching down in D.C. by lunchtime. He'd gone directly to the address he'd acquired for Peter's work, and had been rewarded by seeing his BMW roll out of the lot a few minutes later – by far the most expensive car parked there, in a spot with a sign that said 'reserved' in front of it. He'd followed him and watched as Peter strode purposefully to the entry of an expensive French restaurant in Georgetown. The maître d' greeted him warmly and showed him to a table towards the rear of the restaurant, where an older man had been waiting in the secluded spot.

They sat, obviously in a heated discussion over their lunch, which lasted barely forty minutes, and then the older man rose, agitated, and threw a few bills onto the table before stalking out. Peter had remained behind and ordered a third glass of wine, a look of frowning annoyance on his face.

Neither noticed Alan, who was picking at his filet of sole meunière and sipping a bottle of Perrier as he pretended to study a tourist brochure. The late lunch crowd kept coming and the waiters were eager to turn the tables, but nobody approached Peter, who was taking his time with the wine. He was well known to the restaurant and wasn't to be trifled with. If the man wanted to enjoy his drink, then they would leave him alone to do so.

Alan had accomplished what he'd wanted to do. He'd taken photos of both Peter and the older man, which he would run through the Mossad databases and see if a hit came up. Ryker had told him about Peter, and had intimated that his father was too powerful to take on, but hadn't elaborated, and Alan hadn't cared about his dad. Peter was the one who had directed Ryker to question him and had arranged for the two FBI agents to be present at the coliseum interrogation, and was the one who had put pressure on Ryker to find Alan afterwards – at all costs.

Ryker had admitted that Peter hadn't cared whether Alan was located dead or alive, and had indicated that his preference would be if he disappeared with no trace. While not flat-out ordering Ryker to kill him, the message had been clear – Alan knew too much, and had to be found so he could be silenced.

Alan finished his excellent fish and motioned for the check. He'd seen enough. Peter drove his own car, had no bodyguards that he could see, and seemed to enjoy his booze. The only negative was that Alan didn't know anything about where he lived – but that would change by day's end.

There was a coffee shop on the corner, a hundred and fifty yards from Peter's building, that had free wireless service, which Alan intended to take advantage of while he waited for Peter to leave for the day. Perhaps he could get more information on the older man. Peter's brief dossier hadn't contained anything about his parents – the father was unknown, mother deceased, never married. But Ryker had made a big deal about his father being a power player in D.C., so he would follow that lead through to the end.

Whatever was going on here, Iran factored heavily, and Alan had grown to believe that factions close to, or in, the government had mounted the unsuccessful false-flag bio-attack as a justification for an Iranian invasion. But he needed to know more before he understood what he was up against. Right now all he had were questions.

Peter finished his drink and stood somewhat unsteadily, then pushed through the busy restaurant to the front door. Alan waited a few moments until his quarry was out on the street and then followed him, his car parked only a few stalls away from Peter's expensive BMW.

Alan kept a safe distance as Peter's car wove through traffic, cheerfully ignoring the speed limit as well as the rights of his fellow drivers. It had been the same on the way to the restaurant, so Alan was expecting it and didn't take it as an attempt to be evasive. The man was just a complete prick on the road. Alan suspected the same was true in person.

At the café, he ordered a cappuccino and powered on the computer he'd bought in L.A., then sent the photo to one of his blind email accounts. A few moments later he was on the Mossad servers, uploading the shot and waiting for the powerful facial recognition software to work its magic. He took a gulp of the frothy confection, and then the little window on his computer blinked at him. He navigated to the dossier that was linked to the image with ninety-eight percent certainty and opened it. The cup of coffee froze mid-way to his lips as he read.

The older man was the Deputy Chief of Staff to the President of the United States, and one of the most influential political strategists in the country. His was a household name, even if his image was virtually unknown – he shunned the limelight and avoided publicity at all costs.

And apparently, judging by their body language over lunch, he was connected to Peter in a big way. A paternal way. As he studied the man's image, he could see a definite resemblance, now that he was looking for it.

Peter was a bastard on the road, all right, but that wasn't the only place.

Alan would bet anything that the older man was Peter's father.

CHAPTER 32

When Jet got back to the hotel, Alan was waiting for her, a grim expression on his handsome face. She dropped her backpack on the table and tumbled onto the king-sized bed, exhausted. Alan switched off the television and joined her, resting his head on one hand as he lay on his side, supported by his elbow.

"So tell me everything you couldn't on the phone," Jet said with a weary tone.

"I got to Ryker. He was definitely part of something big. And ugly." Alan then told her all about Peter, his company, his involvement in hunting for Alan, and then saved the best for last.

"I followed him today. He had a lunch meeting. With Dad. This is way, way bigger than anything I could have guessed."

"Come on. Don't hold out. The suspense is killing me."

"Dad is one of the top men in Washington. To call him influential would be to call a hurricane a little bit of rain. The man's legendary. Has advised numerous presidents. The rumors are that he's more powerful than the entire government apparatus combined. He's way too big to take on, and I'm not even sure it would do any good. If he's behind the terrorist strike, then we're hosed. As is Iran, unless they can pull a rabbit out of the hat."

Jet closed her eyes for a few seconds, then fixed him with an unwavering gaze. "Okay, then you have to cut off his operational legs. Which would appear to be his son. Dad connives, and Peter implements. Maybe you can't kill the beast, but you can sure as hell cut the field guy's head off."

"A succinct summary. I got to the same place earlier. Now the question is, how to take him down without getting caught?"

"Same way we worked it in Russia. We have two discrete operations here. The first is Arthur. The second is Peter. We concentrate on the larger problem first, like we did with your Yemen issue, and then we go to the second objective – Peter. I'll help you. That goes without saying. But I think we want this to look like anything but a sanction, which is where the art will come in."

"You're reading my mind."

"Let me put my thinking cap on. Where there's a will…"

"How are you feeling, otherwise? You look beat. Hot as hell, but beat."

"I am, Alan. I need about six hours of sleep to get back on my game. I'm one step above a zombie right now."

He rolled off the bed, her message clear, and rose. "I'm headed out to watch Arthur's place. See if Doctor Evil has any chinks in his armor. When I get back, you can take over. You said six hours?"

"Yup. Do you mind?"

"Not at all. Anything I should know?"

She filled him in on the finer points of her surveillance and the conclusions she'd drawn so far. He listened intently, then nodded.

"All right. I'll change into something more comfortable that won't draw attention and get over to the park. You have binocs?"

She opened her backpack and handed them to him. "Thank you, Alan. I'll call you when I wake up, or you can call me…in at least six hours. We'll figure out what else to do from there."

"Okay. Sleep well. I'll just be a second."

Alan changed out of his button-up shirt and jeans and pulled on a pair of black sweats and a black hoodie he'd bought in L.A., then switched off the lights.

"Goodnight," he said, then slipped out the motel room door, closing it softly behind him.

Jet forced herself up and padded to the bathroom. Reaching into the shower, she twisted the knob and stripped while she waited for the hot water to hit. She rinsed off mechanically, her eyes closed most of the time, and then pulled on some fresh panties and a T-shirt and threw herself onto the bed, her need to rest overriding all other concerns.

Her dreams were troubled. In them, Arthur's scarred face leered malevolently at her as his fingers turned into straight-edged razors and he chased her through a dark maze. Every time she would get close to finding her way out, the labyrinth would change shape and she'd be right back where she started, his twisted grimace the embodiment of evil.

She tossed and turned as variations of the nightmare intruded, and then it changed.

In it, Alan walked down the street, whistling, somewhere in South America, the local color and smells so vivid she felt like she was there with him. He turned a corner on the busy street, and then was suddenly on an empty boulevard, a harsh, cold wind blowing his hair back and making him squint. A baby carriage rolled of its own volition from a doorway and then exploded, shattering the nearby storefronts and shredding him into an unrecognizable carcass.

Somehow in the dream she hovered above him. Something barely distinguishable as an eye looked up at her from the bloody gore, and then the savaged flesh parted and a cloud of black wasps flew from where Alan's mouth would have been, racing directly towards her.

Just as the stinging began, the pain paralyzing, Hannah's voice cried from a second baby carriage rolling towards her. Arthur's tortured profile grinned at her from the darkness of the alley from which it came.

"Mama! Help me!" Hannah screamed, and then the entire dream exploded in a red-orange blast.

Jet bolted awake, her heart racing, her shirt drenched through with sweat, and looked around the room, taking a moment to register where she was. She looked at her watch and calculated that she'd slept a total of four hours so far – not enough, but she was doubtful she'd be able to get any more rest.

She forced herself to lie back down and pulled the covers up, then closed her eyes again, reassuring herself that it was just a dream.

As she dozed, the troubling images faded, and the remaining two hours of slumber were blissfully untroubled, other than a faint background buzz of anxiety, a remnant from the earlier dream or perhaps her time in the park, when she'd been unable to shake the odd feeling of being watched.

※

Standish invited the two men into the house and showed them to the living room, where he usually met with those not specifically invited to Arthur's bedroom suite. Both wore extremely expensive hand-tailored suits and were in their mid-forties. They took seats on the sofa and Standish sat on a loveseat, facing them.

"May I get you anything to drink? Water? Soda? A cocktail?"

The thinner of the two, his balding pate sweating in spite of the mild temperature, leaned forward, his fingers clasped together, and stared at Standish with in impassive gaze.

"Why aren't we meeting with Arthur? We flew in specifically for this."

"Yes, I know, and I appreciate it. Arthur asked me to conduct the meeting. He's not feeling well today. He has his good days, and his...well, his not-so-good ones. As do we all," Standish explained.

"We don't talk to go-betweens," the other man snapped.

"Nor do I. Speaking with me is the same as speaking with Arthur. If you recall, I handled the last three meetings with you, and did most of the talking. So if we can dispense with the protestations, perhaps you'd like to get down to business?" Standish leaned back and studied both men. "The attacks are ongoing, and Papua is in chaos. We knocked out the mine, and the Indonesians have not responded particularly well to the crisis. And now, it looks like the Free Papua movement is gaining a credible shot at independence. If that happens, then I think we can guarantee that the mine will be nationalized and your target will be permanently out of luck."

Neither of the men responded.

"I've been tracking the share price of the company that owns the mine. It's down thirty-eight percent since this started, and every day it drops another few percent. I think it's safe to say that your wise investment in our services has paid for itself many times over by now. Your short position in the stock must have gone through the roof, as have the put options you've been buying, not to mention the credit default swaps."

"How do you know about the CDS pricing?" the bald man demanded.

"Do you take us for fools? Arthur's been doing this sort of thing a long time, and you're lucky he agreed to help you. He has me tracking everything for him. If you were aggressive, just your CDS positions alone would have made your hedge funds billions. And the play isn't over. But Arthur isn't greedy. He appreciates your prompt payment of the hundred million. The question is, what's your end goal here? Because he's interested in being involved in that, as well."

The pair exchanged glances, and then the bald man spoke up. "He's been dabbling in the CDS market himself. There were some suspicious purchases at the time we were taking our positions. Just so you know that we know."

"Of course he was. Do you think he couldn't figure this out the moment he agreed to your request? Surely you can't object to him taking a position. That way he's right in the trenches alongside of you, and shares your objective. I would have thought you would be delighted in this vote of confidence. Besides, he's done everything you asked. Am I missing something?" Standish asked.

"You're not missing anything. He must have made at least another couple of hundred million from his buys."

"I don't discuss his financial affairs, but he's very happy with how the positions have performed. But he would like to understand where you wish to go from here. His ability to impact circumstances over there is now reduced. Whether or not Indonesia bows to international pressure and grants Papua independence is out of his hands."

The heavier man sighed heavily. "We've assembled a leveraged buyout group that will make a tender offer for the company if independence goes through. We figure we can buy it for pennies on the dollar once news of the nationalization hits. That would be disastrous for the company, even though it has other properties it's mining. Obviously its management won't know that we've got a deal to co-manage the mine with the new government. We'll save that little tidbit until after we've acquired the company."

"That's what he thought you were going to do. He asked me to relay how interested he would be in participating in the buyout. Perhaps…a ten percent stake? Something manageable?" Standish asked, not so much questioning as suggesting.

"We'll have to see. That's a big piece. Even with some creative financing, we could be talking about him having to come up with half a billion in order to play. Does he have that kind of juice?" the bald man asked, the discussion having veered into an unexpected direction – one that he was at home with.

"That's in the range he was prepared to allocate to this. I really think you should consider how valuable it would be to have him participate. There are worse people to have on your side. As the results in Papua should tell you."

The bald man's eyes narrowed. "And what about you? What do you get out of this?"

"That's really not anything I can discuss. Suffice it to say that I'm being compensated adequately." Standish had no interest in telling the men that he was seeing a reasonable chunk of the upside. They could infer what they liked. "I was directed to either solidify a deal here, or he would consider his involvement in Papua concluded, as per your agreement. Please take your time, but I will need to go upstairs at the end of this meeting, and tell him…what's the phrase? Deal or no deal?" The traces of a smile flashed across his face.

The men conferred in hushed tones, and then seemed to come to an agreement.

"Fine. You're in for ten percent. But the drawdown will be very fast, and if for any reason he can't perform on demand, his piece will go to someone who can," the bald man cautioned.

They spent another few minutes discussing the deal, and then the two men stood.

"We'll get you a partnership agreement by courier tomorrow," the bald man said, shaking Standish's hand.

"At your leisure. Arthur and I know your word is your bond. I'm sure you wouldn't disappoint him. You've seen what he can achieve. Really miraculous, if you think about it. And you're completely insulated," Standish replied, shaking the other man's hand.

He showed them to the door and watched as their limo rolled down the drive, taking them back to the airport and their Gulfstream jets. His little gambit had just ensured Arthur would quadruple his money, for which Standish would be handsomely rewarded.

Standing on the porch, he shielded his eyes with his hand and looked up at the sky, where a few clouds were gathering. All in all it was a good day. Arthur would be happy.

And if Arthur was happy, Standish was happy.

CHAPTER 33

"Can you be back here to relieve me at four A.M.?" Jet whispered in the dark, watching the house with the binoculars.

"Sure. That will give me six hours of shut-eye. More than enough," Alan agreed.

"In which case I can relieve you again at ten tomorrow morning. I think the six-hour shift is the best way to go."

"Agreed. So what do you think about my plan? With Peter?" he asked.

Alan had filled her in on what he had come up with. Peter would die in a burglary, or commit suicide. How was academic. Alan had a number of possible ways to get to him.

"I like it, but I'm concerned about the timing. We need to take Arthur down first."

"No question. And then Peter meets his unfortunate end, and the threat to me is effectively neutralized. Without his son to run his dirty tricks, his father will be scrambling. If he could have used someone else, he would have."

"I agree. In principle," Jet said. "Let me do a little nosing around in the servers tomorrow morning while you're out here and see what I can come up with. We'll have to do this very, very carefully. And that means no flying by the seat of our pants."

"See you in six hours, then. You need anything?"

"Nope. I'm good."

Alan crawled from his position beside her and then jogged off into the darkness, leaving her to her thoughts. She understood why Alan was focused on terminating Peter – simple self-preservation – but she wasn't sure that he really had to. Alan was dead to the world, so it almost smacked a bit to her of vengeance – a reckoning. Eye for an eye.

There was so much she didn't know about Alan. Would he expose himself to further risk just to even some score only he was keeping track of? Whatever the case, she would help him. But she didn't like operating without all the information, and she felt like Alan was holding back. What it was, she didn't know. But she didn't like it. What you didn't know could get you killed.

An owl hooted in the trees overhead, startling her, and then she relaxed. Her nerves were still on edge from the residual impression of the dream.

Snap out of it, she thought. Find a weakness in Arthur's defenses. Something exploitable that would enable them to gain entry. Because as it currently stood, she didn't see much to get excited about. The airspace around Washington was tightly monitored, for obvious reasons, so a parachute drop wouldn't work – which would have been her preferred tactic if this had been most other places in the world. Drop in, slip into the house, eliminate any threats, terminate Arthur, and then slip out in the ensuing pandemonium after setting off some flash bangs to cover her escape.

But that wasn't to be.

So they would have to figure out another way. The problem being that, at least as of now, there was no obvious way in that wouldn't get her killed.

They needed more information. And she needed to rein in her impatience. Her desire to end this and get back to Hannah couldn't affect her judgment. This would take however long it took.

The hours ticked by, and soon Alan was back, looking markedly worse for wear.

"Did you sleep any? Or were you online, trying to figure out how to get to Peter?"

"Guilty. I can sleep this afternoon. I'm rested. Don't worry about me," he assured her.

She wasn't his mother, so she let it go. He was a big boy, and had as much or more experience as she did. It wasn't her role to nag him. "Fine. I'll be back at ten."

"What are you coming as this time? You've done hippie, jailbait…what's next?"

"I'll surprise you. It'll keep the relationship fresh. I read how important that is in a magazine."

He eyed her. "Try to get some sleep. It won't do us any good if we're both exhausted. Stay off the computer until you wake up. Promise me that," Alan counseled.

"Yes, Daddy."

"I like it when you call me that. Maybe later? And wear the juvenile delinquent outfit?"

She gave him a sweet smile, and then slid away into the night without comment.

❧☙

After four hours of sleep, Jet bolted awake, but whatever had intruded into her psyche flitted away. The more she tried to remember what it was, which she vaguely sensed had been important, the less distinct it was. She hated when her mind did that to her, and she knew that not remembering would drive her crazy.

She sat up, hugging a pillow to her chest, her knees drawn up, thick gray athletic socks bunched around her ankles, and stared at the monotone darkness of the far wall. It had been something to do with the stakeout. With Arthur? No, that wasn't it. Maybe it was about Peter, and the discussion she'd had with Alan about him?

Like a thick fog, reality intruded into her dream state, and as she became more alert the thought, whatever it was, had receded to nothing.

It would do no good to force it. She knew from experience that never worked. It was like a cruel god's way of jabbing her with a sharp stick.

Jet snapped the bedside light on and looked around the room, her eyes eventually landing on the computer. She glanced at the bedside clock. Just after eight A.M.

I will not get sucked into the computer. I won't do it. I will try to get some more sleep.

The mantra failed to work, and obeying a compulsion, she let herself be drawn to the screen. There was so much to do. And the more research she did, the faster they could get the assault on Arthur's over with, be out of the U.S., and back to Hannah. Finally safe, with nobody out to get her.

And then what?

The thought came unbidden, and she brushed it aside. The last thing she needed to do was agonize over the future.

Against her better judgment, she rose and moved to the computer. It couldn't hurt to just spend a few minutes on it. Maybe it would help her remember…the thing. Which she had no idea about now.

Resigned to being awake again, she padded to the shower and turned on the blasting stream, stepped beneath it, and let the spray caress her body. At least something was caressing it. Alan hadn't been around to do much of that since they'd hit the States. Correction. *Any* of that.

After a few minutes of primping, she returned to the table and considered the computer, calling to her with its irresistible siren song. It was pointless to fight it. The computer would win. She'd known that since she'd set eyes on it after waking up.

Jet pulled out the chair and sat, then hit the power button. What was it about the computer she was supposed to do?

Ah. The flash drive. She was going to see whether there was anything in Sloan's records that would help her hack into his company's computers. She'd been so preoccupied with thoughts of Peter, and exacting a terrible vengeance upon Arthur, that she'd spaced out on trying to get into the servers to see what, if anything, the company had on Arthur's complex.

She switched on the TV and turned to a local news program, keeping one eye on the screen while she scanned the records. No reports of Sloan being found yet. That was a positive. But she knew it was just a matter of time until someone became alarmed that he hadn't communicated with anyone for days, and called the authorities. Alan and Jet would need to get to Arthur before that happened, because once Sloan's corpse was discovered, a paranoid shut-in like Arthur would see threats behind every tree. Not that he would be wrong. But it would make a difficult job impossible if he put even more men on the guard detail and stepped up their vigilance.

She tapped at the keyboard and scanned the files, looking for something, anything, that would give her an edge.

~~~

A twig snapping startled Alan from his surveillance of the house, and he exhaled noisily when he saw it was Jet.

"You scared the crap out of me."

"Sorry. Trying to keep you on your toes."

"Not much of a disguise today. What happened?"

"Didn't have time to go shopping for my hooker outfit." She smiled. "You need to get some sleep. Get out of here. I gather that you wrote down all the shift info?"

"Yes, but I'm not sure how much good it will do. These guys are good. Better than most."

"All right, then. Back to the hotel with you. I'm going to go find a new position to watch from. I don't want to make anything easy for them."

"Call me later. Six more hours?"

She studied his unshaven face. "Maybe eight. You look like you could use some serious down time."

He didn't disagree. "Anything on the computer?" he asked.

"I'm working on something. I think I figured out how to get into the company servers. If I can, and they're handling the security, we should be able to get a full breakdown of what we're up against. But I didn't have enough time. I'll do it this evening."

"Okay. I'm outta here. Have a good day."

Once Alan was gone, she hoisted her backpack and moved to the edge of the old cemetery, taking care to spread a towel on a flat patch of ground. She'd opted for only sunglasses and a hat today – no elaborate disguises. Given that nobody had noticed her over the last two days, she didn't feel like she needed one. She lay on her stomach and lifted the binoculars.

At least the weather had held. It would have been lousy to have been doing surveillance in the rain. Hopefully the mild temperature was an auspicious omen – the gods of spying were smiling on their project.

A chill went up her spine and the hair on her arms stood on end as a shadow fell across her. Instantly alert, she rolled as she reached into her bag for the silenced pistol, and whipped it out as a man approached from the woods, dressed in head-to-toe camouflage. Jet trained the weapon on him and then her face registered shock as she struggled with coming face to face with the impossible. She blinked, incredulous, and she fought to keep her face composed.

"You!"

The man kept coming, and then dropped to one knee a few feet from her.

"You really going to shoot me? What kind of greeting is that?" he whispered, his eyes roving over her face. "I only recognized you this morning. The other days fooled me."

"You're alive?" she stammered, lowering the pistol and returning it to her backpack. "What are you doing here?"

Matt nodded. "Looks like the same as you. Only I've been at it for about a week longer. The question is, what brings you to this neck of the woods? Why haven't you stayed gone?"

"You were dead. The beach house. The fire..."

"Three men came in the middle of the night. I managed to get them before they could get me. But I needed to drop out and buy myself time to figure out what had gone wrong. I had no way of getting in touch with you, otherwise I would have. But you'd gone dark. Which brings us to today."

She studied his drawn face, etched with fatigue lines, and felt her eyes moisten, and then she sat up, unsure of how to respond. Seized by an impulse she didn't fully understand, she leaned towards him and threw her arms around him. He drew her close and held her, one tentative hand smoothing her hair, and then the moment passed and she pulled away.

"It's so good to see you. I mean, I...I thought you were dead," Jet repeated, her tone a combination of relief and...something else. Apologetic. "You kind of stink. How long have you been out here?"

"Oh, come on. It's not that bad. I've been sleeping five hours a day, and spending the rest of my time here, looking for holes in Arthur's defenses. Who you were supposed to have killed, if I'm not mistaken." A slight tinge of chastisement in the last words.

"I left him for dead. It's a kind of ugly miracle that he's still alive. Barely, if my information is correct. That will be the last and only time I don't put a bullet in an enemy's brain myself."

"I'm guessing you're here because he somehow found you, and tried to do the same thing that his people tried to do to me."

"Correct."

"But you're fine. And your daughter, Hannah? Is that right?"

"Good memory. She's okay. In hiding till this is over."

An uncomfortable silence settled over them.

"Where were you living?" he finally asked.

"Uruguay. How about you?"

"Sri Lanka. How's Uruguay?"

"Nice. But not for much longer. Time to move after everything that's happened."

"Where to? If you don't mind my asking?"

She stared at the house, lost in thought. "I don't honestly know."

"Huh. I think I'm going to be living in that same neighborhood. Assuming I can rid the world of one scar-faced bastard in the very near future."

"That was my thought, too."

"What's your plan?" Matt asked.

"Beyond killing him? I haven't developed one yet. How are you fixed for gathering intel? Things like blueprints, layout, dossiers?" she asked.

"Pretty good. I still have a few contacts who are loyal to me. They've given me more than you could wish for. But for one person to handle, it's grim. Chances of getting in and out are slim to none." Matt paused, seemingly deep in thought. "Boy, if only I knew where I could find a pair of trained field operatives to help…"

"So you spotted Alan, too?"

"What kind of super spy would I be if I'd missed him?" Matt asked, and then grinned.

She nodded. "It's really good to see you, Matt," she said softly.

He nodded, a faraway look in his eyes. "Same here."

CHAPTER 34

Jet was conflicted as she lay near Matt, watching the house, time flying by, her thoughts in turmoil. She was with Alan; but that spark, that intensity, was still there with Matt, stronger than ever. It was so crazy. All they'd ever done was kiss. It made no sense. And yet her heart was beating like a schoolgirl's, and she felt flustered and flushed.

Why had the universe thrown this monkey wrench into her existence? Weren't things already complicated enough?

"What's your life been like, since..." Jet asked.

"About what you'd expect. Getting off the island, making my way undetected to Bangkok, getting some of the diamonds." He glanced at her profile. "That reminds me. Do you still have the diamonds I gave you?"

Her eyes flashed. "What do you think?"

"I'm betting you still have every one."

"Good bet."

"Anyway, I fell off the face of the earth, and then I got angry. I realized that some of the group's leadership must have made it, and that meant I had unfinished business. I spent a few months trying to ignore what my gut was telling me, and then I got in touch with my contact at Langley who'd helped you out with your operation here...and the rest is history. I got in town two weeks ago, tracked down Arthur with her help, and I've been watching the house ever since. He never leaves, you know."

"I was afraid of that," she muttered.

"It's a tough one. He knows what he's doing, and so do his men."

"Probably has a lot of enemies."

"He should."

"Any idea who those two were that visited yesterday?"

"No."

"And what about the guy in the monkey suit who seems to be there twenty-four hours a day?"

"Name's Standish. His Boy Friday. Does everything for him, handles his affairs, fiercely loyal. He'd gladly take a bullet for him," Matt said.

"I'll add him to the list."

She rubbed her face, and then turned to face Matt. "You've been watching him for, what, a week? Have you learned anything that will help us?"

"Maybe. But there are a lot of pieces that I still need to fit together. I don't have enough information to be confident. Not yet. There are some important details I haven't gotten my hands on – the most critical being the security precautions. The electronics. I've got blueprints for the house, a layout of the lot, but I can't be sure what he's got hiding in the grass."

"Funny you should mention that. I'm working on getting a detailed description of all of it," she said.

He paused. "Say what?"

"You heard me," she replied.

"What are you waiting for?"

"I've been too busy out here. Sorry."

"Can I make a suggestion? Let's combine our resources. We're both after the same thing. Between my intel and yours, we might just be able to come up with a way to crack this nut. It's either that, or I'm going to try to get my hands on a rocket and fire it into the bastard's bedroom. Assuming he's in there. I wouldn't put anything past him. Probably hanging upside down in the basement, like a bat," Matt grumbled.

"I'm game. We're not making a lot of progress as is."

"*We*. Who's the guy you're with?"

Jet thought about how to describe Alan. "Ex-Mossad. Same team I belonged to. It's a long story. Complicated. A lot of stuff happened since I went to Ko Samui to see you that day."

"The day of the fire."

"Yes. I stood and watched them digging through the wreckage. Thinking you were dead."

"I'm sorry. I would have left some kind of a message, but I was busy running for my life. Like I said, I tried to contact you later, but your phone was dead and you'd disappeared into thin air."

"I know, Matt. I'm not blaming you. But things got weird after that. I had more problems."

She told him about Grigenko's son, and Yemen, and the terrorist strike. It took a while.

"Good Lord. So that whole thing was a ruse? Planned by people in the government?"

She nodded, and they lapsed back into silence.

"You're not making this up," Matt said. She didn't answer. "No, I suppose not. You're not really the type to invent drama, are you? Then you're in deeper shit than even I am."

"Like I said. A lot happened, and it's all complicated."

"Sounds like it."

"You don't know the half of it. On top of the Arthur mess, we've got an even bigger problem now."

"What? A meteor heading towards us that will eradicate all life on earth?"

"How about those same powerful people in the government who planned the bio-attack wanting Alan dead, and being willing to kill thousands to do it?"

"What the hell are you talking about?"

Jet took him through the rest of it. By the time she was done, he was shaking his head.

"Maybe I should move over a few feet. Seems to me that it's dangerous hanging around you. No disrespect intended." He smiled, his eyes tired.

"Welcome to my little slice of heaven."

They spent another ten minutes in silence.

"I don't see much reason to stick around here, do you?" Matt said. "After a week of watching the guards, I have their routine down pat."

She looked at her watch. "We might be better off with me getting into the security company's servers, if you've already done all the heavy lifting on the ground," Jet agreed.

"Let me go get my stuff. I want to meet your partner in crime. I can take him through everything I've done while you're there. Kill two birds with one stone. No pun intended."

Jet appeared conflicted and then nodded. "Meet you on the other side of the cemetery in five, Rambo."

She packed her gear while her mind raced over the day's revelations. Matt, alive. An ally with a week's worth of intelligence to add to their pile, as well as access to the CIA's innermost secrets, who was more than a little field-experienced. Things were looking brighter on their chances to get Arthur soon, but she wasn't reassured. Matt being alive raised some difficult issues. Would she have ever gotten involved with Alan if she'd known? She didn't want to consider the answer. Better to keep her eye on the ball until all of this was over. Nothing good would come from dwelling on what might have been.

Matt was waiting for her by the graveyard wall, carrying an oversized backpack.

"How are you fixed for weapons?" she asked as they trudged through the park.

"Good. I have a guy I've known for thirty years. He got me a full-auto M4 with a night vision scope and sound suppressor, and a silenced pistol. He's working on some grenades. Should have them tonight."

"Can you get in touch with him and see if he can get his hands on another M4 suppressor, as well as one for a H&K MP7? And maybe some extra magazines, and some flash bangs?"

"Sure. But how did you get your hands on that kind of firepower? They don't exactly sell that stuff on Amazon."

"It's a long story."

"I've got nothing but time. Try me."

When she was finished, he was quiet.

"I really probably shouldn't have asked. And this Sloan – nobody's found the body yet?"

"No, but that's another time bomb. Once they do, you can bet Arthur's going to go ballistic and call in the Third Army Infantry to protect him, and any chance of getting within a mile of the compound undetected will be out of the question. We're racing the clock on that."

"When were you hoping to go in, then?"

"Tomorrow night, at the latest."

He slowed, pensive. "That's aggressive."

"Now you know why."

Matt picked up his pace again. "I'll make a call. Where are we headed?"

"To the motel we're staying at. Alan's there, sleeping. We've been doing shifts. Six hours."

"So I saw. Not a lot of sleeping going on in my neck of the woods."

She turned to him and glanced at his profile. "You look like shit. You need some rest. After we're done, get eight solid hours. Alan and I can keep watch tonight."

"Thanks. I'll probably take you up on it."

"You got a car?"

"Yes, I bought an Explorer. But it's parked about a mile away. I don't want it being a suspect vehicle after this all goes down."

"Then we can take mine. I'll drop you off."

"Lead the way."

CHAPTER 35

Jet opened the door to the room, Matt behind her, and found Alan standing by the bathroom door, clad only in a white towel wrapped around his waist. Matt took in his sculpted upper body without comment. Jet flushed. Alan froze, his hair wet, the brush he was about to comb it with stuck in mid-air.

"Who's this?" Alan asked, alarmed caution in his tone.

"He's a friend. Don't worry. He's one of the good guys," Jet said.

After a moment of glacial silence, Matt stepped around Jet. "You must be Alan. Jet told me all about your situation. I'm Matt. We go…way back, sort of." Matt moved towards Alan with his hand outstretched.

Alan's face twitched as he registered the words, and then his eyes widened almost imperceptibly.

"Matt. As in, dead Thailand Matt? Ex-CIA spook?" Alan asked. He didn't move to shake Matt's hand for a few moments, and then grudgingly did so. "Congratulations on being alive. I'm sure there's a story there."

"Yeah. You too. Seems to go around whenever she's involved, doesn't it?" Matt said, trying to lighten the tension.

Jet closed the door behind her. "Sorry to barge in on you like this. I tried calling but you didn't answer."

"I was in the shower. I have it on vibrate."

"Alan, Matt was conducting surveillance on Arthur's house, too. He's been collecting data for a week. And he's got access to the CIA's servers, in a roundabout way." She gave him an abbreviated rundown after dropping the backpack on the table. "Looks like we'll have sound suppressors and some ordnance by tomorrow. He's got a line on an arms guy."

Alan regarded Matt suspiciously. "How convenient. And he just happened to be watching the house at the same time we were?"

"Actually, the way I look at it, you stumbled into my surveillance setup," Matt said in a neutral tone. "I was here first. Just to keep the sequence right."

Alan ignored him and addressed Jet. "How well do you know him? This just all seems a little, well, too good to be true, doesn't it?"

"Matt used to work for Arthur. Arthur's been trying to kill him for at least a year. Remember, I told you about the beach house burning? That was also Arthur. So the answer to the next question is that I trust Matt implicitly. Without qualification," Jet said, not liking the direction Alan was going.

"That's good for you, I suppose," Alan said, and then padded to the dresser and grabbed his jeans and underwear. "I'll be right out. Seeing as we've got company, I want to slip into something less comfortable."

Matt eyed Jet with a blank expression, but she could tell his mind was working behind his inscrutable gaze. She wanted to tell him that it wasn't what he thought, but that would have been a lie. She silently wished that she could take back the last week and make it different, but that wasn't in her power, so now she had to suck it up and deal with the fallout.

"A lot happened, Matt. Alan is David's brother. Hannah's uncle," she started, but Matt held up a hand.

"You don't owe me any explanations. Let's just skip all this head-butting and get down to business, okay? I want Arthur dead as much as you do — maybe more. That's the priority. So let's stick with that, shall we?" Matt's tone was professional, but his eyes betrayed him.

"Matt..."

Alan came out of the bathroom and sensed the dynamic, but caught a look at Jet and chose not to say anything. He moved to the little circular table and pulled out one of the two chairs. "So what have we got here?"

"Matt will give you the rundown. He's actually gathered quite a bit," Jet said, and then moved to the computer and began typing at lightning speed. Matt moved to the corner of the bed and sat on it, facing them both.

Ten minutes later, Matt was done with his information dump. Alan said nothing, then leaned back in his chair.

"That's a lot of information, but to my ear it sounds mostly useless. Without knowing what countermeasures they have in place, we're still dead in the water," he said, a hint of derision in his voice.

"I just saved you a week of camping in the woods. 'You're welcome' would be more appropriate," Matt responded, an edge in his voice.

"Big deal. So you have the guard shifts memorized and got Arthur's recent history, and know the players – this Standish character, among others. Am I missing the part where that translates into any kind of a strategy?" Alan fired back.

"Gee, Alan, I'm sorry I didn't come up with your whole assault plan while you were busy sudsing up. Maybe you can go back into the bathroom for a nice soak while I work on it? Then when I'm done, I can clean your guns for you while I'm at it." Matt stood and regarded Jet. "This isn't going to work."

Alan pushed his chair back and stood as well, his hands balling into fists. "Listen to the geriatric. What were you going to do, slip in and gum the guards to death? Beat them senseless with your cane?"

"I'm not all that much older than you, and could kick your ass any day of the week, pipsqueak," Matt warned, his voice almost inaudible.

"Did they have electric lights when you were growing up? Or did you read by firelight? Assuming you know how to read," Alan snarled.

Jet looked up from the computer. "Boys. Play nice. I got into the Nordhaver servers, and the company does run the security for Arthur's house. I've got a complete layout. The bad news is that it's pretty foolproof on first blush," she said, keeping her tone light. "Now, stop it with the testosterone-fest and let's figure out how to take the target out, shall we? Our chances are far better working together than trying to do this separately. Get with the program. The attitudes aren't helping."

Both men stood, facing each other, seemingly unsure how to respond to being dressed down by Jet. Matt sat down first and looked at the screen. Alan followed a second later.

Their concentration quickly focused on the schematic for the electronics.

"Look. Motion detectors," Alan said. "Lasers in the house. Thermal sensors. This is crazy level security – as in, art museum level. Just what I was afraid of."

"There's always a way," Matt said.

"Okay, Mister Viagra, what's your idea?"

"Do you want to continue this juvenile behavior?" Jet said forcefully, throwing Alan a warning look. "Want to go beat each other up outside?

Will you please grow up? I'm not going to say it again. Cut this shit out, now."

Both men visibly relaxed.

"There are backup generators in case of a power outage, so knocking out the power won't have any effect," Jet said, studying the symbols. "They've thought of everything."

"What about if we disconnected the fuel supply for the generators and then killed the power? They wouldn't run. That could work," Alan said.

"They're diesel. He's right. They could be disabled," Matt agreed.

"Mmm, maybe, but look at the sensors around them. They've already thought about it, and positioned the devices to take that into account," Jet said, pointing at the screen.

For another hour, the discussion continued unabated, in a surprisingly civil manner given Matt and Alan's earlier interactions, and then Matt pulled a piece of paper from his bag and made a diagram of the exterior sensors. He stared at it for a few moments, then put his draftsman's pencil down.

"I think I've got it."

CHAPTER 36

"Absolutely not." Alan slammed his hand down on the table after Matt was finished. Both Matt and Jet regarded him curiously.

"What's wrong with it? I think it's a good plan. Maybe needs some refinement," Jet began.

"The problem is that he wants to run the first pass, and he's not the fittest member of this group to do it," Alan said heatedly. "He doesn't have the experience or the physical fitness to pull it off. Look at him," Alan countered.

Matt smiled humorlessly. "Ah, the arrogance of youth. Alan, my boy, I have more field experience than you've got, by at least a decade. That means when you were still playing with plastic cars, making *vroom* noises, I was in combat, and later, running ops for the CIA. Now, regardless of your opinion of the CIA, believe it or not, they don't allow just anyone to work up from a field operative to running an entire country. So with all due respect – I've got more experience than you, it's my plan, and I was here before you even showed up. That means I go in first. That's not negotiable."

Jet's face struggled to hide the trace of a smile that threatened to light it up, and chose an opportune cough instead.

"Nice how you ducked the physical fitness part of the objection, which is what will be the deciding factor between success and failure," Alan sniped.

Matt looked at Jet and then back to Alan.

"I don't have to justify myself to you, do you read me? You may think you're all that, but I'm here to tell you that you're not. You need to learn to share your toys. You may think that having a nano-second-better reaction time because of age makes you superior, but having been there, I can also tell you that experience will usually trump any genetic or chronological advantage. And the fact is, I have easily twice the experience that you do," Matt seethed.

"CIA experience, huh? 'Nough said," Alan replied.

Jet glared at them both. "What am I going to do with you two? What's with the pissing contests? The real truth is that I should be going in first. And you both know it. I'm younger than Alan, so using his argument, I'm fitter. And I'm willing to bet that for all your experience, I've done more of these sorts of missions than either of you, making me the most seasoned at it. So now what do you have to say?" Jet demanded. She was getting tired of the bickering and wanted to put a stop to it. Besides which, she was right, dammit.

Both men stared at her, and then spoke in unison.

"No."

They looked at one another, and the tension finally broke as Matt smiled.

"I guess we agree on something," Alan said.

"You can't do it. It's too danger…you're more valuable going in after, handling the second phase," Matt said, correcting himself too late.

Jet frowned. "Were you going to say it's too dangerous? Was that it? Poor little girl could get hurt? What is this bullshit? You don't have to throw your coat over a puddle for me, buddy. I can take care of myself. And just to prove it, I'm going in first. I'll take that part of the op. No arguments."

"Matt's right. You're better in the second phase. That's more critical, anyway. Let's not waste your talents on the first phase," Alan said.

"Again, bullshit. I don't know why you're both suddenly so protective of me, but I don't need your chivalry. So get used to the idea that I'll handle the first phase. At least that way it'll get done right. And you two can slap fight or have a hair pulling contest while I'm dealing with the target. You'll probably like that. Maybe punch each other unconscious so I have to handle everything myself," Jet spat, and then stood up and walked to the bathroom to get a glass of water and calm down. Both of them were being infuriating.

"Sweetie, I–" Alan began.

"Sweetie? *Sweetie*? Oh, I'm sorry. Why don't you just call me 'little darlin'' and tell me to go make you boys something to eat while you talk business? You're both really starting to piss me off now."

"I didn't say anything," Matt said softly, having registered the term of endearment.

"You were thinking it," Jet said, and then took several deep breaths. "Look. I'm doing the first bit. So no more arguments. We're wasting time. We should be figuring out the second part."

"It's too bad we can't come up with some kind of cell-jamming equipment on short notice," Matt mused. "That's one of the hitches in this idea. It means we'll have to work much faster."

"Fortunately, we'll be in a better position once the security sensors are knocked out," Jet said. "We keep the guards tied up with red herrings while one of us sets fire to the place. Arthur will have to show himself in order to escape the blaze, and then we can pick him off. Either that or he'll burn alive. I don't think he'll choose that option. So really, phase one is the most important part. Can your arms guy get his hands on an incendiary grenade launcher? Can you find out?"

"I'll call him, but don't bet on it. That's more specialized. My take is that he mostly sells to collectors, and probably some of the gangs in the area. Those are the only people that want fully-automatic weapons and silencers. Maybe a few paramilitary groups in the boonies. But I can't see him touching anything that could crank anti-terrorism scrutiny up. Nobody wants to invite that upon himself. And even the most hardened gun enthusiast isn't going to have any call for firebomb rockets."

"Then where did he get the grenades and flash bangs?"

"Probably stolen from an army base. I'm just telling you, don't expect miracles," Matt said, pulling his cell phone from his pocket. "I'm kind of beat. How about we take tonight off, or you two watch the place, and as she suggested" – he motioned with his head towards Jet – "I get some sleep? I don't see us getting this any more detailed tonight, and we'll have all day tomorrow to fine-tune it. Then we go in tomorrow night. Agreed?"

Alan and Jet exchanged glances, and Alan shrugged.

"Agreed," they both mumbled.

Matt gave Jet one final glance and moved to the door. "I'll be back here at seven tomorrow morning, if that works for you." He waited for any protest, then opened the door and exited into the dusk, without looking back.

Alan stretched, rolling his head to loosen his bunched neck muscles, and then winced at Jet as he reached up and rubbed his left shoulder.

"How about we skip the useless all-night vigil and grab dinner, then get some serious sleep? If we're doing this tomorrow night, I'd just as soon be rested," he suggested.

Jet was quick to agree. "He's already done all the work, regardless of your disagreements. What was that all about, anyway, Alan? Matt's really not a bad guy, and he's on our side."

"He's on *your* side. I saw the way he looked at you."

Alan didn't mention that he'd seen the way she had looked at him, too. Maybe he'd been imagining it. He was still sleep-deprived, and his perceptions might be unreliable.

"Nonsense. This is a marriage of convenience. We have the same objective. It makes perfect sense for us to join forces." Even to her own ear, the protest sounded slightly hollow. "Anyway, I don't want to argue about water under the bridge. Let's find someplace, eat something that will stick to our ribs, and then hit the sack. I'm not caught up on my rest, either, and I need to be sharp," Jet said, and then walked to the bathroom. "I want to get cleaned up, and then we can hit it. Why don't you switch on the news and see if any new disasters have struck?"

Alan thumbed the remote as she shut the door and channel-surfed until he found the local news. Fifteen minutes later, Jet emerged from her shower, smelling like a million dollars and looking like two. She grabbed her purse and jacket.

"I'm ready. What do you have a hankering for? Anything special?" she asked.

He bit his tongue. "How about Italian? I saw a place a few blocks away that looked convincing."

They drove to the restaurant and pored over the menu before ordering pasta and fish, making small talk that deliberately avoided the mission and Matt. Alan could sense that Jet was preoccupied through dinner, distant, and knew he should give her the space to do the thinking she needed. Her responses were distracted, but she put on a brave face, finally apologizing for being lousy company because she was tired.

When they returned to the hotel, they took turns brushing their teeth and preparing for bed, and by the time Alan crawled into bed next to Jet, she was lying on her side, with her back towards him, asleep. He reached over and switched off the bedside lamp and then lay back with a quiet sigh, eyes still open, staring at the ceiling, his brain unwilling to relinquish itself to the night.

Jet's eyes were open, too, thin streams of tears working their way onto the pillow. For the first time in forever she didn't know what to do, and felt like a leaf on a roiling rapid, tossed randomly in every direction, powerless to control her emotions. Matt's abrupt and unexpected return had thrown her. Alan was a good man, attractive, strong, honest, and he'd been more than fair with her. Whereas Matt was an unknown, her total attraction based on a few kisses, and perhaps too much time to think during a turbulent time in her life.

She didn't want to hurt either one of them, and yet she knew that whatever happened, one of them would forever feel like he had lost. And perhaps she would, too.

It was a bad situation all around.

And a choice she wasn't prepared to make.

CHAPTER 37

The next day, after breakfast, Alan went to do duty at the house while Matt and Jet drove to a meeting with his weapons source. The sky was partially overcast, clouds blanketing the horizon from a front moving in over the Eastern seaboard. They drove south for an hour until they came to an industrial park and then pulled up to a warehouse that featured a sign advertising wholesale auto parts.

Matt got out and Jet waited in the car while he went inside to see his contact, a burly man in his fifties named Ed – nickname, *Bubba*. Matt had known him for decades, from some of his CIA brethren who used him when they needed weapons that weren't traceable.

He entered through the filthy front office, filled with desultory employees lounging at battered desks in mediocre light answering phones and tapping at antiquated computers, and approached the rear section, where Bubba's secretary, a formerly gorgeous blonde in her forties, a few tall boys past her beauty queen days, sat popping gum and texting on her cell phone. She looked up, vaguely annoyed, and gave Matt a clinically efficient once-over with her eyes, and then softened her stance and moistened her lips.

"Well, hello there, handsome. What can I do with...I mean...*for* you today?" she asked with a chuckle and a smile.

Matt returned the smile. "Is Bubba in? I'm supposed to have an appointment," he explained.

"You betcha. Who's asking?"

"Tom Reynolds."

"Like the aluminum foil, right?"

"Would it surprise you to hear that I get that all the time?" he asked, grinning sheepishly.

"Hold on a sec. I'll beep him and see if he's available."

Her intercom squawked at her after she held down the button like she was shocking an ex.

"What?" a male voice rasped from the tinny speaker.

"Mr. Reynolds is here to see you. Says he's from the Sherriff's office," she said, winking at Matt as she popped her gum again. Her blouse strained to contain her exuberant chest, and Matt wondered mildly how long she took to get ready and put on her makeup in the morning. He guessed an hour, but might have been short by a mile.

"Very funny, Linda. Point him back there. I'm expecting him."

At the rear of the building, an office had been built out of sheetrock, intruding into the warehouse section. When Matt entered, Bubba rose from behind his desk and moved around it to shake his hand, his massive paw enveloping Matt's. Bubba's nickname was fitting – he was a stereotype of rural excess, at least two hundred seventy pounds on his six-foot frame, none of it muscle. He wore a pair of overalls and a plaid flannel shirt, and looked every bit a farmer – except for his eyes, which were cold and calculating.

"Nice ta see ya. What do you think of Linda? Firecracker, huh?" Bubba asked as he moved to a crate in the corner of his office. A dark green duffle bag sat on top of it, zipped.

"She seems to like you," Matt said neutrally.

"Because I pay her ten bucks an hour over what she's worth. But she's got...skills, you know what I'm saying?" Bubba disclosed with a wink, reminding Matt of Linda's similar gesture moments before.

"I'm sure you're getting your money's worth. Is that the stuff?"

Bubba unzipped the bag and looked inside. "Had a hell of a time getting the noise suppressors. Harder than the goddamned grenades, believe it or not."

"I'm not surprised. And the extra magazines?"

"Piece of cake."

"How about the night-vision goggles?"

"Three sets. Everything's there. Six flash bangs, six grenades, goggles, silencers, and magazines. And the cash?" Bubba asked.

"Right here." Matt slipped an envelope to him and waited as he counted it.

"You're good. Now try not to get into any trouble with that stuff. Especially the grenades." Bubba knew better than to ask what Matt wanted them for. His policy was definitely based on don't ask, don't tell.

"I'll remember that," Matt said, and then left the way he had come in.

Jet was listening to the radio when he returned to the car. He tossed the bag into the back seat before climbing behind the wheel and starting the engine.

"All there?" she asked.

"Yes. He's always reliable. Expensive, but so are most things in life these days."

The sky got darker as they moved north, and their conversation was stilted and difficult, the elephant in the room obviously Alan. Eventually Jet couldn't take it anymore, and shifted the discussion to him.

"You know, I flew halfway around the world to Ko Samui to spend time with you. I brought my daughter. I'd bought into the idea of living on a beach in paradise."

"It's not a bad idea. But it is a bad idea if you have a squad of killers come for you in the middle of the night."

"The point is that I came."

Traffic slowed, an accident blocking two of the lanes, and they rolled to a stop among the stalled cars, no exit ramp anywhere near. Matt turned to face her.

"Why?" Matt demanded quietly.

Jet was taken aback. "Why, what?"

"Why did you come?"

"I promised to return the diamonds, remember?"

"That's the only reason?"

"How hard are you going to make this for me?" she asked.

"As hard as it needs to be."

She exhaled. "Fine. I came to see if there was something more waiting for me. With you. Because I felt something…different. Special. When we kissed. And I wanted to follow up on that and see if it was just indigestion, or something else."

"Ah. There. Was that so hard?"

"Matt, what's the point of this? Really? What's going to change? What do we gain by beating this to death?"

"Enter Alan."

"Matt, you were dead. I only kissed you, and you were dead. Give me a break. This isn't some maudlin romantic drama where I sit watching the sea for years after a kiss. Shit happened."

He leaned towards her, and their lips connected. A charge like an electric current ran through her, jolted her, a visceral, powerful sensation unlike anything she'd felt…since David. But different. Very, very different.

A horn honked behind them, breaking the mood, and Matt held up a hand in apology to the driver and pulled forward ten feet, only to be forced to a stop again.

"Like that, you mean? Shit just happened. It keeps happening," Matt said.

Jet didn't have a comeback. Her breath was shallow and rapid, and she forced herself to take deep, measured inhalations.

"If you were married, I'd tell you to get a divorce," Matt said. "Fortunately, you're not."

"It's not that easy, Matt."

"Why? Why isn't it exactly that easy? Explain it to me. I don't understand."

"I…I have something good with Alan…and he's…he's damaged in the same way I am."

Matt regarded her. "That's the reason? 'He's broken?' Hey, I'm pretty scrambled, too. Doesn't that count for something?"

"It's not the same. I'm sleeping with him."

"So stop. It's like quitting smoking. Stop putting cigarettes in your mouth. Easy."

"Maybe for you. It's not so straightforward for me."

"You're right. It is for me. I don't have any hesitation on this one."

She shook her head. "Matt, listen to me carefully. I know we have something here. And yes, I would like nothing better than if you had been there when I went to Thailand. But you weren't, and this happened, and I can't take it back or change it. So do me a favor. Let's get through this with Arthur, and then, when the dust has settled, if there's something to talk about, I promise I'll figure out my feelings and won't leave either of you hanging. But right now, let's not complicate things, all right? For me? Could you just do that for me, please?"

Red lights flashed up ahead, and then they were past the fender-bender and moving again.

"For you, I will. But I'd be lying if I said I was happy. I've been alone for a lot of my life. Never minded it. Never had any desire to change it. But this…it's crazy, but this makes me want something better. That's all I'm going to say. We won't talk about it anymore until this is done. But I'll hold you to your side of the deal. When it's over, you need to do some thinking. That's all I ask. Because I don't believe for a minute that you're going to be happy with Alan now that you know I'm here," Matt finished.

"Don't flatter yourself," she said, but it was empty, her voice lacking any conviction.

He cleared his throat, and they went back to watching the landscape whiz by, the morning's sunlight replaced by an ominous shadow that perfectly matched their moods.

CHAPTER 38

Matt relieved Alan at four, the three of them having agreed on eight-hour shifts, with the assault scheduled for midnight. Alan and Jet returned to the room and went over the plan, which had shaped up to be a decent one. Jet would dodge the sensors and knock out the communications center, which was in the rear of the house. One of the weak spots in the sensor deployment was that it was intended to protect entrances to the house, and the power. But the communications hub, which connected Arthur to the outside world, and therefore to the police and the security company, was vulnerable.

Without access to the electronics schematic, the house would have been more than adequately protected; but with it, she would be able to vault the rear wall and then dart in a specific pattern, first from the wall near the rear service cottage, then south to the junction boxes that had been installed in the basement, accessed by a root cellar door – no doubt because Arthur hadn't wanted the unsightly metal cabinets where they would be visible.

The root cellar didn't have any direct access to the house, so the sensors weren't as densely deployed around it. She'd get in and cut the com lines, which fed the twenty-four hour remote surveillance at headquarters, and buy them a few minutes to breach the security, take out some of the exterior guards at the rear of the complex, and set fire to the house using one-and-a-half-liter water bottles filled with gasoline and the flash bangs. Both she and Matt had three bottles apiece and would soak the siding with gas, forcing the guards to switch from security to fire fighting.

If they failed to contain the fire, the next logical move for the security team would be to get Arthur out of the house and transported to safety – and that would be their opportunity to rid the world of him once and for all. He would be vulnerable for a few moments as he exited the house to a vehicle, and at that point, a few carefully placed shells fired by Alan would finish it: He was a sharpshooter-level marksman more than capable of placing a grouping from one of the M4s in an area the size of a tangerine at three hundred yards. By the time the police and the fire department made it, they would be miles away, their mission completed.

It wasn't a perfect plan, but it was a workable one. The most dangerous point in the entire operation would be the initial breach and knocking out the com hub. Jet had studied the layout over and over, and felt more than ready.

When Alan returned to the hotel Jet was out on a run, burning off any accumulated tension in preparation for the night's operation. Upon her return, she showered while Alan watched the news, and then they went to dinner, this time choosing a seafood restaurant that had looked good.

Once fed, Jet methodically packed her backpack with gasoline, the grenades, one of the silenced pistols, one of the Desert Eagles she'd grabbed from Sloan's, and spare magazines for the MP7. She'd already packed the submachine gun in her trunk, and Alan had done the same with his M4. They were each going to take their vehicles, to increase their chances of a clean getaway in the event they were pursued – a slim likelihood, but one worth planning for nonetheless.

By ten o'clock they were ready. In two more hours they would execute, and it would all go down in a few minutes.

"I'm going to try to get a little rest," Jet said, and lay on the bed fully clothed in her black long-sleeved shirt and cargo pants.

"Good idea. I'm going to stow my gear and hit the market. Do you want anything?" Alan asked.

"No, I'm good. Thanks, though," Jet replied.

Alan lifted his bag and moved towards the door, and then stopped and set it down, and approached the bed.

Jet, sensing his proximity, opened her eyes. "Oh, Alan...no, I'm–"

"Shh." He leaned over and kissed her, tenderly, more so than ever before, and then brushed her hair out of her face with his hand. "Have a good rest," he said, and then he was through the door and gone.

She closed her eyes, any chance of rest dashed as her mind worried over the Alan and Matt dilemma, and after half an hour tossing and turning, she flipped on the television, switching between stations until she found a program that she liked – *Animal Planet*, with a feature on the honey badger. When the program ended she looked at her watch and saw it was already eleven o'clock. Alan should have been back a while ago. He'd probably gone for a walk, she reasoned. Everyone prepared themselves for action differently, she knew from experience – some prayed, some exercised to calm their nerves, others compulsively cleaned and rechecked their weapons.

She switched to the news, and the top story chilled her blood.

"A wealthy security firm CEO was found dead this evening in a gruesome murder that's shocked the residents of an upscale residential neighborhood. The reclusive executive was discovered in the exclusive community of Lake Barcroft."

The story went on to report that the death was being treated as a homicide, but that few details were currently available.

She went to her purse and found her phone, then pressed the speed dial number for Alan's. He answered on the second ring.

"Where are you? They discovered Sloan's body. All hell's going to break loose sooner rather than later. We need to accelerate the plan. I'm leaving right now."

"Okay. Listen, you're going to be really pissed at me, but I'm already in position. I'm going to do the breach on the house, and you can handle the shot to Arthur's head."

"NO! That wasn't the deal. Stick to the plan. Wait for me. I'll be in position in fifteen minutes," Jet protested.

"Sorry. I'm going in. I was going to call in a few minutes and tell you to be here early, but I'm bringing it forward now, and heading out in ten, so you'll be five behind me. I told Matt that we'd discussed it, and you'd seen reason. He'll follow me in once you're here. I'll wait ten minutes from the time I go over the wall, and then I cut the communications."

"Absolutely not. I'm doing it," she seethed, feeling helpless and blindsided by his duplicity. He must have been planning to double-cross her for a while. He sounded completely calm and confident.

"I'm afraid not. Now get your butt over here so you're ready to put a bullet in Arthur when they cart him out of this mausoleum. I gotta go. You have fifteen minutes," Alan said, and then hung up.

Jet stared at the phone, furious, and then grabbed her backpack and ran for her car. The engine started with a whine, and she tore out of the driveway, anxious to trim the fifteen minutes down to ten. Maybe, just maybe, she could make it and cut him off before he did something stupid. She knew the danger involved, and she was better capable of pulling off the first phase than he was.

She ditched the car on the far side of the park and hopped the fence, then ran as fast as her legs would carry her through the brush, pushing herself. When she arrived at the agreed-upon spot beneath Matt's tree, her watch revealed that twelve minutes had passed. Matt looked down at her from his perch in the tree, and then dropped gracefully via a black knotted rope, alighting next to her.

"So, you ready?" he asked.

"Where's Alan?" she hissed in an angry whisper.

"He took off for the target a few minutes ago. I have to admit, he's a fast runner. I'm ready to go in. The rifle is up—"

"Shit. And you didn't stop him?" she demanded, peering through the brush at the house.

"Stop him? Why would I do...wait. He told me you'd switched. Does this mean...?" He didn't finish the sentence. "Guess so. Alan just filled me in on Sloan's being found. It's too late now to stop him, so let's do our best to support him. I'm game on," Matt assured her, and reached into his backpack and pulled out night vision goggles, slipping them over his head before flipping the screen down over his eyes.

"There. Works beautifully. I'm going to go get into position."

"I'm going with you," Jet said.

"No, you're not. You need to be up in the tree so you can plug this shitbag once and for all. Don't deviate from the plan. We need to be calm and collected. Something you aren't right now."

He was right. It was too late to stop Alan.

"Fine. I'll get up in the tree. But I'm not happy."

"I got that. Now give me your gun and the magazines. I left the M4 up there with two extra magazines. Not that you'll need them."

She handed him the MP7 and her spares. He examined the weapon and slipped the magazines into his pants.

"You ever fired one of those?" she asked.

"Actually, it's one of my favorites. I know it well. Good choice."

She hesitated, and then turned away. "Be careful," she whispered, and then he was gone.

Jet scaled the trunk and found the rifle, then peered through the night vision scope at the house. She chambered a round, checked to verify that it was set to single fire and not burst, and then swept the perimeter wall, looking for Alan.

The security men were patrolling in their now familiar pattern, and she watched them move from the back of the house to the front, pausing to talk for a few minutes near the guardhouse before they moved slowly back.

She bit back her anger at Alan pulling this stunt and slowly willed it away. He was just doing what he thought he should – honoring his promise to his brother to keep her out of danger and protect her. In his mind, this was the right thing to do.

He was trying to be honorable.

She understood.

She just didn't like it.

CHAPTER 39

Alan crouched in the lot next door, concealed by the dense vegetation, the lights in the house all off, everyone down for the night. He watched the guards in the dim illumination of the few lamps on the front of Arthur's property, and checked his watch. If they stuck to their pattern, the two men at the front would meet with the two from the rear, hang out for a few minutes, and then return on their rounds. Each patrol took ten minutes, nobody in any hurry. Four more guards lounged up by the gate, there to stop anyone foolish enough to try to crash through the iron barrier.

The guards carried shotguns, which they did after dark, preferring to keep them out of sight during the day and not alarm the neighbors, even though they were all licensed to carry them as part of their job. Twelve-gauge scatterguns, loaded with double-ought buckshot, he knew from Jet's research.

The faint sound of cars three quarters of a mile away on the freeway, an almost inaudible but constant whirring, became louder when an occasional big rig went by. The surrounding trees masked the sound, as they did virtually every noise – something they were all depending on once the fur began flying.

The rear patrol began making its way back to the front gate, as usual, and he waited until they cleared the corner before he sprinted straight for the rear wall and vaulted it effortlessly, his move executed with the grace of a gymnast. He landed squarely on the grass and rolled, then paused on one knee to verify his position. He would need to move ten yards straight ahead, then five to his right near the cottage, and then another twenty straight towards the house, then seven to the left, before completing his final approach. While he would have much rather run flat out, his mind urged caution, and he carefully trotted forward, stopping at the first estimated sensor gap, then turning and taking five more large steps before moving towards the house again.

To anyone watching, he would have looked like he was out of his mind – dressed in all black, his M4 strapped over one shoulder, his backpack cinched tight, moving in an elaborate sequence of steps of no discernible pattern. But he was completely concealed by the bulk of the stately home, so his performance was wasted, no spectators around to view it.

He reached the house without any spotlights going off. He hadn't triggered the motion detectors, which were positioned to allow the patrols to move along the perimeter of the grounds without setting them off, with the focus being the front and back home entrances and the side service entry for the kitchen.

Alan could easily make out the door to the root cellar with the night vision goggles, and he edged along the hedges that ringed the base of the house before arriving at the rectangular form.

And got his first nasty surprise.

A stainless steel padlock was clasped through the eyelets. A big one. Industrial, by the looks of it. He had a pair of bolt cutters in case he ran across a lock, but they wouldn't work on this type – the hasp was protected by its own steel case.

He weighed his options and briefly considered trying to scale the side of the house, but discarded the idea. The wooden siding wouldn't support his weight, and wouldn't have adequate holds for him to make it. The windows on both floors were all wired, he knew from his study of the diagram, so that wasn't a way in, either, if he wanted to avoid detection.

Alan glanced around and mentally calculated how long he had before the guards returned. Three minutes, at most. The choices weren't good. He would have to abort.

And then he saw it: a drainpipe running up the corner to the rain gutter rimming the roof. Maybe he could use it to reach the eaves, and then somehow climb over and in from above. As far as he could remember there were no sensors on the high roof – there was no way to access it, so the designers of the system had felt it was safe.

He glanced at his watch and then steeled himself for the climb. It would be difficult, but he'd done worse. He inched along until he was directly beneath it, and then grabbed the pipe and pulled, trying to gauge its strength. It didn't budge. A good sign.

Alan took a deep breath, and clutching the metal edges with both hands, pulled himself off the ground and clamped onto it with his feet. He willed himself higher, using his legs to keep himself from sliding back down, and was quickly past the first story and moving up to the second. Once he was at the top floor he looked up, and could see the roof edge only four or five feet above. It would be close, but he would be able to make it over the side before the guards returned. From there, it wasn't all downhill, but if there was an attic or ventilation duct and he could gain entry to the house, he might be able to execute Arthur before anyone knew what had happened. Getting out would be harder, but he would cross that bridge...

The pipe creaked and shifted, and Alan froze, suspended two stories above the hard-packed ground, his sole means of support protesting his weight. A rusted bolt that held the top of the pipe in place groaned, but then the movement stopped.

Perhaps it would be all right. He reached up and continued to pull himself up, now being even more tentative so as to avoid vibrating the pipe any more than he had to, and his fingers had nearly reached the gutter when the top shifted again – and the bolt snapped.

The pipe, with Alan, swung away from the house as if in slow motion before it broke halfway along its length, and Alan was falling backwards, trying desperately to spin so he could land facing forward and cushion his impact with his hands and feet. Luck wasn't with him, though, and the last thing he registered after slamming into the ground was four guards running at him, shotguns at the ready, their boots pounding against the dirt as the world spun and he blacked out.

CHAPTER 40

"He's coming to." The first guard's voice sounded distant, as if he was speaking in a tunnel. Alan's eyes flitted open and then closed again, a bright light blinding him.

He tried to move his arms, but his wrists were cuffed behind him, the steel of the restraints cutting into his skin as he strained against them.

A blow landed on his face, a slap, and he opened his eyes again to find himself looking at two bodyguards, and the man he recognized as Standish.

Standish nodded at the guards, and they departed wordlessly, leaving Alan alone with Arthur's assistant. Standish slowly paced around Alan before returning to a position facing him.

"Who are you? Who sent you?" Standish's voice was quiet, but the menace was clear.

Alan didn't respond.

"I asked you a question. It's very rude to ignore a direct question, did you know that?"

Alan closed his eyes again, a wave of dizziness and nausea washing over him.

Another slap.

"Answer my question. Who are you?"

Alan raised his head and opened his eyes. "You asked two questions," he croaked, his voice seeming to be somehow broken. His neck hurt like he'd been slammed in the side of the head with a brick. Something, perhaps more than one thing, was badly damaged.

"Ah, so it speaks. Very good. Now answer both questions, then. Who are you, and who sent you?"

"I'm with the Jehovah's Witnesses. Have you heard the good news of Je—"

Another blow knocked his head sideways, this one harder than a slap.

"Answer me."

Alan grinned, blood covering his teeth from a cut inside his mouth, and spat red saliva at Standish. He needed to stall for time. Give Jet and Matt a chance to get to him.

"That's the best you can do? A little girl punch? Please," Alan taunted.

"Oh, I think you'll find I can do much worse."

"But you won't. Because it's the United States, and it's illegal to torture people here, isn't it? So you'll call the police, they'll arrest me, and that will be that. Now go make the call, pussy boy."

Standish chuckled. Alan didn't like the sound.

"Is that how you think this is going to work? Ah. I see why you're so confident. But I think you have something a little wrong. These men are not ordinary security guards. They're mercenaries. They've all killed many, many times. And they're paid an extraordinarily large amount of money to guard this place. So nobody is going to say a word about your capture. You don't exist. I can do whatever I want to you, and believe me, what I have planned…well, it won't be pleasant."

"You're lying."

"No, I'm not. If you've done any research at all on this house, you know that the owner is ex-CIA. An extremely powerful ex-CIA at that, I might add. Since you're equipped to kill a platoon, I'm going to guess that you're here to assassinate him. So spare me the theatrics and let's get down to business. Who are you, and who sent you?"

"Your mother."

Standish sighed. "How did you get to the house? The entire grounds are wired."

"Not very well."

Standish shook his head. "I don't have a background in interrogation, but I know the head of the security team does. I'd hoped to keep this *entre nous*, but if I'm forced to, I'll bring him into it. And the result is sure to be extremely painful and messy."

"Sounds terrifying."

The two men exchanged hateful glares, and then Standish spun and moved to the door.

"You were warned."

Jet watched the commotion through her scope, and then gasped when she saw one of the spotlights go on and four men carry Alan's inert form into the house, the security men at the front keeping an eye out, confirming that the altercation had gone unnoticed.

Matt reappeared at the bottom of the tree a few minutes later. "Did you see?" he whispered to her.

"I'm coming down." She lowered herself next to Matt, the M4 strapped over her shoulder. "They've got him."

"I know. I was watching," Matt said. "Something went wrong. He tried to climb up the side of the house, but then the pipe he was using let go. He fell at least twenty feet. It didn't look good when he hit. Landed on his back."

"We have to get him out of there."

"Impossible. The guards are on alert now. Even a frontal assault with a full squad wouldn't be enough to make it in," Matt said.

"Shit. This is all my fault. I should have been the one to go."

"And do what? Whatever happened, he couldn't get to the com lines, obviously. So he improvised on the spot. And he got it wrong. How is that your fault?"

She brooded for a few seconds. "It should have been me."

"All right. It's all your fault. Happy? But how does that change the situation?"

She didn't say anything. "It doesn't," she finally conceded. "We need to go in for him. He wouldn't leave me in there. I'm sure of that."

"So he'd make the same kind of stupid decision he made trying to scale the pipe. Fine. But you're not him, and you shouldn't be driven by what he would do. What would you do?"

Jet took her time, thinking, and then turned to Matt, gesturing for him to return the MP7 to her.

"I'd do this the right way."

❧

Jet was just preparing to work her way to the rear of the lot from the park when an engine revved at the house. Matt and Jet exchanged glances and watched as a black Ford Expedition rolled to a stop by the front door and Arthur emerged from the entry, supported by a man at each elbow. He struggled to get into the rear seat before one of the men lifted him and then slid in beside him. She debated trying to get back to the high point in the tree where she would have a shot at him, but it was too late. A second SUV pulled around the Expedition to the front guardhouse, and then both vehicles waited for the gates to open.

"Damn. He's making a run for it. How far is your car?" Jet seethed.

"It'll take me about two minutes to get to it."

"Run. There's only one road out of here. You can pick them up where it lets out. Hurry."

Matt nodded and then tore off, moving flat out down the trail towards the far side of the park. The gates finally stopped moving, and the lead SUV rolled out onto the lane, followed by the Expedition with Arthur in it, moving slowly, no doubt to limit his discomfort.

Arthur had probably panicked when he'd been told that an assassin had been captured, and ordered the men to get him out of there. Wherever they were taking him at this hour would pose its own problems, but they could deal with that after she got Alan out of the house. Now that half the security detail was gone with Arthur, there wasn't anything left to guard, so it would be easier to get in. She hoped so.

Jet slipped across the street a hundred yards down the road, around a bend where the guards at the gate wouldn't spot her, and navigated through the neighbor's park-like estate to the rear of Arthur's lot. The patrols had stopped once Arthur left, which was both good and bad. It meant that their movements were unpredictable, but also could mean that they had let down their guard.

She took a run at the wall and threw herself over, somersaulting as she cleared the iron fencing before landing on catlike feet, then moved swiftly in the same pattern Alan had, but at twice the speed. She was at the house in twenty seconds, and quickly spotted the problem with the lock. Glancing up, she saw a light in what she knew from studying the plans was the main bedroom upstairs, and then another in a room at the far end of the house on the same floor. That would probably be where they were keeping Alan. Had to be. The light had only gone on recently.

Discarding all pretense of a stealthy entry, she felt for a grenade in her backpack and retrieved it, then pulled the pin and tossed it at the back door. It rolled to a stop near the base, and she fished out her other one and hurled it through a window, the glass shattering as it clunked against the living room floor.

The explosion at the back door shattered the night, followed by the living room grenade tearing the downstairs apart. She gave it a few seconds to clear of dust, then dashed to the ruined rear door and ducked inside, the MP7 leading the way.

Two guards were down by the foyer, the blast having knocked them off their feet. She fired two silenced three-round bursts into their bodies as the nearest one tried for his shoulder-holstered weapon. She mentally ticked off the number of men still there. Eight total, if four had gone with Arthur. Four outside at the gate, two dead in the foyer, leaving two more inside. Probably upstairs.

She'd have to make it fast. The police would be on their way after the explosions, and at best she might have five minutes, tops. Then again, the local cops weren't equipped for a military raid, so while they worried her, the guards worried her more. Each was a trained mercenary, and they wouldn't go easy.

A floorboard creaked above her, and she fired up through the ceiling, her silenced rounds tearing through the wood and plaster. She heard a thump from a falling body, and then a thin stream of fresh blood dripped through the bullet holes onto the floor next to her feet.

A round whistled by her ear as she spun to face the stairway and she dropped instantly, firing as she turned, and was rewarded by a man falling backwards onto the stairs, his pistol clattering on the floor at the base.

She waited, listening, her ears ringing from the grenade blasts in spite of having plugged them when the detonations went off, then she moved to the front of the house, her night vision goggles illuminating her way in the dark. She'd need to deal with the exterior guards, by now running down the drive towards her, or risk being overwhelmed by their sheer number. The last thing they would be expecting would be fire from the house. At least, that was her hope.

Jet peered through one of the windows, the glass blown out from the concussion, and spotted two men creeping towards her position along the periphery, by the wall. Her weapon barked twice, and the lead man was knocked off his feet, his shotgun discharging with a boom as his finger reflexively jerked the trigger. The second man was bringing his weapon to bear on her when another burst of death shredded into his torso and he collapsed.

The question was now whether the two at the gate would also try to be heroes, or simply wait for the police to arrive. She could see them ducking down in the guardhouse, and she fired off four bursts to dissuade them from any impulsive acts of pointless bravery.

She didn't pause to see what their decision was, and instead took the stairs two at a time while ejecting the MP7's magazine and slapping another home. At the top of the stairs she got her bearings, the house now dark, the electricity knocked out by damage from the grenades. That was another advantage she could leverage – she had night vision equipment, and the guards didn't, relying upon the motion detectors to turn on the spotlights. Likely a critical distinction she could use in her favor.

Jet stepped over a piece of debris, toed a pistol away from the inert form of the guard she'd shot through the floorboards, and then inched around the corpse before tiptoeing to the doorway at the end of the hall. She stopped outside and listened intently, but didn't hear anything. Gripping the weapon with her right hand, she twisted the knob and pushed the door ajar, then scanned the room with the gun barrel before stopping when she came to Alan, slumped over in a chair, his hands cuffed behind him, his shirt torn open and his feet in a bowl of water with a wire lying next to it, the other end leading to the wall.

"Alan. It's me. Can you hear me?" she whispered, but there was no answer. She tried again. "Alan. Wake up. We need to get out of here."

His chin lifted off his chest, and he struggled to form a word as he came to. She edged nearer.

"What? What is it, Alan?"

His left eye was swollen shut, but his right met hers as he tried again.

"Beee…beh…hin… you…"

She twisted to get her gun pointed at the doorway, but wasn't fast enough.

"Drop it or I'll blow your head off." Standish said from the corner, holding Alan's Desert Eagle, the ugly snout pointed at her chest. "I'll do it. Last chance, and then you're road kill."

She tossed the MP7 onto the oak floor and raised her hands to shoulder height.

"You're brighter than your associate here. That's good. Now, I want you to move over to him and un-tape his legs. It wouldn't do for the police to get the wrong impression when they arrive."

Jet did as instructed, and tore at the tape, pulling it off with effort.

"Now, the handcuffs. I can make out the night vision headgear, so I know you can see. When I toss you the key, catch it, and then unlock them."

"Fine."

She saw the surprise on his face as he tossed her the key.

"A woman? How modern. Unlock the cuffs."

"Then what? You shoot us?"

"You *are* smart. Just unlock them."

She moved around to the back and fiddled noisily with the key, Alan between her and Standish.

"It won't open."

"Don't test my patience, you bi—"

Standish's exclamation was cut off by the blade of the Blackhawk knife piercing his heart, hurled by Jet as she threw herself to the side in order to present a more difficult target. His eyes widened with surprise and then he swung the gun at her and pulled the trigger, but nothing happened. He tried again, and then the life went out of his hand and he fell to the floor, the gun still clenched in his grip.

Jet stepped to where Standish lay motionless and pulled the knife free, wiping it clean on his shirt before folding it closed and slipping it back into her pocket.

"Didn't know how to work the safety, did you, you stupid bastard?" she asked and then leaned down and scooped up the gun, flipping the safety off and then back on before slipping it into her belt and turning to Alan.

"Can you walk?"

"I…I…think… so."

She bent and retrieved the MP7 before she moved to the window and looked out. The guards were still in the guardhouse, keeping their heads down. Smart men. They'd live to fight another day.

"Okay, put your arm around me. You're going to stand up, and I'll support you, and then we're going to go down the stairs and out the back. Can you do that?"

"Yes." His voice sounded stronger.

He struggled to rise, his bare feet brutalized, and then he almost collapsed as she caught him, bearing his weight for a moment before he recovered.

"One foot in front of the other, all right? Easy. I've got you," Jet assured him as they made their way slowly to the stairway. Flames licked at the curtains downstairs and part of the living room was smoldering, threatening to consume the whole house within a matter of minutes. They would need to get out of there immediately, or the old wooden structure could quickly roar into an inferno and trap them inside.

Alan stumbled on the top step, almost taking Jet with him. She stopped him just before he went face first.

"Sorry," he mumbled through mangled lips, his one good eye squinting in the dark.

At the foyer, Jet peered out the side windows but saw nothing threatening. The guards had finally managed to shut off the lights illuminating the front portion of the grounds, plunging the lot into darkness. That would make it easier for her to get Alan to the rear wall and up and over. Her night-vision advantage just got more pronounced, as long as they successfully avoided the sensors.

Her eyes teared freely and she coughed from the smoke blanketing the downstairs, and she held her breath as she led Alan to the rear. At the back door, Jet stopped and whispered to him.

"We're going to stick close to the house till we're by the root cellar, and then walk the pattern again, in reverse. Just follow my lead and we'll do fine."

Alan nodded, and they shuffled together down the back stairs and sidled along the rear hedges until they were opposite the root cellar door.

"All right. Here we go," she encouraged, and they began moving away from the burning building, Jet carefully estimating their progress, keeping them to half a yard per step in the interests of accuracy.

They made it to the point where they needed to turn, and Alan hesitantly followed her, almost falling several times, but making it through until they were at the next segment. The lights hadn't come on, so they'd avoided the motion sensor fields so far and were halfway to the wall.

"Come on. We're almost out of here," she said as they continued their unusual procession, Alan relying heavily on her as what was left of his strength waned. Sirens wailed on the freeway and from town as the emergency response team raced to get there, and her sense of urgency increased. How was she going to get him over the wall in this condition? It would take a miracle...

"What did they do to you?" she whispered.

"Shock. Burns. Beating. Didn't...say...anything," he murmured. "I'm...sorry – stu...pid."

"Stop it. You did what you had to do. Now let's get out of here."

A shotgun blast from the side of the house boomed and Alan pitched forward, the heavy buckshot tearing through his back. Jet dropped with him and twisted, squeezing bursts from the MP7 as she fell. The gunman jerked like a puppet as the slugs slammed into him and then he collapsed onto the grass, his shotgun no longer a danger. Her arm hurt from where she landed on it, and as she scanned the area for the other guard, she felt blood running down her bicep from where a stray pellet or two had nicked her.

She waited a few seconds, but it seemed that the last guard was the most prudent of the bunch and had stayed at the gate. She was seized with the impulse to run to the gatehouse and kill him, but discarded the compulsion as Alan groaned. Jet pulled free of him and looked at his back, a mat of bloody hamburger from the double-ought pellets that had shredded through him, and then turned him over and touched his face, which was contorted with pain.

"Alan!"

"Go...I...I...lo–" He couldn't finish the sentiment as blood gushed from his mouth and his nose.

Jet knew death well enough to know that Alan was finished. Rage coursed through her and she touched his face, which was cold, and then he gurgled and his chest stopped heaving, his struggle over. Tears streamed down her face; she blinked them away, and then the *woop* of a siren pulling onto the street jarred her into action. She swept the perimeter with her gun and, seeing nothing, rose and counted off the yards as she sprinted towards the perimeter wall.

When she reached the base she backed away a few feet and slipped the MP7 into her backpack, then bolted for the wall, springing up and over it in one move, her momentum carrying her onto the grass on the far side, where she landed in a crouch. The sirens sounded like they were almost at the front gate, and she tore off into the brush in a beeline for the lot on her left.

A spotlight punched through the night and the distinctive thumping of helicopter rotors assailed her along with the roar of the chopper's huge motor. The light swept along the rear of the compound and then stopped when it arrived at Alan's body, hovering over his corpse momentarily before scanning the area more slowly, pausing again at the guard's body, crumpled in a heap by the wall.

Jet ran in a zigzag pattern along the elaborately manicured properties until the helicopter's hovering grew fainter, and she thought she'd evaded it when it roared back overhead, the searchlight probing through the thick treetops. A dog barked to her left. The lights in all the surrounding residences were illuminated, the grenades and shooting more than enough to rouse even the deepest sleeper. Her boots smacked the ground and she poured on the steam, and she estimated she'd run almost a quarter mile before the helicopter returned to Arthur's grounds, its searchlight glaring against the surrounding lots in an effort to spot anyone hiding.

She fought back tears as she moved through the woods, pausing before she raced across the road to the park, and gulped air as racking sobs threatened to overcome her. Alan was dead – a good man who'd cared about her and pledged his life to keeping her safe. The only connection to Hannah's father had died with him, and she and her daughter were now alone again. The emptiness inside her felt like a black gulf, a pulsing, hurt thing as vivid as an ulcer.

When she reached her car she jerked off the night vision goggles and tossed them into the passenger seat along with her backpack, then started the engine and rolled away after a final glance at the dozens of police and fire vehicles now on the other side of the park, contending with the chaos she'd left in her wake.

CHAPTER 41

Jet held her cell phone to her ear with her shoulder as she sped along the frontage road in the Focus and waited for Matt to answer. He picked up after four rings, and sounded harried.

"I'm headed south on Chain Bridge Road. We're about five miles away from the house now, moving fairly slow. What happened? Were you able to get Alan out?"

She gave him a brief summary in wooden tones, her speech mechanical, and then made a right on Chain Bridge.

"Stay on the line and tell me if you deviate. I'm going to try to play catch up," she said, after he'd expressed shocked condolences.

"Be careful. Last thing you need is to get pulled over."

"Every cop within ten miles is at the house. I think I'm safe." She floored the gas and weaved around a slower car, the road nearly empty after midnight. The speedometer crawled past eighty miles per hour and held as she gripped the wheel with iron determination, only a few tail lights as far as she could see.

The road widened and she punched the throttle, accelerating to ninety as she flew through the night, Matt silent as they both concentrated on their driving. After a few more minutes his voice intruded.

"We're making a right onto Hampton Road. I'm going to drop further back. There's nothing out here now, and I don't want them to make me."

"How fast are you going?"

"Thirty."

"I should be at the junction in no time at my speed, then."

"You must be flying."

"This Focus will actually do a hundred." The motor sounded like she was about to achieve lift-off.

"I'm slowing. How do you want to play this?"

"You still have your grenades and the rifle?" she asked.

"You bet."

"Let's take them while they're still on the road. It will only get harder whenever they get to their destination. Probably some sort of a safe house, which will have its own countermeasures. I say we knock them out someplace secluded and end this now."

"I'm game. I agree that it will get nothing but harder. Especially with all the shooting tonight. Wolf Trap is now a war zone, and if it was me, I'd have called for backup."

"I won't even tell you about the helicopter."

"Then I won't ask."

Another minute went by.

"Shit. Hang on. There's the turnoff." Tires screeched on Jet's end of the line as she took the corner on two wheels, and then her voice returned. "That was hairy. Okay, I'm on Hampton."

"You should see me any time."

"Oh. I do. You're a ways up."

"I see your headlights," he confirmed, checking his rearview mirror.

"I'm going to shut them off."

"Fine. They're slowing. Their brake lights just came on."

"They must have a house out here."

Both sides of the road were deeply wooded, dense collections of trees in every direction. Jet revved past Matt and accelerated, making straight for the two SUVs. "When they stop, start shooting. Concentrate on the rear vehicle. I'll take Arthur's. Once you can, use your grenades."

"I got it. Good luck. I'm signing off," Matt said, and hung up.

Jet flew past the startled vehicles and then jerked up the emergency brake so her taillights wouldn't illuminate. When she had slowed sufficiently she twisted the wheel and slammed on the brakes, putting the car into a sideways skid. When it screeched to a stop it was blocking both lanes, and she jumped out, pulling the MP7 from her backpack as she hurled herself away from the vehicle, and began firing burst after burst at the approaching SUVs, focusing on the tires, and then the windshields.

The lead truck with Arthur in it swerved as its front tires blew out, and then the glass went white from her rounds and it skidded to a stop. The rear vehicle slammed into Arthur's, unable to stop in time, and she continued peppering the big Ford with fire, pausing only to slap home a fresh magazine as she maintained the assault.

From behind them, Matt's M4 chattered, and then larger caliber shots rang out, the guards returning fire. A boom sounded – shotgun – and then more of Matt's distinctive sputtering, the silencer quieting the rounds to a muffled pop.

A head popped out of the rear passenger side door of Arthur's vehicle and bullets slapped the trees behind her as a gunman fired his handgun. She dropped and rolled in the grass as she emptied the magazine at him, and felt a flash of grim satisfaction when he dropped his pistol and fell back into the truck, the door riddled with bullet holes.

A massive explosion from the rear vehicle blinded her momentarily as one of Matt's grenades detonated, and then the shooting stopped, other than a few final bursts from Matt's rifle.

She felt for another magazine and then realized that she'd expended them all. Tossing the MP7 aside, she reached into her backpack, where she'd stowed Alan's Desert Eagle. Her hand pushed one of the gasoline-filled bottles aside and retrieved the handgun, then she moved back onto the road and cautiously approached the truck.

When she reached the window, the interior was carnage, the driver's head slumped against the wheel, blood drenching what was left of his face and the steering column, the passenger seat occupant's eyes frozen open, four bullet wounds in his head and chest. The guard in the rear seat hadn't fared any better, and the back was soaked with his blood and bits of his skull.

Arthur sat next to him, his labored breathing rasping, hit by at least one stray slug. He pulled weakly against his seatbelt, trying to get it undone, and then his eyes froze on her and radiated malevolence when he recognized her.

"Not looking too good there, Arthur," Jet spat at him, the gun trained on his head.

He didn't say anything, but his stare said it all.

"Couldn't let bygones be bygones, could you? Just had to play God and make my life miserable." She looked around the cab at the slaughter.

"How's the pain management going, Arthur? The agent I injected you with still working? I was told it was a lifetime's worth of agony. In your case, that won't be much longer. I almost hate to end it. Almost."

"Rot in hell, you stinking bitch," Arthur croaked through wormy lips.

"Still a gentleman, huh? Well, that just makes me feel even better about ridding the world of you, you shitgrub." She reached into her backpack and retrieved one of the bottles of gasoline, and using her teeth, unscrewed the top, then splashed the contents into the truck, tossing the half empty bottle into the front seat.

"Rot in hell, did you say? You meant *burn* in hell, I'm sure. Let me give you a little preview of what that'll be like, Arthur. Matt, do you have a light?" she called to her left, where Matt was standing by the other SUV, watching it smolder.

Arthur's scarred brow crinkled at the mention of Matt's name.

"That's right, Arthur, Matt's alive, too. Matt, me, my daughter. So you failed in every respect," Jet said as Matt joined her.

Matt peered into the truck. "Why, hello, Arthur. Looks like you got yourself into a spot of trouble, huh? Couldn't have happened to a nicer guy." Matt held up a flare he'd brought to start the house fire, and tore the end cap off.

"Will you do the honors, Matt?" Jet suggested, and he nodded.

"With pleasure. I traveled around the world for this." He struck the cap with the flare tip and it ignited with a *whoosh*, and then he tossed it into the truck and the gasoline blazed to life with a bright orange-blue flash. They both stepped back and watched Arthur writhe in the flames, his screams otherworldly. After a good thirty seconds it was over, and then she turned to Matt.

"That closes an ugly chapter."

"He was long overdue." He studied her. "Are you okay? Your arm's bleeding pretty good."

"You can dig the buckshot out back at the hotel." She winced as she wiped blood away and gestured with her head. "This is over. Let's get out of here."

Matt spun and hastened back to his Explorer and Jet walked to the Focus, the flames from the SUV illuminating the road with a hellish glow. She slid behind the wheel and took one last look at the Expedition and then put the car in gear and pulled away. The fireball from the gas tank igniting rent the night sky a few seconds later, sending a burst of fire into the air that would be visible for miles. Jet watched the SUV burning behind her in her mirror, then turned on her headlights and checked the map on her phone before increasing her speed, heading to whatever fate awaited her, wherever the winding road led.

CHAPTER 42

"Ow. Take it easy," Jet complained as Matt retrieved the second pellet using a pair of freshly purchased tweezers.

He dropped it into a plastic cup, the bloody ball joining its twin in the bottom, and then held up a bottle of iodine.

"This is going to hurt," he warned.

"Get it over with."

Matt poured a few drops on the two small wounds and Jet's breath hissed as she inhaled through her teeth, but other than that, she showed no reaction. He doused the holes with another liberal application, and then swabbed the bloody tears with cotton balls and tossed the red clumps into the cup with the pellets. Reaching to the table, he unscrewed the top from a bottle of Dermabond and squeezed a drop into the first wound, then pinched it closed for twenty seconds before repeating the procedure with the other.

"There. All done," Matt said, and then loosened the belt he had wrapped tight around Jet's upper bicep, allowing the blood to flow freely again.

"I've been through worse," she said, standing and looking in the motel mirror mounted on the wall over the dresser.

"You'll be good as new within a few days. We just need to make sure there's no infection."

"The antiseptic should take care of that. If it starts bugging me I can always get some pills in Mexico."

Matt stood and picked up the bloody cup. "Mexico, huh? Planning a little getaway to the beaches, are we?"

"Something like that. The border is as porous as Swiss cheese, and the natives don't ask too many questions. Two qualities I like about the place."

"That's the plan, then? We get out of town and head to Mexico?"

"Not exactly. I still have one last item that needs to get done," Jet said quietly.

"Item?" Matt's eyes narrowed.

"An errand."

"That's more important than escaping with our lives from a manhunt?"

"We'll switch motels to something closer to D.C. I'm not worried about being caught. Nobody saw anything, so there's nothing to use to track us other than footprints. Big deal. All the shells were wiped before I loaded them, and I wore gloves. And we're in an extremely densely populated area that has a high crime rate. The fact is, the cops have nothing to go on. We're clean."

"What about the Alan connection?"

"They'll eventually place him as with the Mossad. Or maybe they won't. As far as I know, his prints aren't in any databases. Neither are mine. So they'll be holding a big bag of question marks."

Matt walked to the bathroom and dumped the cotton into the toilet, then fished the pellets from the bottom of the cup and wrapped them in multiple folds of tissue before tossing them in and flushing twice.

"Fine. I'll bite. What's the errand?" he asked.

She told him the detail of the ferry story and Ryker.

"Christ. You offed a Homeland agent?"

"A bent one who participated in covering up a false-flag attack on a stadium full of women and children. And no, I didn't do it. Alan did. But I would have, in a second, without hesitation. That's basically a war crime. I don't believe in due process."

"Right. I seem to recall a lack of tolerance for bad guys in our dealings before."

"I'm thinking about therapy to help with it. I hear voices. Mainly at night."

They looked at each other and laughed simultaneously.

"I'm sure. So what do you intend to do?"

"This Peter turd? I'm going to take him out. For Alan."

"Alan's dead."

"Yes. But this sociopath killed almost a thousand people on that ferry. All to get Alan. Kids. Grandmas. People who never did anything wrong, who are now dead, because this fecal speck decided they were expendable. I'm not going to let that stand."

"You can't right every wrong in the world," he said with a resigned sigh.

"No, but I can get even for this one. And I intend to. Will you help me?"

"I want to go on record saying this idea sucks."

"Noted. Will you do it?"

"What did you have in mind?"

"Alan got some background on him from the Mossad servers, but I could use some more. Could you contact your CIA friend and see what comes up? The more info we have, the better. I'd be particularly interested in plans for his home. The usual stuff," Jet said.

"Let's say I agree. When are you thinking about erasing him?"

"What time is it?"

Matt did a double take. "Really? This soon after Arthur? The town is on high alert. The police think we're being invaded, and they don't know by who. There are more bodies in the morgue than after a ten-car pileup because of you, and you want to jump right back into this and add another to the heap? Are you serious?"

"That's basically it."

"Have I told you that you're out of your mind yet today?"

"I think it came up earlier."

He sat down on the bed and punched the remote control. The early morning news programs were all doing coverage of the gunfight and the fires.

"Fine. Let's say I play along. What then?"

"I go ninja on his ass, kill him, and then we hit the road. Easy, depending upon what kind of security he has in place."

"Do you know where he lives?"

"In Foggy Bottom."

"Oh, good. This keeps getting better and better. That's only a few blocks from the White House."

"I'm not going for the President," she said easily, her eyes on the television as the camera scanned the crime scene tape across the gates of Arthur's compound.

"Probably a good thing for him. You really think you can pull this off?"

"I don't see why not. He's not expecting anything. He's a behind-the-scenes guy, like his father. Thinks he's invulnerable. As you know, those are my favorites."

"His father?" Matt asked.

"I thought I told you about him."

"Tell me again."

When she had finished, he rubbed his eyes, fatigue setting in as the first rays of dawn filtered through the edges of the motel window, the cheap curtains shielding them from most of it.

"So you want to execute the son of one of the most powerful fixers in the country. Less than a mile from the White House, in one of the most exclusive areas of D.C."

She fixed him with a cold stare. "I told you it was simple."

He stood and moved to the room door. "I'm beat. I need to get at least a few hours of sleep."

"Me too. Will you make the call?"

"You're relentless. Fine. Yes. I'll help you. Otherwise I have a feeling you'll just do it by yourself, in which case I'll probably never see my diamonds again."

"Money-grubber."

"Damned right. To quote Oscar Wilde, 'When I was young, I thought that money was the most important thing in life. Now that I'm old – I know it is.' Smart man…"

"Look at you with the literary references. What's next? Iambic pentameter? A sonnet?"

He shook his head. "I like to keep you on your toes. Now get some sleep. Sounds like you're going to need it. Let's hook back up at eleven, and we can figure out our escape route and how to dispose of the guns. I don't think they'll track the grenades back to Bubba, but you never know. He doesn't know my real name, but the last thing I need is that kind of heat. I'd really like to talk you out of this and convince you to get the hell out of Dodge now, if not sooner. That's my money-grubbing self-preservation instinct kicking in."

"All right. Eleven it is. I'm buying. Maybe we can find some pancakes. I love pancakes."

"Drink that orange juice. It'll help you replace the blood you lost." He gestured at a carton of juice he'd gotten at the all night drug store.

"Yes, Dad."

He smiled as he twisted the doorknob and swung the wooden slab open. "Who's your daddy?"

"You are, you big, strong, money-grubbing Matt-daddy."

He chuckled in spite of himself and took a last look at Jet, sitting cross-legged on the bed, wearing board shorts and a black tank top, the most amazing woman he'd ever laid eyes on even after a night of no sleep – and also without a doubt the most deadly. An intoxicating and dangerous cocktail.

He pulled the door closed behind him and walked slowly to his room, exhausted, the vision of Jet ingrained in his imagination, the reality of her lying on a bed only a few feet away.

An intoxicating cocktail indeed.

And one he was powerless to resist.

CHAPTER 43

Two days later, Washington, D.C.

Foggy Bottom was dark at three A.M., the sidewalks empty, the grounds of St. Stephen's Church dark, the residential complexes cloaked in the gloom, with only a few lights on in the windows of the classical façades. An occasional car cruised slowly down Pennsylvania Avenue, the rumble of engines long faded until the next day's rush hour got underway.

Jet, dressed in black, eyed the side of the five-story building near the Spanish Embassy, the turn of the century French design well suited to what she was about to do. She'd been by three times during the day to look the grounds over, each time wearing a different disguise, and she was as ready as she'd ever be.

Her arm was already healing, the shotgun pellets more of an annoyance than anything, and she was confident that the injury wouldn't be an impediment to what she was about to do. Glancing around to ensure she was alone on the street, she rolled down the black knit cap she was wearing, transforming it into a ski mask – an unusual choice for a mild night with lows in the fifties.

With a final look down the street, she sprinted towards the front of the building and ran up the wall, her momentum carrying her eleven feet from the sidewalk, her fingers grasping for a hold on the stone molding that ran along the base of the second floor. She latched onto the two-inch deep impression with a vice-like grip and scrambled with her feet until they, too, found support, and then pulled herself up, hands searching for the next crevice or bump that would carry her higher. At the second story, she swung her legs to the side and pushed herself onto the slim window ledge, then grabbed the top of the elaborate framing and continued her ascent until she hauled herself over the edge of the roof.

Her arm hurt, but it was bearable. And going down would be easier. It always was. She moved to the far side of the building and looked down at the three-story townhouse next door, and then shrugged off her backpack and unzipped it.

Twenty seconds later she had the rappelling cord secured and had tossed the free end over the side. She gave it a pull with her black-gloved hands and edged to the roof lip. After peering over, she gripped the line and then threw herself out into space, her black running shoes pounding against the sheer side as she eased herself down to the smaller building below.

Once on the roof, she moved to the center-mounted access hatch and examined its hinges, then rooted in her sack again and extracted a glass vial half-filled with clear liquid. She twisted the stopper and poured a thin stream onto each hinge, and watched the chemical smoke spiral into the air as the acid went to work.

Four minutes later she was inside the home, her feet gliding soundlessly down the hall to the master bedroom. The door was partially open, and she inched silently into the darkened room where a sleeping figure occupied the far side of the bed.

A floorboard creaked beneath her and she stopped, fearful that she'd roused the target, but after a few seconds she continued to approach the bed, once reassured that he hadn't awakened. She was almost at the foot when the sleeping man lunged for the night table next to him. He fumbled with the drawer but then she was on top of him, and two lightning strikes to the throat sent streaks of pain shooting through his skull as he fought for breath. She rolled him away from the nightstand and retrieved the little Walther PPK he'd been trying to get to. Gazing down at him like an angel of death, she watched as panicked realization registered in his stunned eyes, then she pressed a pillow over his face, pushed the gun barrel into it, and fired twice.

The target's body shuddered and lay still. She pulled the pillow off to study her handiwork, and then tossed the gun next to him and pushed herself away, her feet landing on the hardwood floor with a muffled plop.

Ransacking the bedroom took two minutes, and the downstairs three more, and then she was back on the roof, scaling the side of the building again. Once at the top, she jogged to the far side and jumped off, feeding out line until her feet settled on the sidewalk. She glanced around again, adjusted the backpack, and set out for Virginia Avenue, rolling the ski mask back over her face as she walked, the black wool transformed into a seaman's cap again, shielding her head from the cold.

~~~

The following evening Matt pulled into a motel parking lot on the outskirts of Dallas, and shut off the engine while Jet went and got rooms. They'd been driving nonstop since leaving Washington, and even taking turns behind the wheel, Matt was ready for a decent night's sleep. Tomorrow would take them as far as Tucson, Arizona, where they would spend another night and then drive across the border into Mexico, leaving the Explorer in Hermosillo when they caught a flight to Mexico City, and from there, points unknown.

Jet returned from the motel reception, opened the passenger door, and tossed him a room key.

"You're in 123, I'm in 124. Want to meet back up in half an hour and grab dinner?" she asked, her voice tired.

"Love to. Any complications on the check-in?"

"No. He just glanced at my passport and stared at my boobs most of the time."

"Very effective secret weapon."

"Not so secret. If I didn't need to take a shower before that, I do now."

"Hopefully there are no hidden peepholes in the room," he said.

"Why do you have to go there, Matt? Why put that in my head?"

"You seem too worry-free. It's not like you. I wanted to give you something to occupy your time."

"Thanks. You're all heart."

"Not all. But mostly."

She gave him a tentative smile, then pulled her suitcase off the back seat and rolled it along the sidewalk, Matt watching her as she marched along the row of rooms until she came to her door.

The shooting at Arthur's had created a media firestorm, with every politician in the capital decrying the rising tide of drug violence that was afflicting the nation – the most likely cause of the horrific slaughter at the house, as well as the related killings on the desolate road south of it. The security company whose men had been butchered hadn't been able to shed any light on what they had been guarding against, other than to say that they'd been hired to provide routine security for a reclusive investor who'd been convalescing after a long illness. A few stations had connected the murder of the firm's owner and the shootout, and speculation was rampant that he had somehow offended one of the Mexican cartels invading America's cities – the media's favorite new boogiemen.

The further they got from Washington, the less airtime the shootings received, and once they had crossed into Texas there was no mention of it, the story replaced by the hotly contested semi-final upset of an audience favorite on one of the countless talent shows clogging the nation's airwaves.

Neither Matt nor Jet wanted to chance traveling through an American airport, so they had chosen to drive to the border, where nobody was paying attention to the vehicles leaving the U.S., where the Mexicans welcomed travelers without question, happy that anyone wanted to come into the beleaguered country and spend money.

Matt knocked on Jet's door at the appointed time, and she opened it, her hair still wet, the puckered wounds on her arm less red than they had been the day before. She pulled a long sleeve shirt on over her tank top and then held her arms out, presenting herself.

"Ta-da."

"Very nice. You have to be the best looking assassin in all these here parts," Matt drawled in his best John Wayne.

"Ex-assassin. And I prefer the term 'clandestine operative.' Less pejorative."

"Indeed. Wouldn't want to give folks the wrong idea," Matt agreed.

"Exactly."

"What are you in the mood for? I understand Texas is big on steak, steak, and steak. You up for some steak?"

"Mmm, no, I really had my heart set on macrobiotic vegan fare."

"As long as you don't mind it being made out of beef," Matt said.

"Not at all. My favorite kind."

"We're going to get along just fine, then."

"That was my hope."

They found a restaurant four blocks away that had a packed parking lot and a neon sign featuring a steer's head, and pushed their way in through the cantina-style doors to the dining room, where a leggy blonde with a down-home twang greeted them and led them to a booth with a table made from an old wooden door. They slid in opposite each other and studied the menu, which featured numerous specials containing the word 'Cowboy,' all of which involved some part of a cow.

"You want a beer?" Matt asked as he closed the menu.

"I wonder if they have red wine?"

"Here? They probably add coloring to their white, if you want it."

"Let's ask. I could use a drink after the last week."

Matt flagged down their server, a perky blonde in short shorts and a cowboy hat who assured them that the wine was excellent, and asked Jet if she wanted merlot or cabernet by the glass. She opted for merlot, and Matt ordered a Lone Star beer.

"You can't eat in Texas and not have a Lone Star. I think they stone you or shoot you with a six gun or something if you even try."

"That's probably who makes the wine, too."

"If it's really bubbly and tastes like beer, don't complain."

"Just act natural."

"No sudden moves."

They laughed easily together, both tired but relieved their ordeal was finally over, and when the waitress returned with their drinks they ordered steaks. Jet took a sip of the wine and grimaced.

"Ahh. My favorite. Old socks."

"It's aged," Matt agreed, and then took a pull on his beer. Served in the bottle, of course.

"I think I might have gotten your merlot," he deadpanned.

She shook a fist at him half-heartedly. "Damn you. You always get the better deal."

"It's because I'm pure of body and mind."

"That'll be the day."

When dinner arrived, the slabs of meat more than upheld Texas' reputation for beef, and neither of them could finish the enormous portions. Jet ordered another glass of wine, this time the cabernet, and Matt got another beer, and they lingered over their drinks as they digested.

"What are you going to do about the diamonds?" she asked. "Once I give them to you?"

"Oh, I'm really not that worried about it. I'll just have you hold onto them. There are plenty more where they came from. And it will give me an excuse to go back to Bangkok at some point."

"Do you really believe this is finally over?" she asked in a hushed tone.

"For you? Absolutely. For me? I'm pretty sure my ordeal is finished, too. Arthur was the main driver of the push to get me. Whatever remains of his crew has their hands full trying to salvage whatever they can of the drug business. With the Chinese and Russians at their throats, I'm the least of their problems."

She stared off into the near distance at a black and white photo of a prize bull. "At least the bastard is finally dead."

"What about you? What's your master plan?" Matt asked.

"I don't have one. Just to get Hannah, and find someplace where we'll be safe, and she can grow up healthy and happy."

He nodded. "Any idea where?"

"You ever been to Mendoza?"

"Argentina? Really?"

"It's pretty nice."

"And a long way from anything."

"That too," she agreed.

"I'll drink to that."

They toasted, and Jet grew quiet. Eventually, she finished her glass and stared at it. "I just can't believe he's...gone. Alan."

"I'm so sorry for that."

"He was a very good man."

There wasn't more to add, so Matt stuck to finishing his beer and paying the bill.

They drove in silence back to the motel, and Matt walked her to her door, his key in his hand. He looked down at her, the light breeze stirring her hair. She looked so small, so vulnerable, if only for an instant.

Their lips met and they kissed for a long time, savoring the connection, both needing the other, if only to feel alive for a brief moment. Two damaged souls at the end of a tortuous journey, finally able to rest, their travel almost done.

Jet felt the same incredible energy as each time she'd kissed him before, and she inhaled his essence, the stubble of his face rough against hers.

Inside her, a kernel of hope stirred. Maybe there was a tomorrow she could look forward to after all.

She stepped back, tears rolling down her face, and laughed nervously, wiping them away with her arm.

"I'm sorry, Matt. It's just…it's just too soon. But I could really use some company on my trip to Uruguay. If you're not busy, that is."

He gazed at her deeply, then deeper still until he fell into her emerald eyes, and then nodded and grinned.

"I've got all the time in the world."

CHAPTER 44

The older man stared at the oversized flat screen, his head in his hands, as the black and white footage played on the monitor, the date and time stamp blinking in the right lower corner. A figure in black, sporting a backpack, hurried down the sidewalk from the direction of Peter's home. A woman. For a brief moment, just after she pulled her ski mask off, her face was captured in the frame, and the operator stopped the playback, freezing her image, her white teeth gleaming in the dim light.

"There's no question she killed your son," the operator said. "The timing matches time of death, and there's nobody else on the streets. So it has to be her, sir."

The older man sighed and rubbed his chin, then reached for a plastic bottle of water. He carefully unscrewed the top and took a swig.

"Who is she?"

"We don't know, sir."

"Can we get any better resolution on the camera?"

"No. It's a traffic camera. It's zoomed to the max level. Any more and it gets even grainier."

"Have we run it through the databases?"

"In process. NSA is helping with that."

"When do you expect to have a report?"

"Within the next twenty-four hours, sir."

"Let's see it one more time."

"Of course, sir." This was the twelfth replay.

The footage reversed at hyper-speed, and then the silent film began anew.

"And the police are all over this?" the older man asked.

"Absolutely. They've circulated the photo of the suspect. It's also all over the news."

"Any hits yet?" His voice caught on the hopeful last word, the lie imbedded in the syllable a taunt.

"No. But they're working on it, sir."

"What about the ski mask?"

"They're checking to see how many were sold in the last two weeks in the area, but if it's older, or she got it out of state, or on the internet…there are a lot of variables, but they're following up on all of them, sir."

The older man coughed, a dry hack, and then gestured to the operator. "Again," he ordered, glaring at the screen, wishing the mystery woman dead, as though he could reach out through sheer force of will and crush her with his mind.

"Yes, sir."

The footage played, her gait easy as the mask rolled up her face, and the image of his son's killer burned itself into his visual cortex, taunting him, making a mockery of his power and influence. He had the ability to create and destroy worlds, and yet with all that, he couldn't keep his son alive for a moment longer. When all was said and done, he could move mountains, but he couldn't ever talk to his boy again.

The operator let the footage run this time, and the woman's face turned away from the camera, as though she sensed she was being filmed, and then she was just an indistinct shadow moving along the desolate street.

The operator started when the old man crushed the water bottle with a loud crack and threw the flattened container into the trash, a scowl etched into his features. His fingers worked at the plastic cap in his hand as he watched until the footage went dark and the screen became a jumble of static, and then he set it down carefully in front of him and leaned back in the executive chair, a small sound, a groan, escaping his lips. He looked up from the screen, his expression one of pure misery, and then waved a trembling right hand at the monitor, his eyes locking on the operator's with the intensity of a reactor core.

"Again."

<<<<>>>>

JET V – Legacy is the fifth installment in the bestselling JET series, which follows the saga of the Mossad's deadliest ex-operative, who faked her own death to escape her past. In this novel, JET is called upon to make the ultimate sacrifice in order to keep the ones she loves, and the world, safe.

For preview and purchase details, visit RussellBlake.com

ABOUT THE AUTHOR

Russell Blake lives full time on the Pacific coast of Mexico. He is the acclaimed author of the thrillers: *Fatal Exchange*, *The Geronimo Breach*, *Zero Sum*, *The Delphi Chronicle* trilogy (*The Manuscript*, *The Tortoise and the Hare*, and *Phoenix Rising*), *King of Swords*, *Night of the Assassin*, *The Voynich Cypher*, *Revenge of the Assassin*, *Return of the Assassin*, *Blood of the Assassin*, *Silver Justice*, *JET*, *JET II – Betrayal*, *JET III – Vengeance*, *JET IV – Reckoning*, *JET V - Legacy*, *Upon a Pale Horse*, *BLACK*, and *BLACK is Back*.

Non-fiction novels include the international bestseller *An Angel With Fur* (animal biography) and *How To Sell A Gazillion eBooks (while drunk, high or incarcerated)* – a joyfully vicious parody of all things writing and self-publishing related.

"Capt." Russell enjoys writing, fishing, playing with his dogs, collecting and sampling tequila, and waging an ongoing battle against world domination by clowns.

Sign up for e-mail updates about new Russell Blake releases

http://russellblake.com/contact/mailing-list

Made in the USA
Monee, IL
07 December 2019